P9-BZX-632

TEN
Years
ON

Also by Alice Peterson

Monday to Friday Man

Another Alice

You, Me and Him

Look the World in the Eye

M'Coben, Place of Ghosts

TEN *Years* ON

ALICE PETERSON

Quercus

First published in Great Britain in year of 2012 by

Quercus
55 Baker Street
7th Floor, South Block
London W1U 8EW

A CIP catalogue record for this book is available from the British Library

ISBN 978 0 85738 325 9

10 9 8 7 6 5 4 3 2

Typeset by Ellipsis Digital Limited, Glasgow

Printed and bound in Great Britain by Clays Ltd, St Ives plc

To Robert Cross
(1925–2011)

His reassuring voice
continues to encourage me to write.

PROLOGUE

New Year's Eve, Winchester

'Ten, nine, eight . . .' we all shout in Kitty's crowded sitting room. Kitty is my oldest school friend.

'Three, two, ONE . . .'

I hear Big Ben chiming on the television in the background. 'I love you, Becca,' Olly says, lifting me into his arms.

I'm laughing, so happy. 'I love you too.'

Soon the television is turned off, replaced by music. There's drunken dancing on the sitting-room floor, everyone singing. I hear fireworks.

From the other side of the room, I catch Joe watching Olly and me dance. I beckon him over. He smiles, before being pulled away by one of Kitty's admiring friends.

*

It's three in the morning when Olly, Joe and I stagger back to my parents' home. We cut through the water meadows, the river glistening at night. I'm singing, 'Happy new year.' Olly puts a hand over my mouth, tells me we'll be arrested.

'That could be fun,' I say, pushing him away. 'Who was that girl you were with all night, Joe?'

Olly catches my arm, steers me away from the edge of the river.

'Yeah, I saw you too,' he says. 'She was cute, Lawson.'

'What's her name? Or can't you remember?' I hiccup.

'Juliet, actually.'

Olly turns to Joe. 'You should have stayed, Romeo.' Kitty had urged us to crash there for the night, but Olly and I wanted to head home. My parents are away and my sister, Pippa, is out, so we have the house to ourselves.

'Romeo, Romeo . . .' I pretend to look for Joe from my balcony.

'I didn't feel like staying.' He shrugs. 'I took her number though.'

'Wherefore art . . .'

'Shut up, Becca.'

'. . . thou Romeo?' I finish, twirling myself round the next lamp post.

'Christ, she's a liability,' laughs Olly.

'Let's pretend we don't know her,' suggests Joe.

Back home, we head outside, deciding another drink and cigarette are needed before bed, along with a packet of chocolate biscuits. We sit, huddled, on the bench in the stone-paved area of my parents' garden. I'm in the middle. We raise our drinks to each other. 'To us,' Olly says.

'To us,' Joe and I repeat.

Olly, Joe and I share a flat in Clifton, Bristol. We're in our second year at university. Joe's reading medicine; Olly and I English. Olly and I have been going out for nearly a year. I started to take real notice of him in the second term, after I'd heard his band, 'Stanley', playing in the student union bar. He played the piano. He was tall, slim, wore baggy jeans and somehow made a navy cardigan look cool. His hair was light brown with soft strands that flicked across his forehead. As I watched him play, every now and then he'd turn to the lead singer, flaming red hair and wearing the shortest black dress with lace-patterned tights, and he'd smile, mischief in his eyes. Suddenly I wanted to be her and was determined to attract his attention. Before our next English tutorial I washed and styled my long thick hair, applied foundation, blusher, mascara, lip-plumper . . . wore my suede miniskirt, Wonderbra, low-cut top and cowboy boots. I love those boots – they work every time. Of course, all this grooming meant I was late. I rushed into the crowded lecture room with one other latecomer, saw a seat free, and, oh my God, it was next to Olly. It was fate! I flew towards the desk, plunged my books on the table, dived into the seat . . .

'Back to Bristol soon,' says Joe half-heartedly.

'Let's not think 'bout that just yet,' I say. 'Ugh. Work.' I gulp down some water.

'You don't work, Becca,' Joe points out in that cool, controlled way of his. Even when he's been drinking, rarely does he seem drunk.

'I do.'

'Well, not very hard,' Olly encourages Joe.

I ignore them laughing at me. 'What's the best thing that's happened last year?' I prod Olly's shoulder. 'You go first.'

'Playing in a few gigs, going out with you.'

'Ah,' I sigh, kissing him. 'Me too.'

'Oh God.' Joe stubs out his cigarette prematurely. 'I think I'm off.' He also lives in Winchester, though neither Olly nor I have visited his home over the Christmas break. He says it's about as relaxing as visiting the dentist.

'Sorry, Joe, no more public displays of affection,' Olly promises him, pushing him back down on to the bench. 'Stay the night.'

'How about you, Joe? Top thing that's happened?' I ask.

He runs a hand through his thick dark hair. 'Meeting Olly.'

Olly smiles. 'That was a good night.'

Olly had met Joe at the beginning of our second year. 'Moving into your flat,' Joe continues. He had needed somewhere to live; we had a spare room . . . 'Realizing I'd met a top guy.'

'Shall I leave you two to it?' I say, feeling like a gooseberry.

Joe turns to me. 'And a top girl.'

'Group hug,' I suggest, throwing my arms around both of them. We sit like this for a while, happy, gazing at the stars.

'What d'you think we'll be doing in ten years?' I ask, finally breaking the silence.

'Ten years on?' Olly repeats, as if it's impossible to see that far ahead.

'It'll come round quickly, I bet.' I cross my arms. 'Before you know it, we'll be fifty,' I exclaim, as if fifty is on the verge of false teeth and decrepitude.

Joe shakes his head. 'Can't imagine being fifty.'

'Ten years . . .' Olly thinks out loud. 'OK, I'll live in a London pad with a view 'cross the river, I'll be a famous writer, or maybe I'll be the next Mick Jagger or Bob Dylan . . .'

'Take drugs and trash hotel rooms,' Joe says.

'I'll be far away from here,' I predict, thinking of myself as a podgy little girl, long hair in plaits, on the top floor of my parents' house, painting day after day in the school holidays. 'I want to travel the world, go to India, China, Mexico . . .'

'Uh-oh, she's off.' Olly rolls his eyes.

'I'll live in Florence or Venice . . . speak *Italiano*,' I say, exaggerating my accent, 'I'll learn a ton of languages, and I'll definitely be painting. My work will sell for millions! You, Joe?' I nudge his arm.

Olly and I wait. Joe could do anything he wanted. Like my sister, he's talented at sport; he excels at rugby and has the muscles to show for it. He's handsome in a rugged way: dark hair, stubble, moody grey eyes. He drives women mad because they never know what he thinks of them. Joe has the ability to make you feel like you're the only person he cares about in the world, but in the next moment you're nothing, no one. Christ, I'd hate to be in love with him. I'd never eat, I think to myself as I grab a biscuit. In the short space of time that I've known him, already he's broken hearts. Take that girl tonight. Juliet. She'll be sitting by the phone all day, waiting for him to call. 'Ten years, Joe. What d'you think you'll be doing?'

'Ruling the world.' He lights another cigarette. 'I don't like doing this, Becca.'

'Spoilsport.'

Olly ends up agreeing with Joe. 'Let's face it,' he says. 'None of us know what's going to happen tomorrow, let alone in ten years' time.'

1

Ten Years Later

'He will live on in spirit, forever with us,' Kitty says tearfully. After her reading, she returns to her seat.

Olly's mother, Carolyn, sits next to me, my father on my other side. I stare ahead. This can't be happening. I want to stand up and scream, tell my family and friends to go. There's been a terrible mistake.

'Mrs Sullivan?' I see the policeman standing at our front door that evening. It was late, about eight o'clock, and I couldn't understand where Olly was, since he'd promised to be home by six thirty. 'I'll pick up a bottle of wine on the way,' he'd said in his message.

'May I come in?' the policeman asked.

He refused a cup of tea.

'I'm so sorry, I'm afraid I have bad news,' he said.

'Your husband was involved in a road accident earlier this afternoon.'

Carolyn touches my arm, encouraging me to stand for the next hymn, 'Dear Lord and Father of Mankind'. She looks frail, her fine brown hair scooped back from her face with a comb, tears in her pale-blue eyes. Her skin is ashen. Halfway through the verse she grips my hand, as if we will get through this together. But any moment now, I will wake up and the only touch I shall feel is Olly's arms around me. I'll be able to tell him how vivid my dream had all seemed; how the church was packed with friends and family. How sad Olly's father Victor had looked in his suit and glasses. He appeared smaller, greyer, stooped in grief, and I saw deep regret in his eyes. It was too late for him to get to know his son. There was a price he'd paid for putting work before his family.

'You're making it sound scarily real,' Olly will say.

We'll laugh and hold on to one another, kiss, make love, stay in bed for at least another hour. Then we'll go for a walk in the park, enjoy a lazy lunch, and I won't take anything for granted again.

I am brought back to reality when I hear the sound of footsteps echoing against the stone floor. Simon, Olly's elder brother, is walking to the front of the church, clutching notes. He's a bigger build than Olly, darker hair. He gave up the police force to move his wife and two children to Northumberland a year ago, to be closer to Carolyn and Victor. 'He was always the action man, and the bossy one,' Olly used to tell me.

I like him. He's brave. I could not stand up there today.

'Olly was the musical one in our family,' he begins. 'He started learning the piano when he was six. There was I, busy playing army and building dens in the garden when Olly was playing Chopin and composing music in his head. His other passion was writing.'

I shut my eyes and try to listen, but images of the morning before he'd died keep on coming back to haunt me.

'Surprise!' I'd said.

Olly helped himself to a croissant, saying, 'What a treat.' Rarely did we eat breakfast together before work; I was always in too much of a rush. 'By the way, the shower-curtain rail thingy collapsed, I'll fix it later,' he said.

'Did it? Oh well,' I said, pouring the coffee.

'Becca? Are you feeling guilty? Have you had an affair with Glitz?'

Patrick van Glitzen, or Glitz as I call him, is my sixty-five-year-old boss. In his late fifties he set up a modern British art gallery on New Bond Street. It's now one of the most successful galleries in the country.

'Oh shucks, is it that obvious?' I leaned across to kiss him. 'I've got some exciting news.'

'We don't have to visit your parents this weekend?'

'Cheeky sod. You know Norman Graham?'

'The guy who paints blocks of colour.'

'That sell for thousands. Yesterday I sold a series of six. Six, Olly!'

'That's great. So, you must have got a beefy commission?'

'Yep, but it's even better, Ol. Glitz is going to review my pay *and* give me a small bonus at the end of the summer.'

Olly smiled. 'That's incredible.'

'So, I was thinking . . .'

'Uh-oh, that's dangerous.' Olly poured himself another coffee.

'I was thinking it's time we moved out of here—'

'Not that again.'

'Olly! That's not fair.'

'It's just you keep on going on about it.'

'Well, that's because we live in a shoebox and I'm sick of it.'

'I know,' he said, wounded pride in his voice. Olly felt uncomfortable talking about money. He felt he should be the one earning more, but teaching music and writing a novel in the hopes it was going to get published one day was never going to get us on to the property ladder. So I'd given up my freelance illustrating to work for Glitz. Olly felt guilty that I was the one giving up my dream. I'd been passionate about painting since childhood and had studied art in Florence. He kept on promising that he'd make it up to me. He would finish his script and get a publishing deal.

'There are a couple of witnesses,' the policeman had continued. 'Your husband overtook on a corner . . .'

'No,' I uttered. 'That's so unlike him! He was always careful, he promised he'd be careful . . .'

He nodded with respect, but continued nevertheless. 'He didn't see the oncoming vehicle until it was too late. There was nothing the driver could have done.'

'Olly drew people towards him,' Simon continues, his voice wavering now, 'with his infectious enthusiasm and charm.'

I touch the photograph on the back of the service sheet. Olly is smiling; there's warmth in his eyes. This picture was taken the night we moved into our one-bedroom apartment. It seemed so grand and grown-up four years ago. We were eating takeaway and drinking cheap champagne by the fire.

'It isn't hard to see why he has so many friends here today.' Simon gestures to the packed congregation.

But I know one person who isn't in the church. Joe Lawson. Joe should be here. He was Olly's best friend. The three of us used to hang out together.

And then I destroyed us.

'Oliver was kind,' ten-year-old Barnaby is saying to me, clutching his mother's hand. Olly used to teach piano privately, and Barnaby was one of his star pupils.

My best friend Kitty thanks him for me, saying he'd played his Chopin piece beautifully and Olly would have been very proud.

I move through the crowded church hall, pushing past people drinking tea and eating cake. Mum catches me up, dressed in a simple grey outfit. 'Darling, there you are.' Pippa joins us, holding on to one of her twins, Oscar. Oscar's three. He has chocolate brownie smudged around his mouth. Pippa doesn't know what to say. Nor does Mum. No one does. How can they? I force a smile. 'I need some fresh air. I'll be back in a minute.'

I can feel them watching me helplessly as I walk away.

Outside, I lean against the wall and take a deep breath. I see the policeman again, standing in front of our fireplace. 'He didn't see the oncoming vehicle . . . it was too late.' Why was he so reckless? What was he thinking about? I feel angry, and when I'm not angry I feel so sad, as if I'll fall apart, break into a thousand tiny pieces. I wish with every beat in my heart that I could rewind time, go back to that day. Maybe if I'd waited till the evening to talk to him about moving out of the flat, he'd still be alive.

'We could rent somewhere more central,' I'd said, showing him the two properties that I'd circled in the brochure the night before, when Olly had been out playing poker with his friends. 'I reckon with what we're both earning, and if we tap into our savings, we could afford it.'

Olly glanced at the flats, but was quiet. I watched him put on his jacket. 'What do you think?' I pressed, trying to hide my frustration. 'Both flats are close to the river and to your work.' Olly worked in the music department of a school in Chiswick.

'We could have an extra half-hour in bed,' was my last attempt to get something positive out of him.

'We'll talk about it later.'

'Is everything all right?'

'Fine. Listen, got to run.' He grabbed his motorbike helmet off the sofa. Detecting my disappointment, he came back to me, pressed his forehead against mine. 'I'm tired. Hungover. Entirely self-inflicted,' he added.

I stroked the back of his neck. 'You want to move, don't you?'

'More than anything.' He brushed a greasy crumb from one corner of my mouth, kissed me. 'I'm so proud of you.'

I wipe my eyes with the sleeve of my jacket.

'I've been looking for you,' says Kitty.

'He was keeping something from me.'

Olly had left a message later that morning, when I was in a meeting. 'Look, we need to talk,' he'd said.

'Becca, don't,' she says, leaning against the wall with me.

'Don't what?'

'Go over it again and again. It's not helping anyone, least of all you.'

'But he said we needed to talk.'

'That doesn't mean he was hiding anything.'

'He was distracted, something was worrying him.' I bite my nail.

'Becca, not today, not now.' She rests an arm on my shoulder. 'Come inside. Your father wants to say a few words.'

'Maybe I should talk to Carolyn, see if he'd spoken to her?'

'No! Stop doing this to yourself. Let it go,' she begs.

'I can't!'

She shakes me by the shoulders, looks me in the eye. 'Olly loved you so much, he'd *never* keep anything from you, you know that.'

Tears come to my eyes. 'Do I? I don't know anything any more.'

'It happened quickly,' I hear the policeman trying to reassure me. 'He wouldn't have been in any pain.'

I want to scream. I want to die.

Kitty's arms are around me. I hold on to her. 'I can't live without him, I can't,' I cry. 'Oh Kitty, what am I going to do?'

'Shh. I'm here. I'm here. We're going to get through this, Becca, I promise you. We'll get through it together.'

2

'Right, that's it, we're ready for tomorrow.' I look around the gallery. Paul Lamont's abstract paintings of London landscapes are mounted on the walls, their prices printed out on fresh white cards just waiting to have that red sold sticker in the corner.

I watch as Glitz loosens his tie, slips off his shoes and stretches his legs under the desk. Exhausted, I sit down opposite him. Glitz is handsome, in an unconventional way. He has silvery-grey hair, a long face, large nose and sharp blue eyes that could spot a needle in a haystack. If he didn't work in modern art, he'd make an excellent detective. I can see him in a stylish trench coat with a pair of binoculars.

'You've done an excellent job, Rebecca,' he says. 'The frames work well.'

'You've got a hole in your sock.' I smile at his big toe poking out.

He peers at his feet. 'So I have.'

I play with my pen. 'I didn't have you down for a hole-in-the-sock kind of man.'

He pauses, thinks before he says, 'Life is full of surprises.' He then looks at me for a moment too long, and I turn away, knowing he's going to ask me that dreaded question.

'How are you?'

'I'm fine.' Is it me or is it hot in here?

'Scout's honour fine, or are you crossing your fingers under the desk?'

I show him my hands, fingers uncrossed. After Olly's funeral, six weeks ago, Glitz had suggested I take some time off work, but the thought of being alone in our flat all day was unbearable. I still haven't fixed the shower-curtain rail. 'You see, fine,' I pretend.

'In that case, how about a drink?' Over the past three years Glitz and I have become good friends and occasionally we go to a bar or have something to eat after work.

'Oh my God,' I gasp, reading the scribbled message I had forgotten to give him earlier today. 'Marty called! You have a party tonight. Tom. . .' I try to decipher my writing. 'Tom Bailey?'

'Bugger.'

Marty is Glitz's American wife. She's plump and lovely and wears pale-yellow jumpers with gold jewellery. She'd called me earlier, saying, 'Is His Majesty in a good mood?' When I replied yes, she promptly told me about the drinks tonight, stressing that he couldn't wriggle out of it.

Yet he remains firmly in his seat. 'I can't hear a word at these parties.'

'Well, maybe it's time you invested in a hearing aid.'

'Oh, not you too. I don't need another wife.'

'My father has one, Glitz.' I don't add that he never wears it.

'What?' Glitz smiles wryly. He watches me gather my jacket from the back of my chair. I lose my balance for a second.

'Call Marty right now and tell her I've been mugged.'

'No. You call her and tell her you've been mugged.'

'Can't. The bastards took my phone.'

I laugh.

'I'll give you that Lamont painting you love,' he bargains.

'Ah, now that's more interesting.' I sit down again, feeling dizzy.

'Rebecca? Are you sure you're all right?'

'No.' I rub my eyes. 'I think I need to get home, lie down.'

'I'll call a cab.'

I stand up, lose my balance, grab on to the corner of the desk.

'Rebecca!'

I see black dots swimming before me, like tadpoles.

'Sit down, now!'

'I feel weird, Glitz, faint.'

He rushes to my side, places a hand against my forehead. I'm sweating. Next thing I know, he thrusts my head between my knees.

I groan, feeling sick.

'Not working?' He's now grabbing me under the arms and dragging me down on to the floor.

'What are you doing?' I protest as I crash to the ground.

'Recovery position. Legs in the air!'

Once my legs are stuck in the air Glitz jumps up, saying he'll fetch me some water. 'I feel awful,' I murmur, my vision blurred.

'Hold on,' he urges.

I don't remember him coming back.

*

I'm in hospital. A young dark-haired doctor who looks half my age is taking my blood pressure, a yellow floral-patterned curtain drawn round us for privacy.

Glitz sits awkwardly on a plastic chair by the side of my bed, next to a blue paper-towel dispenser. In the cab on the way to hospital, he told me I had been unconscious for at least a minute and that I needed to see a doctor immediately. I felt he was being a drama queen, but he wouldn't take no for an answer, even when I was feeling more or less back to normal. 'I promised Marty I'd look after you. She told me you shouldn't be working so soon.'

I'd raised an eyebrow. 'This isn't just a ploy to get out of your drinks thing?'

'It's a small ray of light.'

'Blood pressure normal,' the doctor mutters, writing on a piece of paper attached to a grey clipboard.

'So I can go home?'

She nods. 'We've done all the tests we need to do.'

'Great. Thank you.'

'You and the baby are fine.'

'Wonderful. That's great. Sorry, the *what*?'

Glitz knocks his shoulder against the towel dispenser.

'The baby, it's fine,' she repeats, looking curiously at Glitz cursing and muttering in the corner.

I stare at her. 'I'm pregnant?' She doesn't know about Olly. This can't be happening. She doesn't understand! I can't be having a baby.

She nods.

'Sorry, there must be a mistake.' This is a joke, surely.

The doctor shakes her head.

She waits for a sane reaction from Glitz, but he's as stiff as a piece of cardboard.

'Congratulations, er, both of you,' she says.

3

Three weeks later, and Kitty and I are loading cases and boxes into the hired removal van.

The doctor guessed I was nine weeks pregnant. 'You need to leave London, Rebecca,' Glitz had said in my kitchen that night. He'd gestured to the mess in the house, the piles of letters unopened, last night's supper left on the kitchen table . . .

He was right. It was too painful living here, Olly's shadow following me around, and now I had an unborn baby to think about too, but where was I going to go? 'This can't be happening,' I kept on saying.

'It is happening, Rebecca. You need your family. Take all the time you want.'

I shook my head. 'Right now, all I need is a cup of tea.'

He whipped a plug out of its socket, turned round

and stared at me. I'd ironed my dress that morning before I left for work, but I was sure I'd turned it off, hadn't I?

We drive past the Dairy Crest building on the A316. 'Look at the little cows on the roof,' I remember Olly once pointing out.

I can't look at them today. I glance at Kitty, sitting grimly behind the steering wheel, her fiery auburn hair tied back into a ponytail. When we first met outside the school gates I was drawn to her amber-coloured eyes. I'd never seen eyes like hers before. Like me, Kitty grew up in Winchester, though her parents moved to Kent many years ago, to be closer to her brother and their grandchildren.

I stare out of the window, knowing how much I will miss her.

'I'll miss you,' Kitty says, as if she can read my mind. 'Who can I call after another disastrous date?'

'You can still call me.'

'It's not the same. Oh bollocks, I don't want you to go.'

'Nor do I,' I respond, thinking how much I'd taken for granted those nights when the two of us would meet after work, see a film, grab something to eat and laugh about something funny that had happened during our day. On Friday nights, Olly, a couple of his friends, Kitty and I would go out clubbing, followed by lazy breakfasts on a Saturday morning. Often at weekends I'd persuade Olly to come to an art exhibition, and he'd take me to a music gig in the evening. Sunday mornings would be spent fooling around in bed, before dragging ourselves out for a long walk, followed by meeting friends in the pub for lunch. Olly loved Sunday roasts.

Life was simple back then.

'If it gets too much, Becca, I'll buy a blow-up mattress and you can move in with me. Deal?'

'Deal.'

I'm going to miss all my friends, especially Kitty and my old university housemates, Sylvie and Jamie. Sylvie works in a creative marketing company and is currently playing with fire, dating her boss. Jamie runs his own video filming business, recording christenings and weddings. He's a warm person; when I see him the sun comes out.

Sylvie, Jamie and Kitty helped me clear out the flat. I had been dreading touching Olly's things. The paperwork strewn over his desk, his unfinished script, the framed photograph of the two of us on a beach in Cornwall . . . it was exactly how he'd left it.

Kitty was in charge. She works for a careers and education consultant in Piccadilly, specializing in difficult teenagers, but her true gift is her organizational skills. Olly and I used to laugh at the way she'd behave in a supermarket. Before we had even arrived she'd be visualizing the layout of each aisle. 'I'll do eggs, bread, milk; you do fruit, vegetables, cheese . . .'

'I almost expect her to wear a stopwatch and blow a whistle too,' Olly said.

In our flat, she made firm decisions, but at the same time was sensitive and didn't rush me, especially when it came to going through Olly's side of the wardrobe.

Each time I'd open a drawer or cupboard, I'd be haunted by a memory. Everything I touched had a story behind it. I could see the joy in Olly's eyes when I'd given him his vintage record player last year. We'd seen it at an antiques fair in Brighton, and when Olly's back was turned I'd taken the dealer's business card. Olly used to play records while he was writing. Bob Dylan's 'Make You Feel My Love' was one of our favourites. He'd played it on the piano at our wedding. His old and faithful tennis shoes reminded me of our holiday in Spain. Our villa had had two tennis courts right outside our apartment, but Olly had forgotten to pack his trainers so, determined to show off our (non-existent) tennis skills to the other residents, we went on a mission to find a local sports shop and bought them.

Shaving foam in the bathroom made me remember teasing him: 'Isn't it time you joined the twenty-first century?'

His desk, by the window, reminded me of coming home late from work to find him writing, the dirty breakfast bowls and mugs still on the kitchen counter.

If I was in a bad mood I'd throw them loudly into the sink before saying, 'When are you going to finish this book?'

If in a good mood I'd kiss his cheek, and try to persuade him to let me read a little. He'd promise I could when it was done, and I'd bite my tongue to stop myself from asking when that would be.

In the bottom drawer of his desk, I was shocked to see a couple of passport photographs of him and Joe pulling faces in the booth. There was also an old picture of the three of us at Kitty's New Year's Eve party ten or so years ago. I was in the middle, my arms around them both. Had Olly kept the photographs in the hopes that one day he and Joe might become friends again?

Later that night, Kitty, Sylvie, Jamie and I had discussed what to do with his piano, but by then I wasn't thinking straight any more. I'd stored up my tears throughout the day, been brave enough to hide them, but now that the packing was over and the flat looked so empty, it was all too real.

Finally we made the decision to donate it to a local community centre. I knew Olly would have liked that.

I wonder what he would make of me doing this. He used to say he could only manage Christmas with his own family if he took home a bottle of whisky and spent most of his time in his bedroom, drunk.

The last time I saw his parents was at the funeral. I remember Victor's quietness, how slowly he had walked out of the church. I recall hugging Carolyn the morning before they returned to Northumberland. It was as if we were both holding on to a part of Olly, neither one of us wanting to let go. When I'd called to let her know I was pregnant, she was so quiet that I thought the line had gone dead. 'You and Olly,' she said at last, 'are going to have a child?'

It felt as if we'd both been given a lifeline, a branch to hold on to in the storm. 'I can hardly believe it myself, Carolyn, but it's true. We're having a baby.'

A road sign welcomes us to Hampshire. I haven't lived at home since I was eighteen. How am I going to manage living under the same roof as Mum and Dad? What the hell *am* I going to do with myself?

I can't live in our old flat, but I don't want to be shipped home. I must be deranged! We need to turn round. It's my parents' home, their territory, I don't belong there anymore . . .

'Stop.'

'What?'

'Pull over.'

'I can't!'

'Pull over!' I screech now, when I see a sign for the service station.

Kitty steers the van off the motorway, swings into the car park and drives into the nearest parking space. I unbuckle my seat belt and wind down the window, feeling sick that I am letting my old life slip away.

I am sick.

'Heavy night last night, was it, girls?' says a man sauntering by.

We're parked in front of an uninspiring patch of grass. It's drizzling and we're watching, in silence, a man out with his bulldog, smoking. When the dog cocks his sturdy leg against one corner of the litter bin, the man stubs his cigarette butt into the grass and moves on. 'How are you feeling now?' Kitty asks, handing me another bottle of water.

I stare ahead. 'I'm pregnant, Kitty, homeless, no Olly. How am I going to manage?'

She looks away. She has no answers.

'I'm up shit creek.' It was one of Olly's favourite phrases.

At last she turns to me, smiles helplessly. 'Put it this way, things can only get better.'

And for the first time in many weeks, we laugh.

Kitty follows the exit sign to Winchester. My parents moved to St Cross when I was one and Mum was pregnant with Pippa, who lives twenty minutes down the road from Mum and Dad with her husband and their twins. St Cross is on the edge of Winchester, near the famous water meadows where Keats walked and created 'Ode to Autumn'. Jane Austen is buried in Winchester Cathedral. The city is steeped in history.

Kitty and I went to the same school in St Cross. We reminisce about walking the headmistress's pug, Bertie, through the meadows after school with Annie, one of our old school friends. We laugh, remembering how the three of us had all fancied fair-haired and blue-eyed Nick Parker. He had played Robin Hood in our school play and I was jealous because Annie played Maid Marian and got to kiss him. I played Friar Tuck.

Kitty was our director, bossing us about from the back of the stage.

As we turn into my parents' driveway, the nerves kick in again.

'Just remember, it's not forever,' Kitty says.

Mum appears from the back gate, somehow looking chic in beige gardening trousers, a summer blouse and soil-stained gloves, her dark blonde hair swept back in a navy spotted scarf. Audrey, their miniature wire-haired dachshund, barks ferociously until she realizes I'm not an intruder. 'Hello, Audrey Hepburn,' I smile, stroking her when she jumps up against my legs.

'Come in, come in.' Mum calls Dad. 'We'll unload later. I've put you in your old bedroom, Rebecca. Is that all right?'

I nod.

'And Kitty can sleep in Pippa's. Well done you. How was your journey?' She hugs me, pulling away as she doesn't want to get mud on my clothes.

Kitty tells her it was fine, the M3 was deserted. On the hall table is an answer machine, the red button flashing. 'Darling, can you see who called?' Mum asks when Dad appears from the sitting room.

Dad, fine grey wispy hair and dressed in linen trousers with a daring pink cardigan, gives me a warm hug before going to the telephone, muttering that he never hears it these days.

'Because you won't wear your aid!' Mum calls, making me think of Glitz.

'You have one new message,' the machine tells us, as Kitty and I follow Mum towards the kitchen, Mum bemoaning that my father is a stubborn old mule.

'Hi, Mum, it's me,' a voice says.

It's Pippa.

'Got your message. *Of course* I'll come over later. I'm not surprised you're nervous. It's a *huge* deal having her to stay.'

I freeze.

Mum turns, looks at the machine as if willing Pippa to leave it at that.

But Pippa continues. 'I'm dreading it too, but I'll be here to help you and Dad. We'll get through this together. See you later. Love you.'

'Well now!' Mum whips off her gardening gloves, her skin flushed. 'How about a nice cup of tea?'

I have barely strung two words together over supper. The salmon tastes heavy in my mouth. I can't stop thinking about that message. Pippa and me, we're not close. I didn't get to know my sister growing up because she played competitive tennis from the age of ten. At weekends and throughout the summer holidays, she and Mum travelled all across the country to take part in tournaments.

'I'm only thin because I'm always rushing around,' Pippa tells Kitty. 'Oscar and Theo are hard work!'

Does Dad feel the same? Is he dreading having me to stay?

'Love you,' she had said at the end of the message, as casually as saying 'bye'. I can't remember the last time I said, 'I love you' to Mum. I used to say it as a child, especially when given second helpings of Angel Delight, but at some point I stopped. Why? Olly used to say it was simple. Mum invested more time in Pippa and we grew apart.

'More wine?' my father asks Kitty.

'It's delicious.'

'Chilean.'

'Don't feed her at the table, Rebecca.' Mum shoos Audrey back towards her basket.

Pippa places a hand over the rim of her glass. 'Thinking of wine, I tell you who's back in Winchester, Becca. Joe Lawson.'

I drop my knife. 'Who?'

'Joe Lawson.'

'Sorry, what about him?' I play with my napkin ring. It's the same ring that I used to have as a child, engraved with my initials.

'He's opened this new wine bar in The Square – well, it's not quite so new any more.'

My napkin ring is now spinning across the table.

'Todd took some clients there the other day and was really impressed.'

Kitty catches the ring before it falls on to the floor.

'Who's Joe Lawson?' Mum asks, clearing away my barely touched plate of food. I see her twenty years ago, towering above me as she said, 'You will eat your peas, Rebecca, or no ice cream!'

Dad asks if anyone would like coffee.

'You shouldn't drink caffeine from midday onwards,' Pippa points out, and for a second she looks just like Mum, except without the sprinkling of grey in her blonde hair.

'Pah!' he mutters. 'Wasn't Joe one of your old university friends, Rebecca?'

'Um.' I bite my fingernail.

'Apparently you can hire out the cellar at this Maison Joe place,' Pippa enthuses. 'Todd thinks we should have our wedding anniversary party there.'

A silence descends across the table.

'Excuse me.' I scrape back my chair and leave the room.

'Clever,' I hear Kitty say to Pippa, her tone barbed.

Kitty sits at the end of my bed in her stripy pyjamas. 'You never told Olly about Joe, did you?'

I shake my head, an uneasy feeling settling in my stomach.

'Are you going to see him?'

'I don't know. I think I should.' I'm not sure why we're whispering, since Mum and Dad aren't even on the same floor. Their room is on the floor below. 'I wonder why he's back.'

'Didn't his family live here or something?'

'Yes, but he didn't get on with his father at all.'

'You'll have to tell him about Olly,' she says.

Guilt overwhelms me. She's right. The one and only clear thought I had at the funeral was that Joe should be here, among his friends.

Kitty hugs her knees to her chest. 'All that stuff that happened. It was a long time ago.'

'Right.' I nod vaguely.

'Try not to worry, Becca.' She gets up, saying it's bedtime, but before she leaves the room she asks, 'How do you feel about tomorrow?'

'Tomorrow?'

'Your scan.'

'This baby doesn't feel real,' I confide, ashamed I'd forgotten. Nothing feels real any more. I still want to believe I'm going to wake up and see Olly lying next to me. I'll feel his arms wrapped around my waist, he'll kiss me, laugh and say I was sleep-talking throughout the night, that I must have had a terrible dream.

I toss and turn, nearly crash my head against the wall and fall out of my single bed.

Of all the people who could be here, back in Winchester, why does it have to be Joe? How am I going to tell him? Oh God, Olly, I'm so angry with you! How can I tell Joe? You were the one who always knew the right thing to say. Tears stream down my face. I'm so sad. I miss you. God, I miss you.

'I'll be home by six thirty,' he'd said in his last message to me. 'I'll pick up some wine. Look, we need to talk.' Did we need to talk about the flats I'd shown him, or was something else preying on his mind? I know I promised Kitty I'd let it go, but the more I think about the tone of his voice, the more I am convinced it wasn't straightforward.

I take a deep breath.

Maybe I should just avoid Maison Joe altogether for the next six months? I can't drink wine at the moment, so I have the perfect excuse not to go. Joe wouldn't know. It's the middle of June now. I could just hide undercover until I have the baby at Christmas?

I get out of bed and walk to the bathroom at the end of the corridor, splash my face with cold water.

Joe Lawson. I haven't seen him for over ten years.

It's hopeless. How am I ever going to get any sleep?

4

Bristol University, Eleven Years Ago

I drop my library books on to my bed and kick off my shoes. I hear music coming from downstairs. Sounds like Oasis. Who's in the shower? I glance at the alarm clock on my bedside table. It's four o'clock in the afternoon. I bet it's Jamie, the lazy bastard.

I lie down, tired after last night. Olly and I went out; had something to eat and ended up dancing till three in the morning at the Lizard Lounge.

We've been going out now for nearly nine months. I think back to that day when I sat next to him in class. I was in my miniskirt and cowboy boots, hair washed and glossy. It was winter, the beginning of our second term at Bristol.

'I heard you play last night,' I'd said, out of breath

from the exertion of flying into the seat beside him. I composed myself as I continued, 'You remind me of the Rolling Stones, only you're better.'

'Rebecca, is there a problem you'd like to share?' our tutor, Mr Simpson, asked.

'No, sorry,' I muttered, wanting the ground to swallow me up.

But then I noticed him glancing at my legs. Clearly I'd made the right choice with my miniskirt, even if I was freezing my arse off. He raised an eyebrow, before scribbling something down on a piece of paper. He slid the message towards me. 'Aren't you cold? PS Fancy a drink tonight?'

My heart did a somersault. I was going to put that piece of a paper in a frame and keep it, forever.

During our first date Olly told me he wanted to be a journalist, pop star, jazz or classical pianist or maybe a novelist, or maybe a mixture of the whole lot, he'd laughed. I told him I had no idea what I wanted to do with my degree. I was hoping I'd work it out as I went along.

I rub my blistered feet together, sore from dancing last night, thinking about how Olly had walked me back to my halls after our evening. I felt comfortable with him, as if we'd known one another for years. We talked about being away from home for the first time. I told him I was happy, that I enjoyed being free and independent. I'd never felt I belonged in my family, explaining that my mother and sister, Pippa, were both sporty, whereas I was the artistic one. I described how Mum had given me a Slazenger racket for my birthday when I was about eight, hoping I was destined for the giddy heights of Wimbledon.

'She booked me a lesson with the club coach, Kenny. You should have seen me, Olly. I ran *away* from the ball, not towards it.'

He smiled, before saying, 'My father's a bug man.'

'A what?'

'A bug man. Entomologist. It's fine, you can laugh.'

'Sorry, I didn't know what you meant.'

'Shame on you! My dad studies bugs for a living. Didn't you know that there are 1.3 million described species, and that insects account for more than two-thirds of all known organisms . . .'

'I didn't, sorry.' I slapped my thigh. 'What have I been *doing* all my life?'

'And they date back some four hundred million years.'

'Wow.'

Olly looked at me. 'He's an academic, my dad, no good at small talk, lives in his own little bubble. He's not interested in my music, what I'm doing at Bristol, nothing excites him except the habitat of weevils. In fact,' he said, as if he was just realizing this reality, 'he doesn't have a fucking clue who I am!'

Olly laughed, but I could see he felt it deeply, and that was the moment when I knew something would happen between us. 'I've had a great time,' he said towards the end of our date, his face close to mine. 'Why haven't we done this before?'

'What have *you* been doing all your life?' I said, making him laugh.

We kissed that night, outside halls. It was a kiss that promised more, and before I went to bed I called Kitty, saying I'd met the man of my dreams.

Olly and I decided we wanted to live together in our second year, so together with three other housemates, Sylvie, Jamie and Dan, we found a terraced house in Victoria Square, Clifton, with tall ceilings, cheap chandeliers, threadbare carpets and one very damp bathroom. When it came to bedrooms, the five of us drew names out of a hat. Sylvie bagged the biggest. She's reading business studies. She's the punk-rock type: tie-dye T-shirts, tight jeans, uses henna on her long hair, wears thick black eyeliner and heavy black boots. Inspired, I dyed my hair black, but washed it out again when Olly asked me what I'd done to myself. My hair is a rich chestnut, long and thick, with a natural wave. 'It was the first thing I noticed about you, Becca. Well, that and your legs.' I chose the bedroom with the view overlooking a leafy park. Jamie is across the corridor; he's reading history. Dan no longer lives here. He scarpered last week, without giving us any rent, so we're now looking to find a replacement.

Someone's having a long shower, I think, getting up to investigate. Just as I'm about to knock to tell whoever it is to get a move on, the door opens and a tall man with dark wet hair appears, naked chest and a pink fluffy towel wrapped round his lean waist. 'Hello,' he says, a hint of a smile behind his grey eyes. 'I'm Joe. Joe Lawson. How do you do? Olly gave me keys.'

How do you do? Who are you? 'You're wearing my towel,' I point out, trying not to gawp at his naked chest.

'Oh, I'm sorry.' He takes it off and hands it to me. 'I haven't unpacked yet.'

Open-mouthed and holding my towel in one hand, I watch him walk away. Great body, I think to myself, before getting a grip and calling out, 'Sorry, who the hell *are* you?'

*

'Olly, you could have warned us,' I say, when we're having a house meeting in the local pub that night.

He crosses his arms. 'Oh, come on, Becca, what's the big deal?'

'The big deal is *we* –' I gesture to Sylvie and Jamie – 'don't know him! Maybe you should have stopped to ask us first?'

'We needed to find someone urgently,' Olly defends himself.

'I know that, but I think we should all have a say.' I wait for Sylvie to support me, but uncharacteristically she doesn't utter a word.

'Joe wasn't happy in his digs,' Olly continues, 'so I thought I was doing us *all* a favour by asking him.'

'Listen,' Jamie steps in, 'I was talking to Joe earlier, Becca, and he seems OK.'

'Did you know, he took my towel?'

'No! Shocking! He seems fine to me too,' Sylvie adds, before heading to the bar saying we could all do with another drink. 'Besides, he's *hot*,' she calls over her shoulder.

'Exactly. Sylvie's not complaining,' Olly reasons. 'Are you happy, Jamie?'

'It's too late to ask him now!' This argument has

nothing to do with Joe any more. It's more that Olly can't see why I get angry sometimes.

'He'll be a great babe magnet,' Jamie reflects, trying to lighten the atmosphere. Jamie wears spectacles and has a face as round as a snooker ball and a belly like a bouncy castle. Thin would not suit him. He has hundreds of friends, but the girls see him as a cuddly toy, not a Joe Lawson.

Olly agrees. 'He used to play rugby, played for his county or something.'

'You can tell he works out.' Sylvie smiles, returning with the drinks. I grab my beer, ruffled that the others are so easily taken in. 'Come on, Becca, we do need the rent, and I'm sure it won't be that difficult to get to know him,' Sylvie argues, reaching into the back of her jeans pocket to find a crumpled pack of Marlboro lights.

'All you want to do is jump into bed with him, so that'll be fun. Lots of atmosphere in the house.'

'You and Olly are together –' she shrugs – 'and I don't complain.'

Damn it! She has a point. I sit back, can see I'm getting nowhere. Besides, he's already moved in, so short of hurling his suitcase out of the window and changing the locks, there's nothing I can do. Besides, maybe I should give him a chance.

Alone, Olly and I walk home through the square.

'He was starkers, Ol.'

'Just drop the towel, Becca.'

I laugh. 'Joe did that. You should have seen his muscles.'

Olly flexes his arms. 'I have muscles.'

I squint. 'You hide them well.' I walk on ahead of him. 'You'd better watch out, Olly, you've got competition!'

He catches me up, grabs my arm and swings me round to face him. 'Becca, you're right. I should have asked first.'

'Oh, listen, I overreacted too,' I concede. 'I know I get het up about stuff.'

'Do you?' He laughs, pulling me towards him. 'How can I make it up to you?'

'Ah,' I ponder, 'let me think. I'd like a foot massage, crème brûlée in bed . . .'

'How about you and me get an early night.'

We kiss. 'That sounds good. I need to catch up on some sleep.'

Olly raises an eyebrow. 'Who said anything about sleep?'

'What's Joe reading again?' I ask, as Olly unlocks the front door.

'Medicine,' Joe answers for him, dressed in jeans and a white shirt. 'Sorry, overheard.' He clears his throat. 'The room's great. Thanks for letting me stay here, Olly.'

'Not a problem. It's cool.'

'Rebecca?' Joe leans one hand against the front door. There's something so arrogant about this man I want to slap him.

I take off my jacket. 'Yes?'

'You're happy I'm here?'

I give him one of my best smiles. 'Sure.'

'Great.'

'Off somewhere nice?' Olly asks, as if he's a concerned dad.

'Just out,' comes the elusive reply. 'Meeting a couple of friends. I'll see you tomorrow . . . unless both of you want to come?'

'No thanks,' I say, before noticing the hesitation in Olly's eyes.

*

'Where's Olly?' asks Sylvie when she enters the kitchen and finds me alone, wondering what happened to our early night and my foot massage.

'Out. With our new housemate.'

She seems surprised. 'You're OK now, about Joe moving in?'

'Yes, it's fine.' I stretch out my arms. 'Right, bedtime.'

'Becca? What's wrong?'

'Nothing.'

'Becca?'

'It's Olly.'

'What about him?'

'Have you noticed he does exactly what he wants, pretty much all the time?'

'Yes!' She laughs. 'Haven't you? I reckon it's because he's cute and funny and in a band, so he thinks he has some divine right or something, which he does.' She opens one of the cupboards above the sink, takes out a loaf of sliced white bread. 'Toast?'

I shake my head.

'Olly does things without thinking sometimes, that's all. Most blokes are like that – well, at least all the ones I've been out with. I'm sorry I didn't say anything earlier, you know, about Joe. If he'd been some spotty science geek or maths nerd with soup-bowl glasses—'

'You'd have backed me. He does have a great body,' I confide, smiling.

Sylvie pulls up chair. 'Exactly. It's not everyday an Adonis graces our lives. Dan was no oil painting, and he used to nick my crisps.'

I laugh, saying he used to pinch my Snicker bars too.

'Olly loves you, you know.'

'Maybe.'

'No maybes about it.'

'Thanks, Sylvie.' I kiss her goodnight and head upstairs, walking past Dan's old bedroom, the door shut. For a moment I am tempted to open it, just to see what his room's like. Why do I have a sneaking suspicion that Joe's arrival is about to change everything in this house?

5

The sun is shining. It's a lovely warm summer's day, but I miss Kitty already.

'The thing about London, Becca, is nothing changes,' she had promised, as we'd said our tearful goodbyes this morning. 'When you come back, I'll still be living in Earls Court and talking to dysfunctional teenagers about what they should do with their lives, when I have no idea myself what to do with mine. Jamie will still be going out with the awful Amanda and Sylvie will *still* be sleeping with her boss, or maybe not . . . In fact she's the only one who is slightly unpredictable, but you can be sure I'll *still* be going on bad dates.' Kitty had told me how her last date, Richard, Dickie for short, was severely lacking in the hair department, but the final straw was when he said his top film of *all* time was *Sister Act*.

'You'll be fine, just fine,' Kitty had said, hugging me.

'Thank you,' I held her close, 'a million times.'

Mum has booked my scan at the maternity unit of our local hospital at midday. I can't even begin to unpack yet. I stare at all my suitcases and boxes. It's so odd being back in my old bedroom. Opposite me, hanging on the wall, is a framed painting of St Catherine's Hill that I painted when I was eight. I picture my easel by the old dressing-up box, see myself in my red smocked top mixing acrylic paints. I touch my wardrobe and imagine my lime-green and red Flamenco dress still hanging in one corner. I kissed my first boyfriend, Javier, in that dress, at Kitty's tenth birthday party. Javier was Spanish and could only see out of one eye because he'd cycled into a thorn bush when he was little. Pippa said he didn't count as a boyfriend because he couldn't see me properly.

The room used to be papered in Laura Ashley. I chose pale-pink rosebuds with a matching border, but the walls are now painted a soft green and the single bed is decorated with an embroidered quilt. A few glossy country and garden magazines and a bottle of mineral water are on my bedside table. It feels like a guest room.

I find myself going next door, to Pippa's old room,

where Kitty slept last night. When Olly and I visited my parents for the odd weekend, we'd sleep in here because Pippa's room is big enough for a double bed. Pippa also had a sink, because her room was originally a kitchen. I was rather jealous of her sink. I could hear her brushing her teeth and hopping into bed. I, on the other hand, had to pad to the cold bathroom at the end of the corridor, where long-legged spiders congregated for a knees-up in the bath. I'd walk back along the corridor and catch a glimpse of Pippa's shiny tennis medals and trophies mounted on her bookshelf next to her bed, and posters of Andre Agassi adorning the wall. She did need more space, I reasoned. When I had once dared to complain that my room was smaller than hers and I was the eldest, Mum had argued that I had the view looking out into the garden (Pippa's was the busy main road), and I also had the magnificent view of St Catherine's Hill in the distance. I looked out at the view and decided it was special. Looking back, I believe this is what inspired me to paint landscapes. I didn't really mind about the space, just the sink.

I begin to unpack, but there is one box that remains untouched. Inside is a collection of things I put aside when packing up the flat, things I wanted to keep close to me. There's Olly's script, the book he had so nearly finished. 'All I have to do is write the synopsis, work out the pitch and who to send it to,' he'd said with excitement when I asked (in a good mood) how it was going.

I'm not ready to read it yet, but one day I will. I've kept his navy jumper that he always wore round the flat, the funeral service sheet with Simon's tribute typed out for me, a Schubert CD, a collection of photographs including one of my favourite wedding shots in an antique silver frame. We're dancing. I slide the box under my bed and place a framed picture of the two of us in Florence, on our honeymoon, on my bedside table.

When Mum and I enter the clinic I watch a couple leave, holding hands. I imagine them returning home and pinning the sonogram to the fridge. I can hear them discussing whether they should find out the sex next time.

'Oh, that's us!' say a couple seated next to us when a name is called. I glance at Mum. She's wearing a chic red spotted dress with a leather belt clasped together by two small golden owls. I swear she's owned that belt since I was born. A young man sits down opposite me, out of breath. I watch him take off his sunglasses. He tells his wife or partner that he's put a couple of hours into the parking meter.

Olly should be here.

I shut my eyes, see us on holiday, in Spain, two years ago. We're sunbathing on a sandy beach, watching children in stripy swimming costumes and shorts cling on to the hands of their fathers, enjoying the waves. I'm wearing a turquoise bikini; Olly's in tropical swimming trunks. Next to us are a father and son, sitting on a red-checked rug, with remnants of a picnic around them. The boy must be about four or five, with chubby cheeks and Icelandic-blond hair, just like his father's. While he's building a sandcastle, 'Daddy,' he asks, patting the sand into his bucket, 'how many waves are there in the sea?'

The father sits up, looks out to the ocean. 'There are infinite waves,' he replies, 'and there always will be, Freddie, long after we're gone.'

Olly and I gaze at the father, before turning to one another, and I can tell we're thinking the same thing. 'One day I'd love a family,' he says, putting his paperback down.

'Me too.' I take Olly's arm and rest it over my stomach.

'I'd love a boy,' he says.

'I'd love a girl.'

'Well, we'd better have two or three then.'

'Well,' I say, rolling over on to my front and handing

him the tube of sun cream, 'we'd better get started soon then.'

'Well,' Olly laughs as he unclips the back of my bikini and rubs cream across my back. 'What are we doing here?' he whispers into my ear. 'Why aren't we . . . you know . . . ?'

Soon we're grabbing our paperbacks and towels and running across the beach, back towards the villa.

I hear a name being called out. It's not mine.

I notice Mum fidgeting. I sense she wants to say something to me. 'Rebecca, about Pippa's message last night . . .'

'It's fine,' I say, reaching over to the table, picking up a tattered *Take a Break* magazine.

'The thing is . . .' Mum breathes deeply. 'It is going to be difficult, and your father and I, well we *are* nervous, we're getting old and–'

'Mum, it's fine, I understand. I'm grateful to you for having me at all.'

Mum's BlackBerry vibrates. Todd bought it for her. It's an urgent text message from Pippa, saying there has been a drama. The washing machine has flooded. Can Mum pick the children up from nursery?

'No mobile telephones,' says the stony-faced receptionist. Mum whispers that she needs to go outside to call Pippa, just to let her know she's here. 'Won't be a minute,' she reassures me.

I lie down on the examining bed, my bladder now so full I feel uncomfortable. 'You're on your own today?' the nurse says, introducing herself as Sandra. She looks about my age, with dark hair tied back into a practical ponytail and a neat waist held in by an elasticized belt.

'That's what's so wonderful about technology though,' she continues, gathering the ultrasound instruments together. 'You've got the picture, so you can show it to him later. Right,' she begins, smearing gel on to my tummy. 'Now, it's a little cold.'

If Olly were here I'd be telling him exactly how cold it is. Freezing. But he's not here.

'It's always nerve-racking,' Sandra says, sensing my fear. 'Exciting too, but it's natural to be anxious.'

I curl my hands into fists to fight the tears.

'Now if you look at the screen.' Sandra points to something tiny within a funnel shape. That can't be it. I can't even see what she's referring to. I close my eyes, can't hear what she's saying.

What if it's a girl? Olly wanted a boy. But if it's a boy he might look nothing like Olly. What if he doesn't look like him? I'll be searching for Olly all the time, trying to find the warmth in his brown eyes, the small mole I loved so much on his left cheek, the smile that could melt the hardest of hearts. I'd trade this baby to have our old life back. I'd give up the world to see him again. I know our marriage wasn't perfect, but it's only once someone has gone . . .

I look up to the ceiling and start to count the dots. This baby will remind me of the accident every single day. I might shout at my child, be angry with him for not being Olly. I might not be able to care for him. Love him. I won't be a good mum. How can I be?

I hear something exploding inside me. Somebody, stop it! Please stop it!

I place my hands over my ears.

See the coffin at the altar.

Hear the policeman telling me the news.

My baby – our baby – won't know his father. I hear shouting. A door swings open. Someone is gripping my hand, another person restraining my arms. Someone is rocking me in their arms, as if I am a child.

'OLLY!' I scream.

When I open my eyes I see Mum, trying hard not to cry. She lets go of me, though one hand remains firmly around mine. A doctor stands by my side, telling me to breathe, breathe in deeply, everything is fine. I realize then that all this noise is coming from me.

'Those are the legs,' Sandra says.

I'm looking at the screen as she points out the arms, the neck and the curve of the spine. I feel a strange sense of calm now. I can imagine Olly putting his glasses on, squinting at the monitor. I can hear him saying he can't see a thing, it's just a speck.

'Look, that's the heart.' Sandra points to the screen.

I have a little boy or girl with a heartbeat inside me, a part of Olly fighting to be wanted and loved. 'He's perfect,' I sigh.

'So you think it's a boy then?' Sandra asks with a sympathetic smile.

'I have a hunch, that's all.' I turn to Mum, tearful. 'I think you should start knitting something blue.'

6

It's early July, two weeks after my scan, and I'm eating breakfast with my parents in the kitchen. 'You will wear your glasses driving, won't you?' Mum is saying to Dad, dressed optimistically in her tennis gear.

'Oh, do stop nagging,' he replies, carrying on reading the sport's section of the newspaper. He's an avid Wimbledon fan and is looking over the order of play for this afternoon.

Dad is going to Brighton today, to see his porcelain dealer, Mr Pullen. In his retirement he's become passionate about nineteenth-century china. Mum has confided to me her delight that it keeps him busy and prevents him from asking what's for lunch every day. Last week, in front of me, he rehearsed a speech he was giving to the Senior Wives Fellowship. Apparently they all found it riveting, especially hearing about his early Minton with the pseudo-Sèvres marks and the ring handles he loves so much. The great drama, however, was when one of the old ladies fell off her chair during his presentation. An ambulance was called, but thankfully it was nothing serious. 'You must have overexcited her, Dad,' I had suggested, trying not to laugh. 'Sent her into a state of flux over one of your cups and saucers.'

After breakfast I load the dishwasher. Dad ticks me off for putting the wooden-handled knives in. 'It's fine,' Mum overrules him. 'They're so old.'

'I don't like the coffee mugs going in either.' He swipes one from me. 'The colour fades, you see!' He brandishes it in front of me. 'It damages them. And *please*, don't ever put the crystal glasses in.'

'OK, fine,' I murmur.

Finally, when Dad heads off with a tatty empty suitcase, his spirits high, saying he'll be back in good time for Federer's match, Mum and I load the mugs and knives back into the dishwasher, feeling like conspirators. 'But he's right about the glasses,' she says. 'They were a wedding present.' She then hands me a shopping list, saying it would be a great help if I could get the food for her supper party tonight, which I'm welcome to join. Since my scan, a barrier has lifted between Mum and me, but we still haven't talked about Olly. Mum and Dad ask how I am feeling, if I slept well, what am I up to that day, but none of us can bring ourselves to mention his name. I've also noticed how photographs of Olly and me have been removed or repositioned in the house. The wedding picture of us laughing as we cut the cake has been relegated from the mantelpiece to the window ledge, half covered by the curtains. Our engagement photograph, taken on the London Eye, has been covered over with a picture of the twins in a small dinghy with Todd.

'Becca?'

'Sorry?' I say, absent-mindedly.

Mum picks up her tennis racket and a tin of old balls. 'I'm off,' she says. 'Can you bring the washing in if it starts to rain?'

'Yep, sure.' Mum is still staring at me. 'See you later,' I say, refilling my cup of tea and sitting down at the table to read Dad's paper.

'Your mug,' she points out. 'It marks the wooden table.'

I breathe a sigh of relief when the front door shuts. At last, I'm on my own, no one ticking me off. My mobile rings and I consider letting it go to voicemail until I see it's from Glitz. 'Well, we haven't killed each other yet,' I tell him when he asks how it's going. 'What's it like working with Marty?'

'We're heading for divorce. She set the burglar alarm off. Mind you, I was impressed by how quickly the cops came.'

After a trip to Sainsbury's, spent largely hiding behind aisles to avoid bumping into my parents' friends, I walk towards Maison Joe, which is in The Square, close to the cathedral grounds. I've decided to see Joe today. Get it over with. He has a right to know about Olly.

I haven't seen him in over ten years. Why did he quit Bristol without telling Olly? 'Friends don't just disappear,' Olly had said to me, hurt. 'Something must have happened.'

Why is he back here? What will he look like? I picture his thick dark hair, those grey eyes that gripped you. Olly was laid-back and chatty; Joe spoke only when he felt like it, and could be cutting with just one glance. However, on the rare occasions that he did smile, his entire expression changed, his face lighting up the room.

The closer I get to The Square, the more apprehensive I feel. It was about five years ago when Joe called. I was twenty-six and working from home as a freelance illustrator. I'd run out to buy some milk, returned to see the red button on our answer machine flashing. It was an awkward message; he'd tracked us down, he said. He left various numbers to ring him back. He was working in London for some wine shop. That surprised me. I deleted the message. I didn't do it lightly. I thought about it all day, but in the end I was a coward. I feared Joe coming back into our lives; it would only remind me of our past. I felt guilty not telling Olly about the message, but we were in our second year of marriage and happy, so happy that selfishly I wanted nothing to threaten that.

As I approach the Buttercross I see a group of tourists in shorts and sundresses, taking photographs, a plump curly-haired guide saying, 'It was erected in the fifteenth century . . . as you can see it's set on a plinth of five octagonal steps . . .'

The closer I get to Maison Joe, the more I want to turn and run, but something is telling me to keep going.

A section of the high street outside Lloyds Bank is partitioned off. 'Cheer up, love! It might never happen!' one of the builders calls out to me, over the sound of drilling. He's wearing a luminous yellow top with a matching hard helmet. He winks.

'Maybe it has already happened,' says a voice inside my head, as clear as daylight. 'Maybe I have just fallen into a cesspit or discovered I'm sitting next to you on a twenty-four-hour flight, you twat.'

I stop dead. Olly was the only person I knew who used to say the word 'twat'.

Tentatively I turn the corner and walk past a young man with his mongrel dog camping outside a bakery. I move on.

'Talk to him, Becca. He hasn't got leprosy. The poor bloke's starving.'

People are pushing past me in a hurry. I'm imagining it. God, I'm an idiot.

On I go.

'You're not imagining it. Go and talk to him,' the familiar voice persists.

I hesitate; feel for my purse in my handbag. Nervously I look behind me . . .

The homeless man is sitting on a sleeping bag. His hair is greasy; face unshaven, shoelaces undone . . .

'He's all right, Becca, just needs a bath,' the voice goes on, 'a good old scrub.'

Olly would say that. I'm frightened now. I'm going mad. I stand, paralysed, getting in everyone's way.

It's not Olly. It can't be.

But I find myself turning round and walking back towards the man and his dog. Anxiously I peer at him.

Beneath the grime is a handsome man, with pale-blue eyes, who can't be much older than me.

'All right?' he says. 'Nice day.' He doesn't ask for any money.

I ask him what his dog is called. He looks up at me, warmth in his eyes. 'Noodle,' he smiles. 'Go on. He doesn't bite.'

I stroke Noodle. I don't know what to say next. 'Are you hungry?'

'Could murder a fillet steak.'

I look at him, longing to know how his life has brought him to sleeping on the streets. I tell him I'll be back.

'Here,' I say, handing him a couple of Cornish pasties that I bought from the bakery. 'Not quite a fillet steak, but I asked the girl to warm them up for you.' He takes them gratefully, gives Noodle a piece first. I put the change from my five-pound note into his plastic cup. 'He said you were an angel, a top girl.'

I must have misheard him. 'Sorry? Who said that?'

'How rude. I haven't introduced myself. I'm James.' He shakes my hand. 'But you can call me Jim,' he adds as if this is a big compliment. 'Don't look so scared. You've lost someone, haven't you?'

Jim's stare unnerves me. 'How do you know?' I stammer.

'Because he's sitting right next to me.'

'He wants to talk to you,' Jim says, when I return. I have spent the last five minutes walking up and down the high street, telling myself not to go back. I am the first to tell people ghosts don't exist. Nor do guardian angels. It would be comforting to think we have someone out there watching over us, but we don't; it's mumbo-jumbo. Yet, here I am, staying put.

'He's asking why you don't believe he's here?'

This is strange. Walk away, Becca. 'Because he died! He's dead.'

This minor point seems irrelevant. 'He's fine. Safe. He misses you.'

I burst into tears.

I crouch down next to Noodle, as Jim continues, 'He's saying something about a baby? That he's sorry and you need to look after yourself? Does that make sense?'

I bite my nail, my heart pounding in my chest. Jim can probably see I'm pregnant; nothing he's said is convincing enough. 'I'm off,' I say, not wanting to hear any more.

The man looks at me, grins.

'What's so funny?'

'Olly says you always bite your nails when you're nervous.'

'Bye.' I gather my shopping and walk away as quickly as I can, determined to walk away for good this time. This is mad, crazy. I'm not falling for it. But then I stop to catch my breath. How did he know Olly's name?

'He says go and buy a new dress or something,' Jim calls out. 'Your jeans are about to burst.'

I glance down. The button is about to explode.

'He told me you wouldn't believe me; you'd think it was all mumbo-jumbo.'

A small smile surfaces. Boldly I walk back to him. 'Don't mess with my head,' I beg.

'I'm not, I swear.'

'This is weird.'

'Welcome to my world,' Jim smiles. 'I didn't ask to hear these voices, never believed in any of this crap, and if you want to know the truth, I could do without it. But, hey, that's life.' He shrugs with resignation, as if life has dealt him a difficult hand. 'I've never been to this city before,' he continues. 'Noodle and I felt like a change of scene, didn't we, old boy?' He tucks into his second Cornish pasty. 'But now I know. You're the reason I'm here.'

'Will you tell him I love him,' I whisper. 'I miss him.'

'No can do,' he says, finishing off his mouthful.

'Why? Why not?'

'You need to do that yourself.'

In a state of semi-shock I stare down at my banana split. I look around the cafe in a daze. How did I end up here? I can't remember ordering a banana split. I don't even like bananas.

'Excuse me,' says the waitress as I head towards the door. 'You haven't paid.'

'Oh, right.' I head over to the counter and fish out some change with a trembling hand. 'Sorry. How much?'

'Four ninety-five.'

'Rip-off,' the voice says.

As I'm about to leave she calls over to me again. 'Your shopping?' She gestures to the supermarket bags by the table.

I need to go home, make sense of this morning. I definitely can't face Joe today.

I walk past the bakery shop. Jim, his sleeping bag and Noodle have gone. Disappeared.

Did I imagine them? Am I going crazy?

7

The following day I am taking Olly's advice and trying on a green maternity sundress. Then I shall see Joe.

Yesterday, after not eating my banana split, I'd rushed home, raced upstairs and sat down on my bed with my laptop. I googled the word 'medium' and glanced at the flood of information on psychics and people who could communicate and relay messages from the deceased to their living relatives. The information also warned me that there were a lot of fraudsters out there, so beware. I slammed the lid shut when Mum knocked on my door. 'Everything OK up here?' she asked.

'Fine, absolutely great,' I replied, incredulous that I'd almost believed Jim. Imagine if I'd told Mum about my mysterious encounter. They'd think I'd gone mad. I was beginning to think it too.

I look at myself in the mirror. I hesitate to ask him,

chew my lip, bite my nail. 'What do you think, Olly, of the dress?' I whisper.

'Great,' a voice says inside my head.

I lean one hand against the wall of the changing room to steady myself. 'The colour suits you,' he continues.

A shiver runs down my spine. I scan the cubicle, look under the chair. What am I expecting to find under the cushion? I draw the curtain open. The assistant stares at me. I pull the curtain shut again and breathe deeply.

'Can I help you?' she calls.

I clamp a hand over my mouth. She must have heard me talking.

'That dress is lovely,' he says. 'You're a knockout.'

In a frenzy I whip it off, and then slip it back on, unsure what to believe any more.

'How much is this?' I ask the shop owner. She has mad blonde frizzy hair; I'm certain she looks familiar.

'Rebecca?'

'Annie?'

We both laugh, as if to say we have recognized each other for the past five minutes but neither one has dared say anything just in case.

'Rebecca Harte!' She rushes over to me and we hug.

It's pretty Annie Stoner, one of my old school friends, who was a wizard at maths and also an incredible gymnast. She'd fly across the blue games mats in an impressive series of backflips and somersaults that made my eyes water. Annie left our school at thirteen, when her army father was posted abroad.

'Is this your place?' It's a stylish maternity clothes shop with stripped wooden floors and white-painted shelving housing tunic dresses and T-shirts of every colour. There's an island in the middle with a circular glass vase filled with pink lilies.

'Uh-huh. Opened a couple of years ago and on the verge of going bust.' She gestures to the deserted shop floor. 'Are you pregnant? Stupid question,' she adds, rolling her eyes at herself. 'How many months?'

'Just under four.'

'Your first?' She dives into the changing room and returns with a plump cushion. 'Try it on with this. Go on,' she enthuses when she clocks my hesitancy.

I lift up the dress, shove the cushion against my waist and turn to the side. It reminds me of being a twelve-year-old and stuffing socks down my bra. 'I can't believe I'm going to get this big,' I say, examining my profile.

'Oh yes, and if you're lucky you'll get all kinds of other treats like varicose veins too,' she laughs huskily.

'How many children do you have, Annie?'

'Two. Amy and Bella. Six and four. Started way too early! What the hell was I thinking!' She pulls a deranged face. 'Summer holidays soon. Heck!' She's hopping energetically from one foot to the other. 'And you? You haven't changed at all!'

'That can't be true,' the voice says. 'I've seen a few old school pics and you had two long plaits and were a porker.'

I find myself smiling for the first time.

'Becca?'

'Sorry?'

'Are you just down for the day?' she asks, bright blue eyes glowing.

'Er, long story.'

She waits, expecting it to be exciting, or at least hoping it might be.

A young dark-haired woman wearing leggings, flip-flops and a flowery top enters the shop carrying a cup of coffee.

'Listen, you have a customer,' I point out, relieved as I scurry back into the changing room, the cushion falling out of the dress on the way.

'Customer? Don't be daft. That's Lucy, she works here,' Annie calls.

'Oh, right!' I pull the curtain across and fight to get back into my jeans.

'Have you got time for a coffee or a quick lunch?' Annie asks me when I emerge red-faced from the cubicle, telling her I'll take the dress. 'There's this great wine bar in the square . . .'

'Maison Joe?'

'You know it?'

'I know Joe.'

'Lucky you,' Lucy says, impressed.

'Half of Winchester wants to marry him,' Annie confides. 'I just want to have a steamy affair with him.'

'Here we go again,' says the voice, disgruntled.

'How do you know him?'

'University – but we lost touch,' I add.

'Why? I mean, *why* would you do that?' Lucy asks, as if it's as stupid as throwing a winning lottery ticket away.

'Oh, you know how it is.'

'Lucy, it's as dead as a dodo in here, but if by some miracle it gets busy, call me and I'll shoot back,' Annie says, gathering her handbag. 'Shall we go?'

We walk through The Square, past my favourite old art shop and a couple of cafes, a new hairdresser's and a boutique clothes shop. From the distance I can see Maison Joe is a handsome building with a rich wine-coloured awning. Tables with stripy parasols line the pavement and many people are eating outside today.

Annie is saying something about how working in this part of Winchester is dangerous for her credit card. She thinks Cadogan is one of the best men and women's clothes shop; even her husband Richie doesn't mind shopping there. 'Becca?'

'Um?'

'It's a great location too, isn't it?' Ahead of us is the view of the cathedral grounds, with the avenue of lime trees framing the stone paved pathway. Bicycles are chained to the black railings. 'Lovely,' I say, watching students and tourists sunbathing on the grass. A man wearing a straw boater sells ice cream; schoolchildren pile out of the City Museum in a stream of noise, one boy laughing and bending down to stroke a spaniel walking by. The sight of an old couple sitting, hand in hand, on a bench with their packed lunch, touches me.

We enter the wine bar. It's a large open space, bigger than I'd imagined, set on two levels, with stairs leading down to a basement floor. I look around. Now that I'm here I don't feel quite as brave as I did this morning.

How can I tell Joe about Olly? I should have asked him to the funeral. I realize it was not only a mistake; it was unforgivable. I can excuse myself for not being in my right mind, for being numbed by grief, but deep down the truth is I was, I *am*, a coward. I thought about trying to get hold of him but did nothing. What will Joe think of me? What if he hates me? He has every right to.

But there's no sign of him. It's noisy and packed; the sound of clanging plates coming from the kitchen is accompanied by the whirring of the coffee machine in the background. I recognize the music playing. It's 'Volare' by the Gipsy Kings. Olly and I played this song in our holiday apartment in Spain, dancing, laughing and fooling around . . . Don't cry, Rebecca. *You owe this to Olly. You must tell Joe.*

'Relax. Take a deep breath,' the voice says, 'and then when you see the bastard, slap him.'

A young waiter rushes past me, moving in time with the music as he balances three plates of food. 'I'm starving,' Annie says. I don't feel as if I could eat a thing.

Annie introduces me to Edoardo, who's serving behind the bar. He has a mop of dark wavy hair that reminds me of a 1980s Top of the Pops singer and he tucks his shirt neatly into his snug-fitting trousers.

Prosecco is on tap, and behind the bar are wooden shelves lined with spirits and sweet wines. 'This man makes the best cocktails,' Annie informs me, sitting down on one of the leather stools, 'not that that's much use to you when you're pregnant. Where's Joe, Edoardo?'

'Downstairs, teaching,' he says in a strong Italian accent, talking as he serves a couple of customers. 'He has a lunch tasting session on wines from Alsace.'

'You should nip down, say hello,' Annie suggests.

'Maybe later.' I grab a menu and tap it against the bar.

Annie registers my agitation. 'Rebecca? What's going on? You're nervous, aren't you?'

'Not at all!' comes out a high-pitched squeak.

She swivels round on her stool, examines my face, my eyes. 'Rebecca Harte! It's something to do with Joe, isn't it? Why did you two really lose touch?'

I look away, pretending to examine the specials on the blackboard. 'Oh, it's complicated, Annie.'

'Was he an ex? I mean, if he's an ex . . .'

'He's not. He wasn't . . . I mean.'

'. . . oh my God, of *course* it's going to be weird for you seeing him again! I don't keep in touch with any of my old boyfriends. Ugh!'

'He wasn't an ex, nothing like that. We shared a house at university, that's all.'

'Yeah, but what happened next? You said it was complicated?'

When I catch Edoardo listening behind the bar, I ask her if we can sit down. Then I'll tell her the whole story. Or at least part of it anyway.

Annie and I find a table in the corner of the restaurant. We each order a slice of spinach-and-bacon tart with a green salad.

As I tell Annie about Olly and why I am living with my parents, she doesn't utter a word. I don't imagine she shuts up very often.

'Fuck,' she says finally, pushing her plate aside, her food only half eaten. 'I don't know what to say, Becca.' She leans towards me, takes my hand. 'How are you?'

'I'm lucky,' I reply, determined not to cry. 'My parents are being really supportive and my sister lives close by, and at least I will get to know her twins a little better and . . .'

'But how are *you*?' she asks again when she sees tears in my eyes.

I think of the scan, of Olly's voice, the events of yesterday. No one will believe me. 'Alone,' I say.

*

'We met at university,' I tell her. 'Later he qualified, became a music teacher and taught the piano. He was talented, had a real gift with children.' I have kept the letters Olly's pupils wrote to me. Barnaby, Olly's star pupil, who played the piano at his funeral, had drawn an elephant, and along the trunk he wrote, 'I will never furget Olly. He was very speshell'.

'Olly's real passion though was writing.'

'Did he get anything published?'

I picture Olly writing at his desk, music playing in the background. This was the script that was going to be his big break, he'd say. 'You'll be able to paint again, Becca, we can move out of our shoebox. I will make it,' he said, urging me to have faith in him.

'He was about to send . . .' I stop dead when I see Joe striding across the restaurant towards the bar. It's that same confident walk.

'Becca?' Annie says.

He glances across to our table, looks at me. I smile and for a second see a flicker of recognition in his eyes and am sure that he is about to come over, but then there's a blankness in his expression and he walks away. Annie swings round to see what I'm distracted by. 'Did he see you?' she asks.

*

I'm convinced he saw me, though Annie is saying she's sure he didn't, that he's busy running his class, and, 'Let's face it, Becca, you're the last person he's going to expect to see in here after ten years. He might not even recognize you.'

Yet Annie had recognized me. In the past ten years I haven't changed dramatically in looks. I'm still five foot seven, my chestnut-coloured hair is much the same, just shorter, falling a few inches below my shoulders. Skin is creamy, blue eyes the colour of denim, mouth is wide and teeth fairly straight thanks to the help of a cruel orthodontist, and I still have a dimple in my right cheek. I used to have two, but lost one. My father had said I was being greedy and that I had to share my dimples with other pretty girls.

I think he did see me, and he *ignored* me.

My telephone rings. 'Sorry, Annie, I'd better . . . it's my sister.'

Pippa asks if I can babysit tonight. Todd is flying in from New York early and wants to take her out to dinner.

When I hang up Annie asks me if I am OK. 'I mean, stupid question, but . . . are you worried about telling Joe about Olly?'

Yes. He blanked me. 'I've stuffed everything up,' I say, feeling my bottom lip wobble. I think about Joe, our friendship falling apart, the way I'd reacted towards him. I think of Bristol, how we were all so young, with bright futures ahead of us. I remember that late-night conversation after Kitty's New Year's Eve party, what we'd all be doing in ten years' time . . . 'Sometimes I'm so angry with him, Annie. I begged him to sell that bike. Why didn't I stop him?'

'Now listen here, it's not your fault.'

I press my head into my hands. 'I'm thirty-one and what do I have to show for it? I have nothing. Not a bean! I don't know why I'm here, what I'm doing, I'm . . .' I stop, unsure whether to continue, but then something inside me snaps. 'I feel useless not working and I'm terrified of having this baby by myself and I'm angry, *furious* with him for putting me in this position – Why did he gamble with his life? Why was he so distracted that day? – and I miss him, oh God I miss him, it's so . . .'

'Fucking unfair?'

'Fucking unfair,' I say, relief flooding my voice.

'You probably think I have the perfect life too,' Annie says, after we have discussed how some people seem to breeze through with no hiccups. 'Like my sister,' I'd claimed, trying not to sound too jealous, but the truth is, I am, just a little. I think I always have been, but have bottled it up since childhood.

Annie continues. 'You must think I'm one of life's natural breezers. So beautiful and talented . . .'

'Well, you are.' I remind her how lucky she was to be Maid Marian in our school play because she was the one that got to kiss Nick Parker, who played Robin Hood.

'Well, think again. I'll talk you through my life. Are you ready?' Annie leans both elbows against the table as if she means business. 'For starters, I'm married to a dentist . . .'

I don't know why, but I find this funny. 'Ouch!'

'Exactly. In bed he's asking me if I flossed after brushing my teeth – that's about as exciting as it gets between the sheets. And after Richie's played football on a Monday night you can probably smell his stinky socks from Australia.'

I smile, somehow not believing Annie is unhappy with Richie, but wanting her to continue nonetheless.

'My beautiful shop is about to go down the credit-crunch plughole, I feel guilty about not spending enough time with my kids, for being a working mum, so I probably do a bad job at both! Half the time I want to run off, screaming, into the sunset and never come back.'

'Not bad, Annie, but you still can't *quite* compete with me.'

'Rarely do I have a minute to myself to even brush my hair, and speaking of hair, mine must be the most difficult in the whole bloody world,' she says, gesturing to her frizzy blonde curls, which do have a life of their own.

Both of us laugh. 'You still can't compete,' I tell her, my eyes watering.

'I had a pretty fine stab at it though, didn't I?' She offers me a handkerchief. 'Look, it's going to be all right, Becca,' I hear her saying. 'You will get through this, you will . . . it is awful, but you do have something. You have a child. You have Olly's child.'

Edoardo and a couple of the waitresses are clearing up the tables, the restaurant quiet after the busy rush of lunch. Annie had to leave, but we promised to keep in touch. I flick through a wine brochure, glance at a photograph of Joe on the introductory page. 'He's left, Becca,' Olly had said, after he'd visited me in Florence for three weeks before returning to Bristol for his finals. I had left university to study art in Italy for a year. 'I knew he was unhappy, that he was dreading studying next year after we'd all buggered off, but I didn't think he'd leave the country without telling me!' I could hear the hurt in his voice. 'I don't have his parents' number, do you? I don't think his mother's been well, but he's not answering any of my messages. Has he called you?'

'No,' I said, unsettled. 'I haven't spoken to him for months.'

I look at the photograph again and can see how Joe has filled out in the last ten years. His cheekbones aren't as pronounced, and he has flecks of grey that stand out in his dark hair, but it's those slate-grey eyes that I recognize. I read, 'After an Introductory Wine Tasting course at Maison Joe, I guarantee you will be able to dazzle your friends with all your knowledge of the major grape varieties . . .'

I look towards the stairs, and just as I am thinking that Joe's class have been down in that cellar drinking for bloody hours, one by one students start to emerge, some walking in straighter lines than others.

My mouth feels dry. I drink some water.

'Can I get you another peppermint tea?' Edoardo asks, clearing the table next to mine.

What I really want is a neat gin.

Joe heads for the bar. He seems agitated, in a hurry. Maybe he didn't see me earlier.

'I'm off,' he says.

Edoardo nods. 'How is your father today?'

'Not great. Mavis called, said he was trying to play golf in the sitting room.'

'Go over, Becca,' that voice says, 'Find out why he lost touch . . .'

'She was terrified he'd break a window,' Joe continues, heading towards the door. Get up, Becca. Move. This feels like some terrible auction, when I should be making a bid, but instead I'm sitting with my bidding paddle, paralysed . . .

He's at the door. He's not going to turn round . . . 'Back soon . . .'

'Becca, say something!'

'Joe?' I call out, just before the hammer is about to fall.

My heart is racing as I walk towards him, still not sure he recognizes me. Self-consciously I touch my hair. He probably thinks I'm fatter too. 'It's Rebecca. Becca.'

His eyes remain on mine. Is he in shock or does he *still* have no idea who I am?

'How are you?' There's no warmth in his voice, little recognition in his eyes.

'I'm fine.' I smile, trying to appear self-assured.

He glances at his watch.

Unnerved, I ask, 'Do you need to go?'

'Two minutes,' he offers, his tone sharp. Both of us walk back to the bar. I can tell Edoardo senses the atmosphere, but he does well to hide it, humming as he dries up some glasses.

Two minutes . . .

'I was having lunch with Annie . . . I think you know her? I saw you in the distance, but you were busy, I don't think you saw me.'

It's coming out all wrong, and I only have a minute now.

'Wow! This place! It's amazing,' I continue, wanting the ground to swallow me up. I grab hold of the wine list, pretend to read it, saying how impressive it looks and . . .

'You're holding it upside down.'

I redden, turn the list the right way up, laugh at myself.

Oh dear God.

I point out how lovely the decor is.

'Decor? Who ever says the word "decor"?' the voice objects. 'What's wrong with you?'

Joe isn't saying a word; he's just staring at me.

'Excuse me if I appear shocked, but I didn't imagine I'd see you again,' he says finally.

When I dare to look at him I see Joe all those years ago, leaning against the door that very first evening when he moved into our house at Bristol. Then we're in the kitchen, laughing as he's giving me a cooking lesson. I see us in fancy dress, late that night, sitting down on the bench, talking. I picture the look in Joe's eye when I'd asked what he wanted.

The telephone rings. Edoardo tells Joe it's Peta, before taking a cloth and wiping down the tables.

'Tell her I'll call back. I need to go. It was good to see you,' he says in a way that suggests he wants little more to do with me.

'Joe, wait, just one second,' I say, urgency now in my voice. 'The reason I'm here . . .' I clear my throat; start again. 'There's something I need to tell you. It's about Olly.'

'How is he? Is he here?'

'Joe, say something.' Edoardo looks over to us, sympathy in his eyes.

'I'm so sorry, Rebecca.' He curls his hand into a fist. 'He was one of my closest friends. I didn't get to say goodbye.'

'I should have told you. I wasn't thinking straight, I had so much to organize with the funeral and–'

'Don't worry,' he cuts me off. 'We lost touch years ago. I'm responsible for that.'

'It wasn't all your fault.'

'Rebecca, my leaving Bristol, it wasn't just about you,' he says, his tone hardening. 'I left Bristol, I lost touch with Olly, because I was screwed up.'

I take a sip of water. 'Right.'

'How long are you here for?'

I tell him I'm not sure. It's complicated. 'You see, I'm pregnant. I'm having Olly's baby.'

Joe doesn't utter a word. When I tell him Olly died before he knew he was going to be a father . . . 'I'm very sorry, Rebecca,' he says, his eyes softening when he sees my tears. He presses his head into his hands, lost as to what to say. 'I'd like to write to Olly's parents. Do you have their address?' is the last thing he says to me before we part, and I have no idea if I shall see him again.

8

As I drive to Pippa's in Mum's car, part of me is relieved that I have seen Joe and that he knows about Olly, but I also feel uncomfortable at how distant he was. Though what did I expect, especially after they way we'd left things at Bristol? That he would hold me in his arms?

I'm thankful to be babysitting tonight. I need the distraction.

Pippa lives approximately five miles out of Winchester, towards Stockbridge, in a small hamlet called Northfields. One potholed road, called The Street, runs through the hamlet in the shape of a horseshoe, leading back to the main road. She's married to Todd, American and a successful businessman. She and Todd bought a plot of land with a dilapidated barn, which they converted into their large and beautiful home. Pippa once ticked Olly off for calling it a bungalow. 'But it is pretty much a bungalow,' he'd said to me later that night.

Todd and Pippa met in London about nine years ago. Pippa had just returned from America. She was an excellent tennis player, with a world ranking of five hundred and forty-five, but she wasn't quite good enough to play at Wimbledon and other Grand Slam events. She'd also confided in me that she'd lost that hunger to win. 'I'm tired of training, Becca. I want to have a normal life.'

So it was time for her to get a job. She found secretarial work in a jaded sports agency that needed major consultancy help from Todd. He strode into her soulless grey office; they clapped eyes on one another and lightning struck. Todd was thirteen years older than twenty-two-year-old Pippa, and he seemed so worldly-wise and debonair. He was also rich. Flowers and gifts were lavished upon her on a daily basis, but no marriage proposal was forthcoming. 'What's taking him so *long*?' she once asked me.

'What's the hurry? People don't get married young these days.'

'But you and Olly seem close,' she said, almost implying that if it was a race I'd be in the lead.

Olly proposed to me on my twenty-fourth birthday.

He'd taken me to our local bistro, where our friendly waiter had iced in chocolate around my pudding plate, 'Will you marry me?' It was perfect. Todd proposed to Pippa the following week during their Caribbean holiday. They were on the beach when a light aircraft flew overhead, high in the sky, a streamer trailing the words 'MARRY ME!'

'I always knew I'd fall for an older man,' she'd said when she brandished her eye-boggling diamond-and-sapphire engagement ring in front of us, before saying, 'Let's see yours, Becca.'

I can still see her squinting at my finger as she said, 'Oh, isn't it sweet!'

Olly never truly forgave them for casting our engagement into their shadow.

After becoming Mrs Todd Carter, Pippa worked at the sports agency for a couple more years until she became pregnant at twenty-six. After the birth of the twins, they moved down to Winchester to be close to Mum and Dad. Pippa had never really liked London, not like me. She didn't have a strong network of friends, didn't like hanging out in the pub or going to nightclubs, and what with Todd away so often on business, she felt it would be a lonely place to push a pram.

*

I park the car in the gravelled driveway, next to Todd's convertible BMW. I notice how part of the garden is now enclosed, with a trampoline, climbing frame and what looks like a rabbit hutch in one corner.

'Hello!' I call out when I enter through the back door. Todd greets me, dressed in a jacket and tie, glossy brown hair with flecks of silvery grey, kept out of his eyes by designer shades, and teeth as white as snow.

He leads me into the kitchen, the soles of his smart shoes clicking against the stone-tiled floor, opens the fridge, which is almost as large as their front door, and offers me a selection of beverages, from fruit juices to champagne. 'Or I can make you a coffee.' He gestures to the slick silver coffee machine on the breakfast counter. I opt for water.

'Ice and lemon?' He presses a button and ice cubes drop into the glass like magic.

I ask Todd how his recent business trip went. The truth is, I don't really know what Todd does. Nor do Mum and Dad, but they say it's too late to ask him now. We all know he turns companies around, shakes up their finances, but I can't imagine the detail of his life. 'It's a mystery,' Dad says wryly.

'Great,' Todd replies, and that's the end of that conversation, the mystery remaining unsolved.

*

'Uh-oh,' Todd grins, when we hear running along the corridor that sounds like the beginning of an earth-quake. 'Here comes trouble! Now, Rebecca, we don't allow them in the sitting room, and bedtime is in' – he looks at his gold watch – 'approximately twenty minutes.'

When Pippa kisses me goodbye I inhale a waft of honeysuckle perfume. She looks incredible, in a pale-pink evening dress. Pippa is impossibly pretty, with her china-blue eyes, plump cheeks, natural blonde hair and heart-shaped mouth, all features inherited from Mum. I've seen the family albums and she was an angelic-looking baby too, with blonde ringlets. I'm more like my father, with my sharper cheekbones and English-rose skin. 'Have fun!' I call out.

'We won't be late,' she says over her shoulder. 'They can play for another half-hour before bed . . .'

'Twenty minutes,' corrects Todd.

'Oh, and I did promise they could eat the fruit kebabs they made at nursery today.'

'OK!'

'Any trouble, call me.'

'We won't have any trouble, will we?' I say, expecting to turn round to two innocent-looking boys modelling Superman and Spiderman dressing gowns, feet encased in fluffy slippers. They were behind me a minute ago, but . . .

Oscar has plonked himself in his racing car with a Union Jack flag attached to the aerial. He pedals furiously round the kitchen table, screaming and laughing and tooting the horn. Plump Theo is waddling behind, trying to catch him up.

'Hi, boys, why don't we eat those fruit . . . er . . . *kebabs*?' I suggest, having to speak loudly over the noise. Completely ignored, I open the fridge to see if I can find them.

There they are, on a plate on the bottom shelf. Strawberries, pineapple and . . . ugh . . . cherry tomatoes skewered on to sticks.

I drop one of the kebabs on the floor when I hear his voice say, 'Oh, yum-yum! Save one for me.' Slowly I pick it up, brush it off, put it back on the plate, still confused.

'That's right. The boys won't notice,' the voice continues. 'A bit of dirt never did anyone any harm, hey.'

'Olly?' I say. 'Is this really you?'

'Did you ask Joe why he stopped calling me?'

'I didn't. I . . .'

But then I hear screeching. I turn round to see that

Oscar has now abandoned the car and is bouncing round the kitchen table on a bright-blue rubber cow, Theo wailing that it's his turn, it's *his* Happy Hopper.

'Watch out, Becca! Duck!' says the voice.

A toy car is flying in my direction, a distressed Theo about to burst into tears. 'Now that's enough!' They barely look up at me, and it is then that I realize how little I know these boys. My nephews. When Olly and I were first married, we rarely visited Mum and Dad at weekends, nor Pippa and the boys, partly because we were having too much fun, mainly because I don't think Olly felt completely at ease. 'I'm sure your Mum wishes you'd married a reliable solicitor like your father, or another Todd,' Olly would say. I told him not to be silly, but deep down I sensed it too. I'd make up all kinds of excuses as to why we couldn't visit them at weekends, one of the main ones being that Olly needed the time to write. I think Mum thought Olly's head was in the clouds half the time, that his writing would always be just a hobby, and her disapproving tone made me feel protective of my husband. I look at the boys now. I don't know them at all. There is a price to pay for distancing yourself from the family.

*

'Now, it's nearly bedtime, so let's eat these and then why don't I read you a story?' I suggest, hardly recognizing my hearty-hearty sing-along voice as I kneel down to hand both boys their kebabs. 'These look scrummy!'

Theo shoves the stick my way, offering me a bite, a squished strawberry precariously close to my lips, which I refuse a little too quickly, before saying, 'No, no, they're all for you! So, you made these at nursery? Aren't you clever!'

'I've made kuss kuss too,' says Theo, chomping into a strawberry, half of it falling on to the floor.

'Couscous. How delicious,' I titter merrily, thrilled by how the evening is progressing. With Pippa and Todd's genes, I decide they are handsome boys. Wide foreheads like Todd, saucer-shaped blue eyes and cherubic curls. Oscar is slighter in build and has a reddish tint in his hair, a little like mine. Theo is rounder-faced with a dimple like mine, and he's pure blond, like Pippa.

'What would you like me to read to you?' I ask.

Oscar stares at his kebab, thinking, a wicked glint in his eye . . . Next thing I know, he's flicked it towards the kitchen window, *splat*, tomato seeds dribbling down the glass.

'Hey!' I protest, grabbing a J Cloth. 'What did you do that for? That's naughty!'

SPLAT! A strawberry now hits the glass, followed by hoots of laughter coming from Theo, who has copied him. 'No! Stop it!'

Roars of laughter! They couldn't care less!

The telephone rings, a flash machine with so many buttons that I daren't touch it. It's Todd's office, Todd's mobile, Todd's this and that.

'They *bleep* each other in the house?' There's a smile in his voice.

Eventually I hear Pippa's voice on the answer machine. 'Hi, Becca, hope everything's OK and the boys are behaving.'

Splat.

'Stop fussing,' I hear Todd murmuring in the background as frantically I wipe the mess off the window.

'Just to say, we left some Waitrose goodies for you in the fridge, so help yourself to whatever you want, see you later, and really hope those monkeys are being good.'

Another *splat*.

Theo and Oscar are in bed, teeth brushed. Earlier I read them a story about a blue kangaroo, we played games, both of them hiding under their duvets. 'I think Oscar must have gone on holiday to Barbados,' I'd said, pretending to search for him. Theo found this touchingly hilarious.

I scan the shelf of DVDs in the sitting room. I can see why the boys aren't allowed in here. It's spotless: no toys, no clutter, a sanctuary for Todd and Pippa. The walls are covered with modern paintings (expensive but not my taste), the sofas are cream, there's an antique coffee table in the middle of the room, and by my side an Italian glass lamp base with an art deco shade. Oh dear God alive, I am going to have an Oscar or a Theo in five and a half months. My life will change in every way. Olly and I had talked about having a family, but we'd wanted to be more financially secure. 'We have all the time in the world,' he had said.

'All the time,' I say emotionally, kneeling down to slot *Pretty Woman* into the DVD player.

'Oh, come on, Becca. You've watched it about a hundred times,' he says. 'Go wild. Watch *Avatar* instead.'

I wake up with a start. Where's my mobile? Who's calling me at this time of night? It might be Pippa? I haven't even checked on the twins . . . I hunt for my mobile; finally find it wedged between the sofa cushions.

'Hello,' I say, standing up and catching a look at myself

in the mirror. My face is lined and crumpled from sleep; my hair looks as if I have just put my finger in a plug socket.

'Rebecca? It's Joe.'

Joe. Oh God. Wake up. It's Joe.

'I feel terrible,' he confides. 'I didn't know what to say earlier . . .'

'Don't worry. I understand. It was a shock.'

'I wondered if we could meet? There are so many things I didn't ask.'

I don't say anything for a long time.

'Rebecca? Are you still there?'

'I'm here,' I say, and I can sense his relief. 'I'd like that. When?'

'How about tomorrow?'

After the phone call, I open the boys' bedroom door. They're scrunched up into tiny balls, fast asleep under their superhero duvet covers. I kiss them goodnight. 'Life gets complicated when you're older, so make the most of it now, sweethearts,' I whisper, perched on the end of Theo's bed, gently stroking his hair. 'Maybe don't flick any more fruit kebabs against windows, and *always* be kind to your old aunt, but have lots of fun, laugh and be happy . . .'

'Because you can never go back. God, how I wish I

could rewind, go back to that day,' the voice continues inside my head. I stand up, abruptly. 'I'm sorry, Becca, for being so careless. I'd taken one of my short cuts, it was normally a quiet road . . .'

I rush out of the room, closing the door behind me. I pace the corridor, thinking about Jim and his dog, Noodle.

'Talk to me, Becca. You know it's me. I'm here.'

I look into an empty space. 'What do you mean you're here? You're not. You're not!'

'Not in that way, but–'

'I'm having your child. This wasn't how it was meant to be.'

'You'll be a great mother,' he says quietly. 'I have faith in you.'

'Oh Olly. I miss you.' I turn round and stop dead when I see them.

I don't know how long Pippa and Todd have been standing there; I'm not sure how much they have heard me say. Todd looks at my sister with concern.

'I'm hearing his voice,' I confess. 'And I'm scared. Really scared.'

9

Bristol University, Eleven Years Ago

After Joe moves into our house the buzzer rings every five minutes, medical students dressed in skimpy skirts and revealing tops file in to see our new housemate. When my friends visit, they look over my shoulders to see if he's around, or pretend they need the bathroom for the fifth time in the hope that they will have a chance encounter with him on the landing.

Sylvie wants to sleep with Joe. She flicks her dark hair in front of him, leaves shirt buttons undone to expose sexy underwear. The house smells of Chanel perfume. I watch in fascination as she bends down seductively to reach for the butter in the fridge, lacy thong on display. Jamie appreciates it. Olly can't help but notice. Joe appears immune. Maybe he's gay? But deep down I don't believe that, so I advise her to use another tactic; ignore him. Yet Joe still isn't interested. I only know this because Olly and Joe go out to the pub on Monday nights, after their rowing session. 'What do you *talk* about?' I ask, because Joe isn't exactly chatty.

'Oh, everything,' Olly says. 'He's a top guy. By the way, I've tried to convince him Sylvie's fun. I reckon she'd be wild in bed.'

'Olly!'

He laughs, tells me Joe is shagging someone else anyway, she's called Zoe and they're in the same anatomy tutorial. Joe says it would get messy and complicated sleeping with a housemate.

'Phew. So I'm safe.' I smile.

It's Sunday morning. Chicken and potatoes are roasting in the oven. Pudding next. 'Five large eggs, tick. Caster sugar, tick,' I continue, assembling everything on to the kitchen table. I'm cooking Sunday lunch for Olly, who's still in bed. Stanley were playing in a gig last night; they were the last band on, and by the time they played everyone was too drunk to care, and then the nail in the coffin was when the sound system packed up. At one point a meathead guy threw a beer bottle at Olly, shouting, 'Loser!' Joe left my side and approached the man saying, 'Don't be a dickhead all your life. Apologize, please.'

'Apologize! Who the fuck are you? His dad?'

'His friend, and you're a fucking wanker.'

When he tried to punch Joe, he was so drunk that he staggered into a table instead. The entire pub clapped and cheered Joe on, especially the women.

I still think Olly needs some serious cheering up though, and the one thing he says he misses about home is his mother's Sunday roasts.

'Cornflour . . . tick.' I jog on the spot, as if warming up for the next exercise. 'Olly's going to be blown away by my newfound culinary expertise,' I say to myself. 'White wine vinegar . . .'

'Tick?' Joe suggests, standing at the door. I turn to him. How long has he been watching me?

He enters the kitchen, asks me what I'm doing. He's dressed in his rugby gear, a patch of dry mud encrusted on to his thigh.

'Cooking.'

He raises an eyebrow. 'You never cook.'

'It's for Olly. Thanks for sticking up for him last night.'

'Olly would have done the same for me.' Joe glances at the recipe book.

'Raspberry meringue roulade. That's ambitious.'

'Easy.'

'Peasy lemon squeezy.'

I look at him, surprised.

'Will there be any left over for me?' He opens the fridge and takes out a carton of orange juice.

'If you finish off my assignment.' I think of my books upstairs, unread. 'And take a shower.' I crack an egg into a bowl.

'Funny. Hang on! What are you doing?'

'Cracking eggs into a bowl.'

'But you've got to separate them.'

'Separate them? Why?'

He looks incredulous. 'Haven't you made meringue before?'

I grab the book. 'It says here, beat the eggs . . .'

'The egg *whites*.' He walks over to the table, picks up the bowl and chucks my previous effort into the sink, before taking two clean bowls from one of the cupboards. 'Look and learn, Rebecca Harte,' he says, with that arrogant smile. I watch as he cracks the egg against the side of the bowl. 'I'm separating the egg into two shells,' he comments, 'moving the yolk back and forth . . .'

'I can hardly contain my excitement.'

'Watch.' The egg white falls into one of the bowls,

he drops the yolk into the second bowl. 'You see? Separated.'

'OK. I can do that.' I take another egg from the box and crack it against the side of the bowl. He's standing so close to me that I feel nervous of mucking up. Slimy egg white drips into the bowl and down my hand, the yolk wobbles from one half of the shell into the other. 'Did it,' I jump up and down proudly.

He grabs my arm. 'Before you get too carried away,' he says, handing me another egg, 'only three more to go.'

'How come you're so good at cooking?' I ask. Joe is the only one in the house who uses the steamer and saucepans, and he's just bought himself a wok.

'My mum taught me. When I was growing up, she'd always be telling me how she'd cooked the chicken with cider or tarragon, or how she'd marinated the lamb, and then Dad would be telling us why he'd chosen a certain wine to go with our meal. As boring as it sounds, it did make me appreciate cooking and tasting food.'

'Are you close to your mum?'

'Very. Becca, watch out!'

'What?'

A blob of yellow has landed in the egg white mixture.

'Oh fuck! Oh no.' I stand back from the disaster. 'I'm going to have to start all over again, aren't I?'

'Let's see.' Joe stands next to me, our arms brush for a second as meticulously he uses a piece of shell to pluck out the blob of yolk from the egg whites. 'It's a blow, Becca, but it's not a knockout.'

As I whisk the egg whites, Joe and I talk about home and how little we visit our parents, considering Winchester is only an hour and a half down the M4. 'I love my mum, but it's too intense,' Joe confides. 'All I can hear is the ticking of the grandfather clock. I can't lounge around on the sofa or watch TV. According to Dad, television is a waste of time.'

Our parents live only five minutes away from each other, but their lives have never crossed. Joe's mum and dad are quite a few years older than my parents, which could explain it. Joe's father, Francis, was forty-six when Joe was born. Francis was a scholar at Winchester College, and wanted his son to attend too, so put Joe's name down practically before he was born, hoping Joe would be bright enough to secure a scholarship. 'I sat the exam when I was thirteen,' Joe tells me, 'but didn't get the scholarship.'

'But look at you now' – I pose in my apron – 'around such elite students at Bristol.'

Joe looks at me in a way that suggests he's unsure about that.

'Have I whisked the eggs enough?'

'Tip the bowl upside down.'

'What?'

'Tip it upside down.'

'No.'

'Like this.' Joe wrestles the bowl away from me, both of us laughing. 'Perfect,' he says. 'You see? No damage done. The egg whites remain intact.'

'You're lucky, you know,' I tell Joe as I smooth the meringue mixture into my prepared baking tin.

'Lucky? Why?'

'With medicine, it's pretty clear-cut, isn't it? It's like law. You read law or medicine, you become a barrister, lawyer, doctor, whatever. It must be a relief to know what you want to do and–'

'I don't want to be a doctor. I hate medicine.'

'What? Why are you doing it then?'

'My father's a surgeon, breast cancer.'

'I know that.'

'He's a god. The things his patients give him. A holiday in the Caribbean, a crate of Burgundy; you should see his wine cellar. He can do no wrong,' Joe says, anger rising in his voice, 'and his son, come what may, will follow in his grand footsteps.'

'But you don't have to,' I suggest, slotting the baking tray into the oven. 'I mean, if you wanted to do something else–'

'You don't know my father,' Joe interrupts me, and for a split second I see vulnerability in his grey eyes. 'I'm an only son, Becca; there isn't anyone else he can mould but me.'

'What about your mum?'

'They have a strange relationship. I'm sure Dad plays away. He goes on so many conferences. Mum just turns a blind eye. No one's ever stood up to him.'

'But Joe, you could do anything. You're bright and talented . . .'

'I'm average,' he says sharply.

'Surely if you talked to him. If you–'

'You don't understand.'

There's a pause. With Olly and me, we're perfectly happy in silence, but with Joe sometimes I feel this need to fill it. 'I'm the same, you know,' I tell him. 'When I was growing up I had these dreams of being an artist and living in a beautiful studio in Italy, the sun streaming in through the window. I'd paint the olive trees and the vineyards, or there'd be a cafe outside where I'd sketch the locals drinking and playing cards. I'd have my own exhibitions in the market square. But I decided to listen to Mum and Dad's advice, give up art and get a proper degree. Shows what an independent spirit I am.'

'I like that painting of yours, in your bedroom,' Joe says. 'The lemon tree.'

'Thanks,' I say, glowing inside at the compliment. 'So, if you hate medicine, what *do* you want to do?' I ask, pulling up a chair and sitting close to him.

'What do I want to do? You mean right now?' he asks. I think he's about to kiss me, and for a brief insane second I want to kiss him too.

'Hi, guys,' Olly says, entering the room. He's in his blue dressing gown, soft hair ruffled from sleep. He drops a kiss on my head, tells me something smells amazing. 'What's up? You two look serious?'

'Becca was grilling me on what I want to do with my life.'

'Yeah? And?' Olly sticks the kettle on.

'I have no fucking idea.' He turns to me and smiles, a full proper smile this time, and it is in that moment that I understand what everyone sees in Joe. On the rare occasion that he lets down his guard, it feels like a gift from heaven.

'You could do anything, Joe, anything you want,' Olly says, before thanking me for cooking. 'I'm starving. Aren't I lucky to have the best girlfriend in the world?' he says, pulling me towards him.

I wriggle free from his arms, telling him I'd better check on the chicken.

'Very lucky,' says Joe, leaving the room.

'Becca?' Olly asks me, when we're alone.

'Yes?'

'I'm sorry about last night, for being in a mood.'

'That's OK. I understand.'

'I was thinking I might give Stanley up.'

'Really?'

He nods.

'Oh come on, Ol – you're good and you'd miss it. Don't let that one idiot put you off.'

'Becca?'

'Um.'

'Do you find Joe attractive?'

I busy myself round the kitchen. 'Do you fancy bread sauce? Why are you asking me that! I could pop out . . .'

'Stop. Look at me.'

'Olly, what's this all about?'

'I don't know. It's just . . .' He pauses. 'Well, every girl I know does, so . . .'

'He's good-looking . . .' I chuck the mixing bowl into the sink, 'but he's not my type.'

'You promise me?'

I walk over to him. 'I promise. Cross my heart.'

'Good,' he responds to my kiss. 'Because I've told him, if he ever tried it on with you, I'd kill him,' Olly says with a smile, but I can see he means every word.

10

I find my father in his hut at the end of the garden. When he retired from being a solicitor, Mum feared they'd get on each other's nerves if they were both in the house, so they decided to build him a shed, where he could keep his mounting stock of porcelain and carry out his admin, as well as keeping a framed print of his pin-up, Audrey Hepburn, after whom the dog is named. Normally I find Dad asleep in his armchair, a hardback book about the D-Day landings or the Russian Revolution open on his lap, but this morning he's fresh-faced from his recent porcelain-buying expedition with Mr Pullen.

'Oh, Dad, how much did you spend this time?'

'Shh,' he tuts. 'Isn't this divine?' He holds up a small porcelain figure wearing breeches and mustard-coloured stockings and buckled shoes. He's playing some kind of brass instrument. 'The French horn,' Dad informs me.

'He's one sexy dude,' Olly says, making me smile.

'He's enchanting, isn't he? Staffordshire. Dating from 1800.' Dad lifts an accompanying figure out of the box, a girl playing the tambourine.

'Very smart hat, can see you in that,' Olly continues.

I'm trying not to laugh now. Dad asks me what I'm up to today.

'I'm popping round to Janet's,' I say. Janet is an elderly neighbour. 'And then I'm meeting Joe for lunch. Joe Lawson.'

'Now, Joe is the one who owns this lovely wine bar? I really should take your mother there. Colebrook Dale.' Dad holds an ornamental basket encrusted with flowers and leaves in front of me. 'It's battered, but I couldn't resist.'

Olly laughs. 'Mr Pullen couldn't believe his luck! He hadn't shifted that basket thingy for years.'

Dad asks me what's so funny. I hesitate. How do I begin to tell him about Olly's voice in my head?

Last night Pippa had told Todd that I was exhausted, emotional, grieving *and* pregnant: a toxic combination. She said the imagination can play tricks. I don't believe she's right. I don't think I'm going crazy, but would Dad?

'Dad?'

'Um.'

'Recently, well, recently I've been hearing–'

'Turkish,' he states, gleefully holding up a rich blue-and-green glazed jug. '*Izink*.'

On my way out of the house. 'Please put that picture back where it used to be,' Olly says, when I see a frame poking out from beneath the blue chintz curtain. It's a picture of the two of us taken on Bamburgh beach in Northumberland, near to Olly's parents' home. His arm is around my waist, my hair's windswept, we're laughing at something. I remember that weekend. It was the first time I'd met his parents. I was a nervous twenty-four-year-old, not sure what to expect. Victor was hibernating in his study, wearing a tweed jacket, half-moon spectacles and trousers too short in the leg. He had wispy hair, with only a few signs of grey, but it was the brown eyes I noticed before anything else because they were just like his son's. I found him charming, if eccentric. He showed me his enormous collection of weevils in various wooden cabinets that he'd accumulated over the years, and in each collection I marvelled at how he'd written in such tiny writing the date they were found accompanied by a small description of their breed. Carolyn, his mum, was the normal one, as Olly put it. She loved gardening and growing vegetables. When we stayed the occasional weekend, she'd always be dressed in cords, holey jumpers and wellington boots. Fashion had bypassed her, or perhaps that was because Victor wouldn't notice if she wore a bin bag. But, like her son, she was musical, taught singing and still does. I have been in touch with her recently to let her know how the first scan went. She'd wanted to know if I was going to find out the sex at my next appointment. 'I'm unsure what colour wool to choose for a cardigan, Becca,' she said, her voice growing in strength. She and Victor have promised to help the baby and me financially, in whatever way they can.

'Don't cry, Becca. Honest to God, I'm not worth it,' Olly says as I place the photograph of us proudly back on the mantelpiece, where it used to be, next to the French clock.

'Becca?' Dad says. I hadn't noticed him entering the sitting room.

I turn to him. He glances at the photograph. He seems ashamed, out of his depth as he rattles the loose change in his trouser pocket. 'Your mother and I, we weren't sure you'd want to see pictures all over the house, we didn't know . . .'

'He did exist,' I say. 'My wedding dress used to be in Pippa's wardrobe too, Dad. It's not there anymore.'

He nods. 'We put it in the loft.'

'You don't need to protect me, Dad. Olly's gone, but I want to keep his memory alive.'

'I know. Of course. We were wrong. I'm so sorry, Rebecca.'

Armed with a cottage pie, cooked by Mum, I feel like Jane Austen's Emma taking food to the poor and needy, as Audrey and I set off to Janet's.

'Only your family could have a dog that doesn't like walks,' Olly says, when Audrey stops in the middle of the pavement, refusing to budge. Olly loved Audrey, but when she got just a little too close, he'd pull back, saying she had to have the worst fish-breath in England. 'Why stop at England?' I'd replied, laughing.

'Come on, sweetheart,' I say, tugging at her lead. Reluctantly she shuffles on.

Janet lives only two minutes away from my parents, in a small house off a winding narrow road called Whiteshute Lane. Growing up, Janet was a regular guest at Christmas. She had no family close by, since her husband had died and her sister lived abroad. She would have been in her sixties when she first joined us to sing carols at church, wearing a smart coat, fur wrap and a hat with a jaunty feather. Pippa didn't like her invading our Christmas. I remember her being put out one time when Janet chomped on yet another silver coin wrapped in foil in the Christmas pudding. I, on the other hand, enjoyed her visits. She lightened up the room when she arrived with her presents and box of crackers. She'd give me sketchbooks and paints and she always wanted to see my art too. 'You have a gift, Rebecca,' she'd say. Janet was a dog-breeder, so I'd often visit when one of her dogs had had puppies. Pippa preferred cats.

Mum tells me Janet has macular degeneration now; that she's been losing her sight since her early seventies. She's now eighty-four.

When I knock on the door, a dog barks. I wait. And I wait.

'Well, I'll be jiggered!' she says. She's dressed in an autumn-coloured tweed skirt that falls just below the knee and a longish pale-blue cardigan with deep pockets over a cream silk blouse, but I'm sure Trinny and Susannah would have something to say about her brown sheepskin zip-up slippers that finish off the look.

'Come in, come in!'

A miniature schnauzer wags his tail and approaches Audrey, only to be snapped at. 'Audrey! Be nice!'

'Audrey Fish-Breath really lets the side down,' Olly says, making me smile again.

Janet leads me down the hallway, past rosettes, doggy medals and paintings of her dogs hung on the wall. Mozart's Requiem is blasting in the background. 'That was Jaxmins Claudicus Maximus.' She points her white stick towards a painting of a giant schnauzer hanging above her fireplace. With his beard and droopy moustache he looks more like an aristocrat than a dog.

Janet feels the buttons on her music machine, turns Mozart off. Next to the CD player is a section of the newspaper. 'Ah! You might know!' she bursts out, peering at the crossword puzzle through her magnifying glass. '"Poker Face" and "Paparazzi" singer, four-four, beginning with L.'

'Lady Gaga.'

Janet juts her chin out. 'Hmmm?'

'Gaga. Spelt g, a, g, a. You know, as in I'm going gaga.' I pull a mad dotty face. 'Lady Gaga,' she writes carefully in the boxes. 'What a wonderful name! I should like to meet her.'

After I have popped the cottage pie in the fridge she leads me back into the sitting room. It's more like a museum, each table covered with ornaments. Her telephone with enlarged numbers is placed on a Dutch marquetry table next to a framed photograph of a married couple walking away from a church. When I look more closely I see it is Janet, who is dressed in a long white dress with fur-lined sleeves, her veil swept off her face. She's striking, with dark hair cut into a shoulder-length bob. He is significantly older.

'Gregory,' she says, knowing which picture I'm looking at. 'We were married for twelve years.'

'What was he like?' I ask, realizing I know so little about Janet and her past.

'A saint.' She laughs. 'He'd have to be to put up with me. He was in the army in the Second World War, in the Coldstream Guards. Never talked to me about it though. A brave man. We lived in Cambridge when we first married. He was a lecturer in history, loved reading more than anything in the world. He was a lovely letter-writer too. He'd be reeling in his grave with Facebook this, and Twatter that.'

'Twitter,' I correct her, smiling.

She looks at me. 'Now tell me, how are you?'

Why is it that whenever someone asks me how I am in that sympathetic voice, I want to cry.

She twists a sapphire ring round her bony finger, misshapen by arthritis. She doesn't say how much I must miss him, or what a shock it must have been, or how time heals. She waits, aware I am trying to hold it in. 'We don't cry or whinge, we pull our socks up and get on with it,' I can hear Mum saying to me as a child, when I'd asked her why she was always with Pippa in the summer holidays. Janet helps me out. 'It's hard, isn't it? For the one left behind.'

Over a cup of tea I find myself telling Janet about my decision to move home. 'I'd been denying his death in London, Janet. I thought I could go to work, put a no-entry sign in my head, not think about Olly. I thought I'd be much better off working than staying at home wallowing in self pity, but the thing is . . .' I hesitate, not sure how to put it.

'Grief catches up with you.'

I nod, remembering Glitz telling me I needed to go home. 'I wasn't coping, and then when I found out I was having a baby, you can imagine the shock. Oh, Janet, I have to be strong. This is a gift,' I tell her. 'Breaking down isn't an option when you're pregnant. I want to be a good mother.'

'You're a brave girl,' Janet says, dabbing her own eyes. 'You and the baby are going to be just fine.'

After a second cup of tea Janet talks about her life

with Gregory in Cambridge. She shows me photographs and letters he wrote to his sister during the Second World War. I ask her to remind me about the brooch, a silver-shaped star with a red cross enamelled in the centre, pinned to her cardigan. As a child, I remember her wearing it all the time. She tells me it is the Coldstream star. 'I never take it off, makes me feel close to him. "*Honi soit qui mal y pense.*"' She taps the engraving. '"Shame be to him who evil thinks."'

The grandfather clock chimes twelve times, reminding me I must go. I'm meeting Joe in half an hour. 'Are you going anywhere nice for lunch?' Janet asks.

I mention Maison Joe and the wine tasting school. 'Oh, I love wine!' Janet says, leading me towards the front door, Audrey following behind. 'I know nothing about it though. That was always your department, wasn't it, Gregory?'

Startled, I stop and turn to her. 'Do you talk to him, Janet?'

'Oh yes, often,' she says with a wave of her hand, as if it's the most natural thing in the world.

'And Gregory – does he reply? Do you hear his voice?'

'Gosh no. I wish I did.' She studies me. 'But I know several people who do hear voices, and it's nothing to be scared of. Still, I like to chatter away. I can sense him ticking me off when I put the heating on all day; he was a right old Scrooge.'

I want to ask her more, but it's late and I need to leave. But just as I'm about to head out the door . . . 'Janet, I'm so sorry,' I exclaim, touching her arm.

'Whatever for?'

'When you used to visit us for Christmas . . . I never realized what you were going through, losing Gregory.'

'You were young!'

'And I think I gave you a box of homemade fudge every year for Christmas, didn't I?'

'Not *every* year. Sometimes it was truffles.'

I laugh. 'Probably disgusting too. Cooking has never been my strong point.'

'Enough of that, Rebecca. I always enjoyed seeing you and looking at your lovely paintings. Please visit again,' she says, 'and make it soon.'

11

Joe leads me down to the cellar. It's an open-plan room with long oak tables and wooden benches running down the centre, and a library of wine decorates the shelves, plus Joe tells me there's more storage space round the back. 'I couldn't believe my luck when this place came up for rent,' he says. 'I wouldn't be able to run wine tasting courses without this incredible space.' There's a PowerPoint on a screen at the far end, with a graph of different regions and the wines they specialize in. 'It's all very new,' Joe says. 'I was worried that in the recession no one would sign up, but thankfully they've proved me wrong. Here, let me.'

'Oh, thank you,' I say, slipping my jacket off and handing it to him. I sit down at one of the tables and admire the lunch before me, a selection of cold meats and salads. 'I'm not surprised people want to taste wine,'

I tell him. 'It's miserable, cutting back on all the best things in life.'

'So . . .' we both say at the same time.

'Sorry, you first,' I say.

'I've written to Olly's parents.'

'They'll appreciate that.'

There's a silence. All I can hear is the noise upstairs, coming from the restaurant.

'How are your parents?' he asks, his tone formal.

'They're well, thank you.'

'And doesn't your sister live here? I think I've met her husband. The American.'

'That's right. Pippa. She has two boys. Twins. Oscar and Theo. They're lovely – well, they're little rascals really.'

I tell Joe about the flying fruit kebabs, quickly wishing I hadn't. Joe's eyes have already glazed over.

'What did Olly do?' he asks, wisely moving on.

I tell Joe he was a music teacher.

'I remember Stanley . . . and how good he was at the piano.'

'He used to play Chopin and Schubert while I was in the bath. We lived in a flat about the size of this bread-basket,' I say, holding it up, 'so I could hear him loud and clear.' I don't tell Joe how insane it drove me at times, and how desperate I was to move somewhere with more space. 'Sometimes he'd play while I was cooking.'

'Cooking?' Joe raises an eyebrow. 'I remember one night catching you tip some baked beans over pasta.'

'I was in a hurry. To get to the pub,' I add. 'I did make Sunday lunch for him once.'

'I taught you how to separate egg whites. Our roulade was pretty good.'

'You see,' I say, 'not such a hopeless cook after all.'

Joe is now thinking about something else. 'That couple in the curry house? It was just the three of us.'

'After that party.' I know exactly what he's talking about.

Joe, Olly and I had left a party early. Starving, we stopped off at our favourite curry place on the way home. Sitting at the table next to us was a middle-aged couple, not saying a word to one another, nothing but their food and a dried-up carnation in a white vase between them.

'You must be related?' I'd suggested to Joe at the time.

'I talk when I have something interesting to say.'

'Hey, you two, simmer down, simmer down,' Olly ordered.

'I'm not in the least bit heated up, Ol,' I retorted, glancing at the menu, though I always ended up having the same old chicken tikka masala.

The three of us then had a drunken debate about how long this couple had been married. At what point did they run out of conversation? Were they like this at home and with friends, or was it just with each other that they couldn't think of a word to say?

'The day I run out of things to say is the day I die,' Olly had announced, before leaning across to them, Joe attempting to pull him back, but once Olly had an idea in his head . . .

'I know I shouldn't be eavesdropping,' said Olly, 'but fascinating, really *fascinating* . . .'

'We had to drag him out,' I say, 'before the restaurant banned us.'

'Do you remember when you forgot to bring your heels to that black tie?'

'I told Olly I couldn't go, everyone would be staring at my trainers.'

'So he carried you across the garden and into the marquee.'

'I danced barefoot.'

Another silence.

'You might not know this,' Joe begins again, 'you

were in Florence at the time, but my father came to Clifton. It was my birthday and he was determined to take us all out to the smartest restaurant in town.'

'Wish I'd been there.'

'No. No, you don't. We'd have felt much more comfortable in the pub. Jamie called my father by his first name, which went down like a lead balloon. When Dad raised his glass and said how much he looked forward to my success in the surgical field, do you know what Olly said?'

I shake my head.

'Mr Lawson, isn't it up to Joe what he specializes in? He might not want to slice people up for a living.'

I laugh, proud of him. 'A lot of us tiptoe round one another,' I say, thinking about Mum and Dad hiding the photograph and my wedding dress, 'but Olly always said exactly what was on his mind. He had no fear like that.'

Joe pushes his plate aside, pours us both another glass of water. 'The only time I saw him scared was when you left.'

'What do you mean?'

'He wanted you to go to Florence, he knew it was something you had to do, but the idea of you meeting some tall, dark Italian opera singer and forgetting all about him – that terrified him.'

I nod, building myself up to the question. 'Why did you disappear, Joe? Leave Bristol without saying a word?'

'At last,' says Olly's voice.

'My mother died.'

'Oh. I'm so sorry.'

'She had cancer of the pancreas. They found it much too late. Even with the best medical care she had no chance.'

'Why didn't you tell us? Especially Olly?'

'You were both in Florence. You'd just got back together.'

I nod. Olly had flown out – a last-minute surprise – during the Easter break. I hadn't seen him for over six months, and during this time we'd both been seeing other people. I was going out with Luca, a chef. He was handsome, but he didn't make me laugh, not like Olly. I don't think it would have worked since we didn't have enough in common, but it was fun at the time. When I met Olly at the Duomo all my old feelings for him flooded back. It was clear we both still loved one another. He stayed with me for three weeks, before returning to Bristol for the summer term and his finals. Joe had vanished.

Joe clears his throat. 'I didn't want to rain on your parade and–'

'He was your best friend. He would have supported you. So would I.'

'Really? I seem to remember you saying you hated me, that you never wanted to see me again.'

I twist one corner of the napkin, guilt creeping into my veins.

'I helped Dad with the funeral, but after that I went off the rails. I did many things I'm not proud of. The one and only thing I knew was I didn't want to study medicine any more. I was so angry with Dad; I blamed him for Mum's death. Vice-President of this, chairman of that – but he couldn't even help his wife, my mum. Part of the reason I wanted to leave Bristol was to hurt him. Throw my education back in his face with all the hopes he'd had for me, because they were his dreams, not mine . . .'

'But why didn't you talk to Olly? Why did you ignore his messages?'

'I wasn't a good friend.' He looks at me directly. 'You know that more than anyone. When he called to tell me you were back together, I wanted to be pleased, I did . . . but . . . I never stopped caring about him, or you . . .' He trails off, 'but I couldn't find it in me to be happy. I was too messed up, too focused on myself. Olly deserved better. He didn't need me. He had you, his music. He had so many friends,' he says, trying to justify it.

'He missed you. I can't believe we didn't know your mother had died, that you went through it alone.'

'I took off, went to Australia to stay with my uncle,' Joe continues, as if he doesn't want to think about the hurt he caused by cutting Olly out of his life. 'I had to leave. I can't explain it, I'm not doing a good job, but all I knew was I needed to clear my head and make a new start. I ended up staying with Uncle Tom for three years, working in his vineyard and learning about the wine business.'

'How's Tubster?' Joe asks towards the end of our lunch, both of us in need of some lighter conversation. 'Tubster' was Olly's nickname for Jamie.

'He's dating someone called Amanda. She's awful,' I confess. 'Calls him Jamie dearest, and orders him about, almost treats him like her child.'

'I once had a girlfriend called Amanda, but it was over the moment she told me it was my bathtime.'

I smile, more at Joe's deadpan delivery.

'And Sylvie?'

'Works in marketing. Going out with her boss.' I fold my napkin in half, then halve it again.

'You used to do that with crisp packets too.'

I look up, blushing. 'And you? Are you married, Joe?' As I ask him, I recall Annie saying he was the most eligible bachelor in town.

'I have a girlfriend. Peta.' His eyes warm up. 'She's an actress.'

'How did you meet?'

'Here. She's lovely. We haven't known one another for long but I like her, a lot.' He runs a hand through his hair. 'Rebecca, if you don't want to talk about it, I'd understand. But how did it happen? The accident?'

I tell Joe he was on his motorbike. 'He was taking a short cut, thought he could overtake . . .' I breathe deeply, remembering how I'd been waiting for him to return, but knowing something was wrong the moment I heard the loud knock on the door.

I press a hand to my forehead. 'What hurts is it was so avoidable.'

'We're all guilty of taking stupid risks,' claims Joe. 'Doing a quick overtake or going through a red light because we're in a hurry. We never think it's going to happen to us.'

I nod.

'And then you discovered you were pregnant?'

'Yes.'

Joe looks awkward, unsure how to comfort me. 'I wish I'd seen him,' he says. 'I tried to call, some time ago now. I tracked you down, left messages. I never heard back from you so I assumed you still didn't want anything to do with me.'

'We've all done things we regret,' I say, 'me included.'

I cycle home. 'What did you want to talk to me about that day, Olly?' I'd promised myself not to go over and over the same question, promised Kitty not to torture myself, but talking to Joe has brought it all back. 'You were quiet over breakfast. What was worrying you? Why were you so distracted?'

'He called?' Olly says. 'When? Why didn't you tell me, Becca?'

I pedal faster; under the arch by the print shop, past the Wykeham Arms pub. 'You haven't answered my question, Olly. I need to know.'

'You haven't answered mine. Why did you hate Joe? What happened between you two?'

12

Bristol University, Ten Years Ago

Alone in my bedroom I tear open the letter. It's from the director of the art academy in Florence.

I read it and reread it, just to make sure. 'We are pleased to inform you . . .'

I do a little dance before rushing downstairs to phone Kitty. After she's congratulated me, she brings me back down to earth with a bump. 'You'll have to tell your parents now.'

I twist the telephone cord with one hand.

'Olly will miss you too.' There's a pause. 'You have told him, haven't you?'

'Give me a chance. I've only just found out.'

'Yeah, but he knows you applied, right?'

Kitty understands the meaning of my silence.

*

Olly will be happy for me, I tell myself, dread in my heart, as I head for the library, hoping to find him revising. Summer exams are looming. He'll understand this is an incredible opportunity. I want to follow my dream and be an artist.

I look back to that day when my father showed me some old sketchbooks belonging to his Aunt Cecily. 'That's your great-aunt, Becca,' he'd said, carefully lifting some leather books out of a box. We were alone in his study on a Sunday afternoon because Mum had taken Pippa to a six-hour tennis-coaching session in Slough. The books were worn at the edges and inside the paper was fragile, but they smelled of adventure. Underneath each work of art she had written neatly in pencil the scene and date. That afternoon, Great-Aunt Cecily took me to cafes in Barcelona, beaches in Cornwall, fields of cows in Somerset, deserts in Egypt, and I remember being mesmerized by her pictures of African wildlife. 'Cecily loved architecture,' Dad told me, showing me exquisite ink drawings of Corinthian columns, Norman archways and church doors; there was even a sketch of the west side of Winchester Cathedral. Dad explained that that was how he'd first known about Winchester, because this is where she had lived too. I loved the Winchester paintings because they were familiar. My favourite, however, was a picture of the hilltop basilica of San Miniato al Monte in Florence. Dad told me it was a magnificent Romanesque church, with an adjoining Olivetan monastery. When he pointed to the mosaic of Christ enthroned between the Virgin Mary and St Minias I said, 'Wowee, Dad!' thinking it looked so splendid in gold. I can remember my relief after seeing Great-Aunt Cecily's work. Old aunts can often be associated with mothballs, but Cecily was an explorer. 'She would have been twenty-eight then,' Dad told me when we saw she'd visited Florence in 1917. I vowed to myself that when I was grown-up, I would go to Italy and see it for myself, with my own sketchbook.

I pass the library cafe, head for the stairs . . .

Students are working in enclosed cubicles, but there's no sign of Olly. There's only one other place he might be.

'You're very lucky, Becca, that you enjoy painting so much too,' Dad had said, 'It's a wonderful hobby.'

'Hobby?' Olly had commented later, when were lying in bed, my head resting under the crook of his arm, listening to 'Supergrass'. We were nineteen, going on twenty, and had been dating for nearly six months. I'd invited him down to Winchester for the weekend. 'That's patronizing, isn't it?'

I went on to tell him how Pippa's tennis wasn't a hobby; my parents, especially Mum, had great dreams that she'd play at Wimbledon. My art, on the other hand, was fun, but no one makes a living out of painting. 'Look at Andy Warhol,' Olly protested.

'He's dead.'

'Yeah, but he made a fortune. How about David Hockney? He's laughing all the way to the bank!'

He stroked my long thick hair, curled it round in his fingers. 'I've never seen your paintings, Becca. Can I?'

I reached for my black portfolio folder on top of the wardrobe.

Carefully he leafed through my work. I pointed out my favourite painting, a stylized cafe scene which had won first prize at college. 'What's this one?' he asked, hooking one foot over mine. 'Oh my God,' I said, memories flooding back. 'There was this competition, for five- to nine-year-olds . . .' Olly was distracting me, rubbing his foot against mine, his touch tickling, 'and we had to draw a natural disaster.' Before us was a picture of a red house, the bricks crumbling, and in the background were mountains and bubbling lava, but it was the figure in the foreground that made Olly and me smile because his legs looked so odd. I'd wanted the man to be running furiously, away from the disaster, but I couldn't get his leg action right. He looked as though he was doing the splits. From the top of the house, I'd screamed with frustration. 'Oh, is that all,' Mum had said, when she rushed in to see what all the drama was about. She didn't even look at my painting. I told Olly, 'I was so angry that I scrunched it up and threw it in the bin. That's why it's so creased now.'

'Do you miss painting?'

I nodded. 'But they're right. It's a hard way to make a living.'

As I gathered my drawings together Olly gripped my wrist. 'Becca, I want to be a writer, and no one is going to tell me I can't do it. They can fuck off. Don't listen to your parents!' He put the folder on the floor and kicked the bedroom door shut. 'You've got to do what makes you happy. It's your life. Come here.'

Soon we were kissing. I raised my arms; Olly pulled off my T-shirt. Next his hand was expertly unhooking my bra; he'd had a lot of practice by this time.

'You're amazing and talented,' he murmured, as I pulled off his jumper, my hand now reaching for the buckle on his belt.

'Rebecca, supper!' Mum called up to us.

We paused for a second, our mouths pressed against each other, but next we were stripping off. 'Have you got something?' I murmured. 'We've got to be quick . . .'

'I can do quick.' Olly jumped off the bed and grabbed his wallet from the back pocket of his jeans.

I run down the corridor, the sound of music filling the air.

Where is he? He must be here . . .

Olly is in the last room. Quietly I open the door and stand in one corner. He has his back to me. His body moves with the music, his head tilts from side to side, his fingers ripple over the keys, gaining speed as the piece becomes livelier.

Tears fill my eyes when I realize how much I love him. Am I prepared to give that up, to go away?

When the piece comes to an end he stands up and bows, as if he were in the Royal Albert Hall.

I clap and wolf-whistle, call out, 'Encore!'

He turns to me, cheeks glowing with embarrassment. 'Becca! How long have you been standing there?'

'Long enough to know you are quite brilliant.' I perch on the end of the stool. 'That was beautiful, Ol. What was it?'

He sits down next to me. 'Schubert.' He starts to play another piece, enjoying the audience now.

I glance at the music sheet. It's Schubert's Impromptu in G-flat major.

'Who do you imagine you're playing to?'

'Cameron Diaz.'

'Hey!' I nudge him before striking a key.

'Naked,' he finishes.

'I always know something's wrong when you bite your nails,' Olly says, as we walk back home together.

'What do you think about me going to art college?'

'What do you mean? When?'

'I've been accepted on to this course.'

'What course?'

'It looks amazing, Olly. It's a foundation in drawing, painting and sculpture, and the teacher sounds so inspiring. Many of his students have gone on to become professionals and—'

'Becca, slow down! I think it's a great idea, but . . .'

'This autumn.'

Olly stops. He lets go of my hand. 'You'd leave Bristol?' We cross the road.

'Um.'

'Right. Can't you finish your degree and then do it?'

'My heart's not in it, Olly. If it weren't for you . . . Anyway, if I applied next year, I might not get on.'

'Where is it, this course?'

This is the part I've been dreading. 'Florence.'

Don't look at me like that.

'How long would you be away?'

'A year . . . but you could visit all the time.'

His pace picks up. He digs his hand into his pocket, finds his house keys. 'Why didn't you tell me?'

'I didn't think I'd be accepted. I thought if I told everyone–'

'I'm hardly everyone, Becca. I'm your boyfriend.'

'I thought if I told you, it would curse my luck,' I say, catching up with him. 'It's like when I took my driving test. I didn't tell anyone, so that I wouldn't have to explain if I failed, which I did – on my emergency stop. Pressed down hard on the accelerator instead.'

He doesn't find me funny this time. 'Have you spoken to our tutors?'

'Not yet.'

'Parents?' Olly opens the front door, dumps his books on to the side table, next to an army of empty wine bottles that we've collected in the last few days. 'My marks haven't been great,' I say, justifying my reasons to give up my course here. 'I can't get away with drawing pictures down the margins any more.' When I was at school, to make up for my average essays, I'd accompany them with sketches of Vikings in their warrior hats.

'Do you have to go abroad?' he interrupts me in the middle of my warrior hat story. 'Aren't there colleges over here? There's even one in Winchester, isn't there?'

'Yes, but this is my one chance to do something different,' I say, following him into the kitchen. 'I want to work all summer, save up and . . .'

Olly turns to me. 'I can't believe this, Becca. You're always having a go at me about how *I* do what the hell I want half the time without asking you, but here you are telling me you're about to move to another country! You could have at least have told me you'd applied.'

He leaves the room. I shut my eyes when I hear the front door slam.

'What's wrong?' Joe asks. I don't know how long I'd been sitting at the kitchen table, thinking about what Olly had said. It must have been a long time, since it was now dark outside.

'I'm leaving Bristol, Joe.'

He heads to the sink, pours himself a glass of water. I tell him about the course. I mention that I'd kept it quiet until I knew I'd been accepted.

'I see. And Olly's mad?' Joe pulls up a chair, sits down next to me.

'Furious. Maybe I should try and find him, tell him I'm sorry. I should have told him, Joe.'

He touches my shoulder. 'He won't be mad for long, Becca. Talk to him when he's calmed down.'

There's a long silence, which I break finally. 'And you, Joe? What do you think? Am I doing the right thing?'

'Only you can answer that.'

I wish I could read Joe's mind. Since that moment when I thought he was about to kiss me, we haven't spent much time together alone, just the two of us. Subconsciously, perhaps, I have been avoiding him.

'Maybe I shouldn't go.'

'This course . . . is it what you really want?'

I nod, slowly.

'Well then,' he shrugs. 'I mean, if you were sitting here telling me you wanted to quit Bristol to become a pig farmer in New Zealand, I'd say your relationship was over but . . . If you and Olly are meant to be, you'll work it out.'

I take his hand. 'Thank you.' His support warms my heart. 'I needed to hear that.'

'Right.' Joe withdraws his hand and stands up. 'I need to get ready. I'm going out with Liz.'

Liz is the current girlfriend.

'Have a good time.'

'Olly will come round. He's only cross because he loves you and he'll miss you.'

'I know.'

'Oh, and Becca–'

I look up to Joe, now standing at the door.

'Your Mum called. They've bought a puppy, a miniature dachshund or something, and your father wants to call her Audrey.'

I smile, telling him my father has always loved Audrey Hepburn.

'I can see you living in a studio in Italy,' Joe says finally, 'painting the cypresses, sunlight streaming in through the windows.'

'I'm sorry,' says Olly, late that night when he returns.

'I'm sorry too,' I say tearfully.

We rush to hug.

'You're the one that inspired me, Ol, said I should follow my heart.'

'Bollocks. I wish I hadn't opened my big mouth.' He strokes my hair, tucks a strand behind my ear. 'Oh, Becca, if it were anyone else . . . but it's not.' He holds me in his arms again. 'You're right. Of course you should go. It's a great opportunity . . .'

There's a 'but' in his tone.

'But where does that leave us?'

13

'She's been at home for a month now,' Mum whispers in the kitchen, 'and just locks herself in her bedroom.' I'm standing outside, listening.

'What? Speak up,' Dad says. I can hear coffee being poured, toast popping up and the sound of my father turning the pages of his newspaper.

'She needs a reason to get out of bed,' Mum says, turning down John Humphrys on the *Today* programme. 'She's still in bed, Harvey. It's like having a teenager in the house again. Do you think we should suggest counselling?'

'Hmmm?'

'Why aren't you wearing your aid?'

'It makes a horrid noise. Can you pass the marmalade?'

'I've heard her, talking to herself upstairs. I'm worried, Harvey.'

'Let her be.' Dad sighs. 'What do you expect her to be doing? She needs time to grieve.'

'I know.'

'Did I tell you I bumped into Jeremy at Sainsbury's?'

Jeremy is an old family friend.

'Eleanor has broken her ankle – she slipped on a cattle grid,' Dad continues. 'She's in hospital.'

'How awful. We must send her a card, or flowers. Which hospital?'

'I don't know. He didn't say.'

'How long will she be there?'

'I don't know.'

'It must be a bad break, if she's in hospital.'

'He didn't say.'

'Well, you should have asked! I'll give him a ring. I'm still worried about Becca,' she adds.

'It's going to be a long hard road.'

'She's talking to herself. I can't hear what she's saying but—'

'I talk to myself, in my shed.'

Mum laughs. 'Yes, but come on, it's different for you. You're an old man. Marjorie was asking if Becca would like to help her.'

My shoulders stiffen. Marjorie is one of Mum's tennis friends who runs an online business called Country

Knick-Knacks. Country Tat, Dad calls it. I hide from her when I see her in town.

'I might call her . . .'

NO! I scream inside.

The pinger rings. Dad's boiled egg is ready. 'No,' Dad argues. 'Don't rush her. Our job right now is to be here, that's all.'

14

It's mid-August, the morning of my twenty-week scan. I have been living at home now for eight weeks. Mum, Dad and I have slotted into a routine. I take Audrey out for walks, often with Janet and Woody. Sometimes Mum joins me with the twins, which makes the walk an event.

There's a contest between them as to who opens the small white kissing gate leading into the water meadows. Often there are tantrums, and it's usually Oscar who refuses to walk, sitting down, *splat*, in a cowpat in his newly washed and ironed combat trousers. Theo then copies him. I don't know how Mum looks after them on such a regular basis while Pippa works at the tennis club. By the end of the day she is snappy and hits the vodka bottle an hour early, skipping a cup of tea.

I'm in touch daily with friends. Jamie was just as

shocked as me when he heard Joe was living in Winchester. Sylvie is curious to meet him again, although they were never close at Bristol. She doesn't know what happened between Joe and me. None of my friends do except for Kitty. Carolyn and I talk regularly. She tells me about the vegetables and herbs she's growing, adding how she loves the long summer evenings when she can do her planting. I imagine her garden is her sanctuary.

I've been helping Mum cook, yet even that isn't quite as simple as it sounds. 'Oh, that's interesting,' she said last time, when I'd added lime juice to my chicken marinade. 'Clare Francis says lemon works better *and* you should add the zest.' Clare Francis is Mum's friend and cooking guru.

I talk to Olly. Sometimes I hear his voice inside my head, sometimes I don't. He continues to say that nothing was worrying him on the morning of the accident. I wish Mum, Dad and I had the courage to mention his name across the supper table.

'No, Pippa, I'm sorry, but I can't,' I overhear Mum say down the telephone, as I finish reading an email from Glitz.

My heart lifts when I read: 'I've worked out a bonus for you, plus maternity leave, and then, after you've had the baby, we can review. I'll be sending the cheque shortly.'

Lovely Glitz. What a supportive boss and friend he has become. This money will give me a sense of security. After my appointment, I'll call to thank him.

'I miss you,' he finishes. 'Marty and I think of you often. Good luck with the ultrasound. Love, Glitz.'

'I know it's still the holidays, but it's Becca's scan,' I overhear Mum saying. A couple of minutes later she puts the phone down.

'Come on, Rebecca, you can read that later,' she orders, and for a second I feel like I'm ten years old and being told that if I don't get a move on, I'll be late for school. Still, it's good of her to be coming with me, I remind myself. 'What did Pippa want?' I ask.

'To look after the boys. I can see it's difficult for her, but . . .'

'I can go on my own, Mum.'

'No. I can't always be at her beck and call.'

Why don't they get an au pair? It's a question that's been on my mind for some time, but I don't ask Mum. I don't want to rock the boat just as we're about to go to the hospital.

Mum and I gaze at the monitor screen. This time we can make out the shape of my baby.

I watch the nurse's expression carefully as she studies the screen. I know how much I want this baby now because I am terrified that she will detect something wrong, but so far she is telling me all the measurements of its head and abdominal circumference and the thigh bone are just as they should be.

'Would you like to know the sex?' she asks.

Mum has advised I keep it a surprise, but I can see from the way she's stopped knitting that even she is a tiny bit tempted.

'It's a boy, isn't it?' I say.

She nods. 'It's a boy.'

Mum and I look at one another tearfully. I reach for her hand, but then withdraw it just as quickly.

'Mum! I felt him kick!' It was like a little tap, an air bubble inside me. He kicks me again.

'He's saying hello, introducing himself.' Mum smiles.

'I'm going to cook supper tonight,' I announce to Mum. 'You go and put your feet up.' Mum stares at me as if I've just told her to go paragliding. 'I'll make some spaghetti, if we have mince.' Lemon chicken and spaghetti bolognese are about the only things in my repertoire.

I open the fridge, locate a packet of minced beef

behind a bowl filled with half a chicken fillet, a few tired-looking green beans and a couple of carrots soggy from gravy: last night's leftovers.

'We can eat it for lunch,' Mum says, protesting when I suggest we bin it. 'Or Audrey can have it as a treat.'

I peel off the outer layer of the onion, slice off the stem and root and start chopping. Mum is back in the kitchen only minutes later. I glance at the clock: six thirty on the dot. As she heads over to the vodka bottle . . . 'Oh,' she says. Soon she's hovering over me like an eagle and I can feel my shoulders tense and my hackles rise.

'You do it like that?' Mum looks down at my onion.

'What?' I sniffle, wiping away the tears.

She pushes me out of the way as she peels the second onion and cuts it in half. 'I slice it horizontally, three times towards the root,' she says, before swiftly spinning the onion towards her and slicing it, she counts out loud, 'one, two, three, four, five, six times, from top to bottom, *comme ça*,' before swivelling the onion round again, holding it tightly with her thumb and forefinger, 'and then,' she says, as if this is the *pièce de résistance*, 'you slice it over the top, and look! What neat little cubes, plus I'm not crying. Clare Francis tells us . . .'

'Oh, stop banging on about Clare Francis,' I say. 'You make her sound like the Messiah.'

Mum laughs. 'Sorry. But she is good. You should come with me to her next lesson.' She dives into her cooking files, on the shelf above the bread bin. 'Here we are: "Hassle-free Entertaining".'

'We'll see.'

After supper, Dad picks up the television controls and stabs at a button. He lets out a giant groan when nothing happens, Mum and I exchange a secret glance. Eventually he finds the right channel. He is keen to watch a programme about the plight of tigers and how we must do everything in our power to save them from extinction.

Quietly I leave the room, deciding to make a telephone call. 'Can I borrow the car?' I ask Mum when I return, Dad already fast asleep.

She looks surprised. 'Are you off somewhere?'

'Annie's.' As I'm about to head out the door, Mum still knitting, I feel a tug of affection towards her; the wall between us is being chipped away, even if she irritates me in the kitchen. 'Thanks, Mum.'

'What for?'

'For coming with me today. It meant a lot, and I know

Olly would have been glad I wasn't alone too.' There. I've said his name out loud, and it felt good. Liberating.

'It meant a lot to me too.'

'Maybe we can go shopping soon,' I suggest, thinking of Glitz's forthcoming cheque. 'I need to start thinking about prams and cots and . . .'

'I'd love to.' Tearful, she holds up her half-finished matinee coat. 'I can hardly believe he'll be as tiny as this,' she says.

15

Annie lives in St Cross, in a small street tucked behind St Faith's Road, close to our old school and the water meadows. She opens the door in a bright-blue dress, the colour of an exotic bird. 'Come in,' she says, leading me down a narrow hallway and into an open-plan kitchen with an island in the middle. A small table is at the end of the room, in front of the double doors that lead out into the garden. 'I'm on my own tonight. Richie's at some conference on gum disease.' She rolls her eyes. 'So I'm glad you called.' She lifts the kettle. 'Tea, my darling?'

I'm enjoying getting to know Annie again. I've discovered she used to live in Islington, worked in recruitment, but was always determined to run her own business. She lost her virginity on her twenty-first birthday to a two-timing monkey called Christian. 'Late starter,' she'd laughed, 'but don't worry, I've more than made up for it since.' She lived with Richie the dentist for a year before realizing she'd fallen in love with him.

Annie gives me a quick tour of the house. 'Winchester was the one place we both loved,' she says, walking into the sitting room, a cosy space with cream sofas and a guitar on a stand. 'Can you play?' I ask, impressed.

'Badly. I was in a band for a while, in London.' It reminds me of Olly. 'My dream was to be famous and marry a rock star. I ended up working in a shop and marrying a dentist!'

'Well, mine was to be an artist. I ended up selling other people's art instead!'

Olly's dream was to be a writer.

'Maybe we shouldn't have dreams,' I suggest to Annie.

She shakes her head. 'If you don't have dreams, you don't have hope,' she says.

Over a cup of tea we reminisce about our school days. She rushes out of the room and returns with a photograph. 'Oh my God!' It's our school play. There's Annie, wearing a red medieval dress that drowned her, with a matching headdress, looking miserable. I'm in the background, Friar Tuck, donning a brown hooded robe with a makeshift rope belt around my substantial waist. 'It was no wonder they gave me that part. I look pregnant!' I gasp.

'D'you remember our music competition, singing the Frog Chorus?'

'*We all stand together*,' we sing out, and I'm laughing properly for the first time in ages.

Annie says she's longing to meet Kitty again. She remembers her being teacher's pet, the swot sitting at the front of the class, waving her arm in the air, desperate to answer every question. The teachers often had to tell her to give someone else a chance. I tell Annie she works for a leading careers consultant in Piccadilly.

'Single? Married?'

'Single. She hasn't had much luck with men.' Her last internet date had been with a guy called Phil. 'He had a head the size of a peanut,' Kitty had lamented, 'and mean little eyes. He didn't pay for my drink either.'

When Annie asks how I'm doing, I tell her about the scan. 'It's a boy,' I reveal.

'A boy,' she sighs. 'Your first is exciting. I'll write a list of all the things you'll need if you like.'

I tell her Pippa has already done this, though her list was as long as a marathon. 'I'm halfway through,' I joke, pretending I'm out of breath, 'not sure I'll reach the end.' I accept Annie's kind offer. Besides, it might be interesting comparing.

'And if there's *anything* else I can do . . .'

I take a sip. Go on, ask, she won't bite. 'Well, there might be.'

'Oh?'

'I'm a little bored.'

'That's an understatement,' Olly's voice pipes up.

'I don't have enough to do.'

'Christ, I wish I was in your position,' she blurts out, before apologizing. 'Oh fuck, it wasn't supposed to come out like that . . .'

'Annie, don't worry,' I smile, putting her at ease. 'You don't have to tiptoe around me. I get enough of that at home.'

'Tact has never been my strong point. Right. What could you do?' Annie strums her fingers against the table. 'Join a few societies?'

I pull a face.

'Learn French?'

'Not sure,' I say, knowing I don't want to learn a language.

'Japanese?' She bows her head towards mine.

I bow my head back. 'No!'

'Swahili?'

'Fluent already.'

'Have some singing lessons?' She tells me an opera singer lives next door and she wakes up to *The Marriage of Figaro*. 'Join a choir. It's the latest rage!'

'I'm tone deaf,' I laugh. When I had piano lessons, the teacher soon told Mum it was a waste of money.

'Knit some tea cosies and flog 'em on a market stall? I know! You must join my bookworm club, though that's hardly going to keep you rushed off your feet. Often we don't even *read* the book. How about salsa classes? Hang on – not such a great idea when you're pregnant.'

I'm going to just have to come out with it. 'Annie, I wondered if you needed an extra pair of hands in the shop.'

'Ah, I see,' she says, chewing her lip. 'Oh, Becca, you saw how empty it was that day you came in, like a morgue. Oh God, I'm so sorry!' She claps a hand over her mouth.

We end up both laughing helplessly.

'It's so quiet that *I'm* going to have to look for a new job soon,' Annie declares. 'If I could employ another person you'd be top of my list, but . . .'

'It was a bad idea, I'm sorry.'

'No. Don't be.'

'I'm sorry work's so quiet for you too. You must be worried.'

'If the worst comes to the worst, I can always sell my body on the streets. Or maybe not.' She stretches out her long pale legs. 'Look at my varicose veins, and I swear I have bikinis that will never see daylight again. What can you do?' she goes on thinking to herself.

I confide how I am now an expert in daytime television. '*Come Dine with Me* is a favourite. I even watched *Celebrity Cash in the Attic* the other day, and I could keep you up to date with *all* the goings-on along Ramsey Street.'

'Is *Neighbours* still on?' she asks, the question of a busy woman.

'Oh yes, twice a day.'

'Look, I'll ask lots of friends, and Richie can ask around too. I know! I'll send out a mass email, I'll Facebook and tweet it and everything. I'll become a social-media hussy.' She clenches her hand into a fist. 'I will get you a job, come what may.'

'Thanks. I'll do anything. Stack shelves, type letters, stuff envelopes, serve coffee, I really don't care.'

A smile slowly spreads across her face. 'I've just remembered something.'

'What?'

'I was in Maison Joe the other day and overheard Edoardo saying something about some girl who couldn't help out on Joe's course. That's right – his next wine tasting course thing starts in a couple of weeks and they've got no one, and Luis and Edoardo were complaining that they're overstretched.'

'I'm not sure.'

'Hang on,' she says, when she hears a child's voice calling for her. 'Back in two ticks.'

When she's out of the room I think about her idea. What have I got to lose? But do I really want to work for him? Am I that desperate to keep busy? But then again, it could be fun, and I do need the distraction. I'm five months pregnant, not an invalid. I can't sit at home doing nothing until the baby arrives, and there are only so many glossy magazines and baby books I can read.

At the end of our lunch, weeks ago, Joe and I had agreed to put everything in the past. 'Come and see me again,' he'd said outside as I was about to leave. I wasn't sure if we were going to hug or shake hands. We ended up doing nothing, but I'm sure I saw kindness in his eyes. But I haven't called him, or dropped by.

'Becca?' Annie taps my arm. 'You're a world away.'

'I was just thinking.'

'About Joe? The job?'

'I'm not sure,' I say again. 'I don't think so.'

'But Maison Joe's perfect. It's only two days a week so it wouldn't be that demanding.'

'Stop biting your fingernails,' Olly says. 'Why don't you want to work for him?'

'Becca, tell me to shut up if it's none of my business, but what exactly happened between you and Joe?' Annie asks.

'You see. And it's about time you told me too,' Olly butts in.

16

Bristol, Ten Years Ago

I lean against the door, eavesdropping. 'I can't be ill, not tonight,' Olly groans.

He and Joe have organized an end-of-term leaving party for me, this evening.

Joe pops a couple of pills out of a packet. 'Take these, right now.'

'Doctor, doctor . . .' Olly collapses on to the bed in a crumpled heap. 'I think I'm a biscuit.'

'This isn't a joke, Olly. You've got a high temperature.'

'You're *crackers*!'

Despite himself, even Joe laughs. Olly lies down; Joe yanks his shoes off and tosses them across the floor. 'Where's Becca?'

'Getting ready,' Joe replies. 'You know how long women take.'

I'm about to barge in and protest that I was ready ages ago, but then decide it's more fun listening. 'Pills,' Joe repeats, and from the crack in the door I can see him handing Olly a glass of water.

'I can't miss her party.'

'I don't think she'll mind. To be frank, you're not much company right now.'

'*To be frank?* I love you Joe, but sometimes you talk like a stuffed shirt.'

'I love you too, but sometimes you're a pain in the arse.'

'We've been arguing lately,' Olly continues. 'Not about Italy, just stuff. Becca's right. I know I can be a selfish arse.'

'It's exams. Everyone's been stressed out.'

'She called me a hypocrite, said that if I had the chance to go to a music academy or whatever, I'd be on that plane tomorrow, but . . . do you know how much I don't want her to go?'

'I know, Olly. None of us do.'

'He's a stubborn patient, isn't he?' I whisper, after I've kissed Olly goodnight.

'He has to be half dead before he misses out on a party.' Joe's expression softens. 'But it's bad luck he's missing yours.'

I nod. 'You're the only one he listens to, you know. It's nothing serious, is it?'

'Flu.'

In the run-up to the end of our second year exams Olly had become increasingly stressed, and was actually sick before he sat any paper. Even though I'd officially left Bristol I found bar and waitressing work locally so that I could be in the flat, pay my rent and support him. We have been arguing, but Joe's right. It's the anxiety of exams, and even though I'm excited about Florence, I'm also nervous about change and leaving this house behind. Olly and I haven't spoken about 'us'. I don't know if we want to have a long-distance relationship, but the uncertain future hangs over us like a dark cloud.

Joe surveys me in my lace corset and tight black jeans, my blonde wig backcombed and styled with a whole can of hairspray. Olly and Joe had organized an eighties night and I am trying to pass myself off as Madonna. I want him to tell me I look good. Instead he tells me he needs to get ready. People will be arriving soon.

*

The buzzer rings. Friends pile in dressed as Duran Duran, Boy George, Michael Jackson and Blondie. Music blasts out from the sitting room, but everyone migrates towards the booze in the kitchen. Sylvie and I lean against the fridge, down a couple of vodka shots. Joe enters the room dressed in a leather jacket, T-shirt and ripped jeans. I laugh at his hair, coiffed like George Michael's.

It's close to midnight when I check on Olly again. Finally, despite the noise, he's asleep. Heady from vodka, I make my way back downstairs, weaving in and out of the crowd blocking the hallway. I enter the kitchen, now misted by smoke, find Joe uncorking a bottle of wine, George Michael's 'Wake Me Up Before You Go-Go' playing in the background.

'George.' I smile, approaching him.

'Madge,' he says, handing me a glass. 'So, you're off.'

'Yep, off and away!' I make drunken movements with my arms, as if they are wings. I stop, realizing I'm drunk. Very drunk. I give it some thought, before coming to the handy conclusion that I don't care. It's my party. I can be as drunk as I like. Sylvie and Jamie join us. Sylvie's dressed as Tina Turner, her hair wild. She sits down on the window ledge. Jamie cracks open another beer, asks us what we're talking about. He's wearing an alarmingly tight-fitting 'Frankie Says Relax' T-shirt.

'Nothing,' Joe replies. I get the feeling he wants them to leave.

'Just that I'll miss you all,' I sigh. 'I love you all.'

'Oh fuck, how much has she had to drink?' Sylvie asks Joe, before handing me her half-smoked cigarette and dragging Jamie away.

A new crowd comes into the kitchen, one guy dressed in a military-style jacket and leather trousers, face paint smudged across his nose and cheeks. 'I don't know who half these people are,' I whisper to Joe.

'Nor do I.'

Mr Adam Ant lookalike pushes his way in front of me. 'Hot,' he says, eyeing me up and down. I edge towards Joe, before Adam Ant shouts, 'Arsehole!' His jeans are now soaked in an unfortunate place by Joe's wine.

'Oops. Accident.' Joe's holding an empty glass. He grabs my hand. 'Come on, let's get out of here.'

'I'm sorry we didn't get off to the best of starts,' Joe says as we walk into the small square opposite our house. Even though he's been drinking, he's in control as always.

'You stealing my towel, you mean?'

Joe steers me in a straighter line. 'I thought it was Olly's.'

'It was pink.'

'I thought it was Olly's.'

I laugh. 'I thought you were the arrogantest man *ever.*'

'There isn't such a word, Becca. You say, *most* arrogant.'

'You see. That's why I gave up English.' I turn to him. 'You always have to be right, don't you?'

'Always.'

'You drive me mad, Joe.'

'Good.'

We walk on. 'I hope you'll be happy,' he says.

'You too, Joe.'

His expression suggests that's never going to happen.

'I don't understand you,' I say, plonking myself down on the bench. He sits down next to me. 'You have *so much* going for you, Joe. If you don't want to read medicine, do something else. D'you remember that conversation you, me and Olly had, 'bout what we'd be doing in ten years' time?'

'I don't like looking ahead.'

'Well, you should. If you don't see yourself being a doctor, then stop wasting your time . . .' I prod him on the arm. 'Do something you love, because we only live once, Joe.'

'Great lecture.' He claps. 'A-plus.'

I cross my arms, indignant. 'You act big, all tough, but when it boils down to it, you're just a coward.'

'Excuse me?'

'You heard me. You're a coward, Joe Lawson.' I smile, as if it all makes perfect sense now. 'If you're not happy, change. Do something about it.' Alcohol has loosened my tongue. 'What are you scared of?'

He reaches into his pocket for his cigarettes.

'Are you scared of failing your dad? My parents aren't exactly thrilled I'm going, but at least it's my decision,' I continue. 'I think you're terrified of letting him down; you're so scared of mucking up, you make out you don't care.'

'Becca . . .' he says in a warning tone.

'You go out with loads of different girls . . . there was Fiona, Zoe . . . what happened to Liz? None of them last because you don't want to deal with real feelings. It's much easier, isn't it, keeping it simple, just carry on pretending . . . ?'

He covers my mouth with his hand. 'Enough! Enough,' he repeats, looking into my eyes. I've seen that look before. How can I pretend I don't recognize it? I hold his gaze, knowing I'm in trouble. I'm crossing a line. What are we doing here, alone? I think of Olly, asleep inside. I move away from him. 'Let's go back,' I say quietly.

By the time I go to bed it's four in the morning. I slip off my heels and fling my blonde wig on to the dressing table. I unpin my long hair; it falls against my bare shoulders. I wipe the scarlet lipstick off my mouth. There's a knock on the door. When Sylvie comes in I realize that I'm disappointed.

'Major hangover tomorrow,' she says as we kiss each other goodnight. 'Shame Olly was ill,' she adds.

I sit down on the bed, confused. Joe and I, we're friends. I'm with Olly. I love Olly, don't I? Soon I'll be gone. Just forget about him, why don't you?

I see us dancing in the early hours of this morning. I see that look in his eyes again, his face so close to mine, his hand pressed against my back . . .

Stop it! It's Joe. Joe Lawson. Olly's friend. I don't have feelings for him. He's cocky, arrogant, always thinks he's right. But there is a lovely side to him too. He takes me by surprise, can say things that touch my heart. Ironically he's given me more support than anyone about Florence, but then again, that's only because Olly loves me and wishes I was going to an art college in this country. At least Olly's honest enough to say that. With Joe, it's hard to know what he thinks. Most importantly, he's Olly's *best* friend. What am I thinking? I will not be another name on his list of conquests. He only wants me because he can't have me. Is this some game he's playing? Well, I won't play.

I stand up, attempt to undo the bow at the back of my corset, desperate to get out of this tight thing and into my pyjamas, but it's impossible to undo the buttons with these stupid fake fingernails. My mind wanders back to Joe again. Maybe I'm a *tiny* bit attracted to him. I can't deny I haven't thought about kissing him. I'm sure Olly fantasizes about other women, it's only natural. What is going to happen when I'm in Italy? Can we both remain faithful? 'Come on,' I mutter, hopping up and down with frustration when I hear another knock on the door. I freeze. 'Who is it?'

'Joe.'

Adrenalin charges through me. Cautiously I move towards the door. 'I'm really tired,' I say, turning round and leaning against it, squeezing my eyes shut.

'Let me in,' he says softly. I hear the door handle opening.

I move away. Joe enters, barefoot. He's in jeans and a loose T-shirt, hair damp. 'What is it?' I ask, my heart pounding.

'You know why I'm here.'

'Listen, I'm really—'

'Tired? So am I.'

He walks over to me, kisses the nape of my neck, unhooks the lace corset. 'I'm tired of pretending,' he says, as it falls to the floor. He turns me round to face him. I'm standing almost naked in front of Joe. *Tell him to go*, I'm thinking, his face only inches away from mine now. I close my eyes.

But then I push him away, just in time. 'What are you doing?'

'I'm sorry. I thought you felt differently. Clearly I was wrong.'

His sense of calm irritates me. 'What do you mean, felt differently? I'm going out with Olly!'

Anger flares in his eyes. 'You think I don't know that?'

'I'm going to check on him,' I say, grabbing my dressing gown. I put it on, pulling the cord tightly around my waist. I open the door; Joe slams it shut. I fight to push past him, but he blocks my way, edges me against the wall. 'Becca, don't you dare pretend you haven't been aware of something between us.'

Trapped, I'm still unable to meet his eye.

'Olly's a good friend,' he continues, 'he's the last person I want to hurt, but I can't pretend any more, I can't just act as if I've got no fucking feelings. Why do you think I can't commit to anyone?'

He holds both hands firmly against my cheeks, forces me to look at him. 'Why, Becca? You know why.'

'Joe, we can't do this.'

He lets me go. 'You're right. Forget about it. My mistake.' He walks away, out of my room, along the corridor.

'Joe!' I call out.

When he turns to face me I drop my arms by my side. We rush towards one another, he takes my face firmly in both hands again, but this time he kisses me urgently and I kiss him back. We head back to my bedroom and shut the door. I pull off his T-shirt; he unbuckles my belt. I wriggle out of my trousers, his hand slips inside my red silk knickers, his touch teasing, but soon they are peeled off and we're on the bed, naked, kissing, our hands exploring one another. 'I've wanted you for so long,' he says, lifting my legs to wrap round his waist.

We fall asleep in each other's arms, our clothes strewn across the floor, daylight already creeping in through the window.

17

Lying in bed late that night I feel relieved I've told Annie the truth.

It was a long time ago, yet when I shut my eyes I can see the following morning so vividly. I woke up hearing Olly calling my name. Events from the night before flashed in front of me. I shook Joe awake.

'Becca!' Olly groaned. I could hear the sound of footsteps coming towards my bedroom.

Head pounding, I slipped on my dressing gown, shut the door behind me and met Olly outside the bathroom. 'I feel terrible,' he said.

'Go back to bed,' I urged, guiding him back to his room. 'I'll bring you a cup of tea.' I felt sick, as if my head was about to explode.

'What would I do without you?' he murmured, as I propped him up on the pillows.

'You'd be better off,' I said, fighting hard not to cry.

'I had weird dreams last night,' he recalled. 'You were with someone.'

'What?' A shiver ran down my spine.

'In Florence. You'd fallen for a Luigi, or was his name Giuseppe?'

'Olly, just rest.'

'He was serenading you in his gondola.'

I smiled faintly. 'That's Venice.'

'I'm sorry I've been crap . . .'

'You haven't.'

'I haven't been much support, have I? Things haven't been that great between us . . .'

'It doesn't matter.'

'We still haven't spoken about what happens when you go. Do you think long-distance relationships can work?'

'We'll never know if we don't give it a try,' I replied, guilt streaming through my veins, 'but let's not talk about it now.'

'I love you, Becca,' he murmured, before shutting his eyes.

When I returned to my room Joe was sitting up, but he was still in my bed, undressed. I wanted him out, gone. I couldn't bear even to look at him. 'You need to leave,' I said quietly, terrified of waking the others.

'Becca, we need to talk.'

'No. No, we don't. Just go. Last night was a mistake, Joe.'

'No, it wasn't.'

How could he be so calm? So controlled? Didn't he feel guilty?

I picked up his clothes off the floor, gathered them into a bundle and shoved them at him. 'You and me, nothing happened,' I said shakily. 'What we did, it's wrong, all wrong.'

Joe pulled on his jeans.

'What's Olly done to deserve friends like us?' I asked, disgusted with myself. 'I was drunk! I didn't know what I was doing . . .'

He stood up and faced me. 'Don't say that. I'm not saying it was right—' he took a deep breath 'but I knew what I was doing, and I think you did too.'

'No!' I lashed out, hitting him on the chest. 'You shouldn't have come into my room. All of this – it's your fault!'

'That's not fair.'

'I hate you!'

He took me into his arms. For a moment I stayed there. 'You don't hate me, Rebecca.'

I pushed him away.

'I'll go,' Joe said calmly. 'But later we can talk–'

'There's nothing to talk about!'

'Becca?' I heard Olly calling.

Joe and I froze, a painful silence filling the space between us.

I heard Sylvie's door opening . . . footsteps heading to the bathroom.

'Leave. Please go,' I begged tearfully. 'We can't see one another ever again.'

Joe walked out of my room and out of my life. That was the last time I saw him . . . until we met again in Maison Joe, ten years on.

'I'm so sorry, Olly, I should have told you,' I whisper now, 'but at the time I was so confused and scared. I was a coward. I didn't love Joe. It was one night, just a one-night stand. We had an attraction, I can't pretend that we didn't, but he wasn't you. I know that doesn't make it any easier, or excuse it in any way. I love you.'

I hear nothing. I tell myself that it isn't real when I hear his voice. I imagine it. Grief does strange things to you. Yet deep inside I know I'm not hearing him now because his silence says it all.

The following morning my body aches with loneliness, my heart dreads the empty day ahead. I realize I can't work for Joe. What was I thinking, even considering it? I force myself out of bed. I'll feel better when I've had a shower, I tell myself.

'Call him.'

'Olly?'

'You can't keep on watching *Come Dine with Me*.'

'You're not angry?'

'I am angry. Of course I'm angry. You two went behind my back.'

'I know,' I say, ashamed.

'I trusted you both.' He pauses. 'If I'd known about it then, you would have broken my heart. But I can't do anything about it now, can I?'

I launch into another apology, but he stops me. 'I think part of me was always scared you'd fall for him.'

'I didn't fall for him, Olly. I wouldn't have married you if I'd loved Joe, but I'm sorry that I didn't tell you, that it destroyed your friendship. I can't help thinking–'

'Becca, stop! If we haven't learned that life's too short, then we've learned nothing at all. Enough damage has been done already. Be friends with Joe. You need all the friends you can get right now.'

Tears roll down my face.

'Why are you being so forgiving?'

'I've done many things I'm not proud of.'

'Like what?'

Silence.

18

I walk into the crowded bank and fill in a paying-in slip before joining the queue.

Clutching Glitz's cheque, I work out that my bonus has given me enough to buy the essentials for the baby and put down a deposit on a rental place plus my first month's rent in London. My maternity cover helps too, and if I combine this with our savings, I have enough to keep me going for approximately six months. After that, who knows?

I shuffle forward in the queue. It's my turn next.

Thinking of money and work, I still haven't decided what to do about Annie's suggestion of a part-time job at Maison Joe. Should I drop by on my way home to see him? When I saw Annie two days ago, she said his course started soon. If I want the job I need to do something about it now.

'Cashier number five,' says the recorded voice, in a tone that suggests I've just won a prize. A car would be nice. Or a house. No. All I want is Olly back.

'Good afternoon,' the cashier says, dressed in a cream-coloured blouse and navy jacket, plump lips covered in pink gloss. 'How are we today?'

'Great.'

'How can I help?'

I slide the cheque underneath the barrier. 'Can I deposit this into my savings account, please?'

'No problem. Do you have the details?'

She enters the account number into a keypad, a delicate gold bracelet sliding up and down her wrist. Then she slots the cheque into a machine. 'When's it due?' she can't help asking me.

'December.'

'You must be excited.'

I nod.

'You should go on holiday with this, whoop it up, because once you have a baby you can kiss goodbye to any social life . . . but it's all worth it,' she adds, smiling, to end her story in an upbeat way. *Tap tap tap*. 'Right. Well that's been deposited for you. Is there anything else?'

'Can I check the balance, please?'

'No problemo.' She swivels the monitor screen towards me. I look at the figure, puzzled. It seems a little less than I'd remembered. Then I stare at one of the transactions made about six weeks before Olly died. It was a withdrawal for a thousand pounds. What did Olly need a grand for? Why didn't he tell me? We made a pact not to touch our savings unless there was an emergency. This money, before now, was our deposit on a house. I can feel the colour draining from my cheeks. Was he having an affair? What did he buy?

'Is there anything else I can do for you today?' the assistant asks.

'No. Nothing.'

'Tell me, Olly,' I mutter under my breath, walking home as quickly as I can. 'What did you need that money for?'

'I packed in my job,' he says, finally.

'You what?'

'I left. Quit.'

I cross the road. I can't have heard right. 'You mean you lost your job?'

He says nothing.

'You resigned!' I burst out, much to the alarm of a passer-by, but right now I don't care if people think I'm mad.

'I was unhappy. Tired of being a teacher. I was desperate to finish my novel. All I ever wanted to do in life was write. I felt this was my last chance.'

I open the gate. I'm seething. I unlock the front door with a trembling hand. 'I wanted to paint, Olly, but sometimes we have to grow up, you know, do the responsible thing in life and work to pay the rent!'

'Becca, I feel terrible.'

'So was I just going to bankroll both of us until you finished your script?'

He doesn't answer. I sit down at the kitchen table, trying to make sense of it all. 'What with my bonus and our small savings,' I'd said to him that last morning, 'we could move out of here, rent something more central. Look Olly. This flat is perfect!'

'There was me going on about renting a place close to your school,' I say, 'and you weren't even working there any more.' I shake my head. 'Why didn't I see this? I'm such an idiot.'

'No. I'm the idiot. I should have told you.'

'What if you'd received another rejection? What then, Ol?' I chew my nail remembering how I'd dread seeing his scripts returned in those brown stamped addressed packages. 'I won't give up,' he'd say to me, sensing my doubt.

'I don't know,' he speaks softly. 'I let you down.'

I drop my head into my hands. 'So this is why you were distracted on your way home? You were terrified of telling me?'

Silence.

'Oh Olly, it was only a job,' I reflect, my anger subsiding. 'Only a flat.' Tears come to my eyes. 'I would have forgiven you. Nothing is worth losing your life for. Nothing.'

That evening I yearn to tell Kitty, but if I do I shall have to explain about how I hear his voice, and I can't. Not yet. I decide to keep his secret to myself. I wouldn't like my parents to know either. I fell in love with Olly because he had so many dreams. I look back to our first date, when he'd told me he wanted to be a pop star or a famous writer. I sense Mum and Dad thought Olly unrealistic chasing too many dreams.

Deep down I know I'd started to feel that way too.

19

'You want this job?' Joe asks down the telephone the following day.

'If you haven't found anyone else,' I reply, aware Mum is pretending to read the business section of the newspaper.

Joe is silent. Perhaps he's thinking the same thing: won't it be as awkward as hell? But I know now I have to get this job. I can't stay at home any more. I need to keep busy, keep sane.

'I can't pay much,' he says. 'The budget on these courses is tight.'

'That's OK. It's not really about the money.'

Joe tells me his wine tasting course doesn't start until the first week of September. That's in just over a fortnight's time. It runs for eight weeks. 'Can you work until the end of October?'

'Yes.'

'And I can always do with an extra pair of hands behind the bar.'

'Fine. I can work at least a couple of days a week. I'll start tomorrow, if you like.'

'In that case, Luis will show you the ropes.'

'What did he say?' Mum asks the moment I'm off the telephone.

Luis is half Spanish, in his mid-twenties, with short dark hair, eyes the colour of coffee beans and olive-coloured skin. When I arrive he puts me at ease immediately, showing me round the open-plan kitchen and introducing me to a couple of the chefs, Bruno and Luke, who look young enough to be my children. I attempt a trial cappuccino and make a mess of the frothing switch, milk sloshing everywhere. 'I have done a bit of waitressing before, believe it or not.'

'You surprise me,' he laughs.

I smile, explaining to Luis that I had worked briefly in a restaurant in Chiswick, and this is where I'd met my art gallery boss, Glitz, for the first time. I had just turned twenty-seven.

'When I served him a mocha instead of an espresso,

he shooed me away with his napkin, shouting at me that it wasn't rocket science.'

'Oh yes.' Luis nods. 'We get a few of those in here.'

'It's the spoilt kids I don't like,' adds Bruno, 'tearing round the place.'

'What happened next?' Luis asks, touchingly gripped by this minor drama.

'I told him he was rude. He then told me that he was in a foul mood because his third assistant in a row had walked out on him. I confided I was in a bad mood too, because I was an artist but my work had dried up, so I was going to have to think of an entirely different career. He offered me the job.'

'Just like that?' Luis clicks his fingers.

'Well, not exactly. He asked me what I knew about modern British art, and I told him I knew more about the Renaissance because I'd studied in Florence.' He had also asked me who my favourite artist was. I told him I loved Cezanne's landscapes, Jean-Antoine Watteau's paintings of musicians and fêtes galantes. I loved Mark Rothko because each time I looked at one of his paintings I felt at peace. 'It was pure luck meeting Glitz, because at least working there had something to do with art,' I say. 'And you, Luis? How did you end up here?'

Luis tells me he read engineering at Barcelona, but it was the wrong subject for him. 'I was seventeen! Who knows what they want to do at that age?' he exclaims in his strong Spanish accent. 'It is like plucking something out of a bag.' He makes a disgruntled sound. 'A degree, it is just a piece of paper. That's why I think Joe employed me. He likes to give people a chance. I am passionate about wine. He does not care about qualifications.'

'He's a top bloke,' says Bruno. 'When my mum was poorly, right, he gave me time out, said I must be with her.'

'How do you know Joe?' Luis asks, just as a customer walks in. 'It's a long story,' I whisper, tying my hair into a ponytail and making sure my navy striped apron is on properly. 'What can I get you?' I ask, praying it's not going to be a cappuccino.

*

The wine tasting session starts in thirty minutes, but the room is already filling up with students. The cellar looks romantic in the nightlight. I have laid the long oak tables with plates of cheese biscuits, crisps and nuts and tasting glasses.

Two smartly dressed women in their mid to late forties arrive in a waft of perfume. As I sign them in and take their jackets, I imagine their husbands at home, told to stick the chicken pie in the oven at a hundred and eighty degrees, while they go out and have some fun. Their names are Felicity and Diane. They take their glass of champagne, and totter off in their strappy heels to find two seats together.

I sign in Scott, a young and handsome Australian with tattoos on both arms. A businessman walks in next, newspaper under his arm. The next student staggers down the cellar steps, as if drunk already. In his sixties, he looks like a mad inventor, with his wild grey hair that sticks up like mini beansprouts. His name is Henry. 'Bravo,' he says when I take his tweed jacket and hand him a navy Maison Joe file filled with course notes for each session, accompanied by a list of the wines tasted, which Joe sells in the restaurant. He shuffles towards one of the tables, planting himself next to an exotic-looking blonde Italian woman in a pinstriped suit and designer glasses called Monica. She glances at him, an expression of acute disappointment written on her face. I can't help but smile when I hear Olly telling me that her plans of sitting next to a single tall, dark and handsome stranger have been cruelly shattered.

I'm so busy watching Monica edging away from Henry

that I don't hear the last student arrive. 'Hello!' he says, shaking my hand enthusiastically. 'I'm Adam.'

Adam is wearing a blue shirt and bright yellow tie with koala bears on it, half his shirt hanging out of his jeans.

'Oh, and by the way,' Joe had warned me last week, 'there's this one guy on the course, Adam. He's Mavis's son.'

'Mavis's son?'

'She looks after my dad. Adam's twenty-two, doesn't have a proper job as such. He went to a special-needs school, but Mavis says he's passionate about food and wine, so I promised her I'd give him a place.'

Adam beams at me. 'You look just like Julia Roberts, only prettier.'

I blush, before complimenting him on his tie.

'Do you have a boyfriend?'

Joe brushes past us, telling Adam to find a seat, before saying, 'Adam's a ladies' man. You'd better watch out.'

'How many of you here don't believe you can taste and describe wine?' Joe asks, starting the lesson.

Many hands go up.

'Well, the good news is you can. We all have the same equipment.'

Adam turns round and waves at me. I wave back.

'Tasting wine just takes practice, and, to be frank, I can think of a lot worse things to practise, can't you?'

'Still talking like a stuffed shirt then,' Olly says.

'It's not like going to the gym!' calls out Henry, plumping out his chest and nudging Monica playfully in the ribs.

'Exactly,' Joe says. 'Even the doctor prescribes one glass of red wine a day for a healthy heart. So, what you're here to learn for the next eight weeks is what style of wine you like and why. *Why* is what counts. It's not always the most expensive wine that you're going to love. If you're lucky, you may well love the cheaper wines . . .'

'Here's hoping,' calls out Henry.

'OK, as you can see, my assistant Rebecca,' Joe gestures to me, 'has laid out in front of you some tasting glasses, a bottle of water and some light snacks. There's also a spittoon. It's up to you whether you want to spit out or swallow. I guess it depends on whether you've caught the bus or driven here.'

Adam sticks his thumbs up at Monica, saying he's caught the bus.

'But before I get started on the grape varieties we're covering tonight, Rebecca is going to pour you all a glass of Chilean Merlot.' I circle the tables, filling each student's glass with a small amount. 'Don't drink it yet!' Joe orders Henry, before continuing, 'So, imagine this. You've ordered your wine and the waiter asks if you would like to taste. Many people feel rather embarrassed and rush this, but the whole point is to check the wine's condition.'

'Condition?' asks handsome Scott. He's tanned, light-brown hair streaked with blonde from the summer.

'Yes, you want to make sure that the wine isn't "corked". Who knows what I mean by corked?'

'Compost,' calls Adam, holding his nose.

I find myself laughing.

'Yes, Adam, that's right,' Joe says. 'It smells "off". It's basically a taint in the cork that reminds you of a dank attic or wet cardboard. If Rebecca and I come across a corked bottle over the next eight weeks, I promise you we'll keep it and hand it round. Right,' he claps his hands, 'first things first – you sniff the wine.'

The students sniff.

'Next you swirl the glass, and this isn't about pretension. We swirl to release the aromas.' I watch Joe as expertly he spins his glass. 'My Uncle Tom, who inspired me to learn about wine, says it's like a wine helicopter,' he says, Monica gazing up at him, already transfixed.

*

An hour and a half later everyone has gone and I'm washing up the glasses.

'Adam was a character,' I say.

After the lesson had ended he told me that he worked in the local library and volunteered at the homeless shelter, dishing out tomato soup.

Joe turns off his laptop. He'd been showing a film on grape-picking in Alsace. 'Mavis worries about him. It's hard. Where do people like Adam fit into this world?'

As I continue to wash up, Joe talks to me about how his passion for wine began.

'After my grandfather died, Uncle Tom left his insurance job in England and went travelling. He ended up investing his inheritance in a farm in Western Australia. When he flew over for Mum's funeral, he persuaded me to return with him. He had a successful business by then and he knew my heart wasn't in medicine. Dad hated it, of course; told me I was throwing my life down the gutter. He wouldn't speak to Tom after that, felt his brother had betrayed him.'

'So what happened then?'

'After three years I moved back to London, found work in a wine merchant's, took the exams for the two-year diploma while I was working . . .'

'And your father?'

'We didn't communicate much. He was lost without Mum. I think he'd had numerous affairs, but she'd always been at home waiting for him with his dinner on the table. He missed that, and he wouldn't forgive me for abandoning medicine. It wasn't until I found a decent job in the wine trade that he began to take me seriously.'

'Why did you move back to Winchester?'

'Dad. He's not well.'

'I'm sorry. Is it serious?'

'Dementia.'

'Oh God, Joe, I'm so sorry.'

Joe grabs a drying-up cloth.

'That's why I need staff I can trust. Luis and Edoardo understand why I have to shoot off sometimes and they don't ask questions.'

'Does he live with you?'

'No. He's in our old family home, but he has live-in help. Mavis is my favourite. She looks after him beautifully. Money doesn't make you happy, but at least it gives you options.' He slots the dry glasses back into their storage boxes, telling me they're called Riedels, and they're the best tasting glasses, since they're sturdy enough to be washed over and over again and again.

'I did think about putting Dad in a nursing home,

especially since we haven't been close for years but . . . I don't know,' his voice trails off.

'Joe?'

'This might sound mad . . . you'll think I'm crazy . . .'

'Go on.'

'I sensed my mother talking to me, asking me to forgive him and be there for him, and then this place came up. I'd wanted to run my own business for a while. The timing seemed incredible. It felt like she was telling me to stay.'

I don't say a word.

'Joe!' Luis calls from the restaurant. 'We need you a minute!'

'I can't believe I've just said that, I haven't told anyone, not even Uncle Tom. I've spooked you. You think I'm mad . . .' he says, halfway up the stairs.

'No. I don't think you're mad, not at all.'

'You were great tonight,' Joe says when we're alone in the bar at the end of the evening. It's the first time since I've been working here that we've had a chance to really talk, and I've enjoyed it. 'Especially putting up with Adam's advances.'

'He thinks I'm prettier than Julia Roberts. I'd say

that's quite a good night for an old pregnant frump like me.'

'Sit down,' he urges. 'Let me get you a drink. You've been working hard. Luis and Edoardo say you're a natural behind the bar, by the way.'

I'm about to tell him that at last I have mastered the cappuccino machine, when I place a hand over my stomach. 'He kicked!' I am overwhelmed with relief, because during the past few days he's been quiet. Mum told me that was quite normal but I can't lose this child, not now . . .

'He? Do you know the sex?'

I tell him it's a boy.

'What does it feel like?' I hear Olly's voice.

Tears come to my eyes. I can't stay mad at Olly for long, when he's the baby's father and he's missing out on this. 'Olly would have made a lovely father,' Joe states, as if reading my mind. He curls his hand into a fist. 'I wish I'd seen him. I let him down. I know why you ignored my message, so I did the easy thing. Pretended I'd tried, decided to move on. I shouldn't have given up.'

'It wasn't all your fault,' I say to him. 'If I'd had the courage to tell Olly about that night . . . I didn't handle it well. I ruined everything between the three of us.'

'I wish I could talk to him, say how sorry I was for being such a bad friend.'

I have to tell him.

'Joe? There's something you need to know.' I fiddle with the strap on my handbag.

Joe waits.

'When you said that thing about your mother, that you sensed her talking to you . . .'

'Yes?'

'I hear his voice in my head. At least, I think I do.'

'What do you mean, you think you do? Who else is talking to you if it's not me?'

'Whose voice?' Joe asks.

'Olly's.'

'Rebecca . . .'

'I know it's weird!' I say in a rush when I see his shocked face. 'That's why I haven't told anyone, not even Kitty or my parents. But when you said that thing about your mum . . .'

'What's he saying?'

A small smile surfaces as I listen to Olly. 'You've put on weight.'

'Bastard!'

'One too many peanuts at the bar?'

Joe looks at me incredulously, and I can read what he's thinking: that's exactly what Olly would say.

Yet he goes on to suggest that I could be imagining it. He didn't actually hear his mother talking, only sensed her presence, and the fact that this place came up for rent could have just been a coincidence. In the face of doubt, I explain about Jim and Noodle. I haven't seen them since that day. It was as if they came to deliver a message and now they've gone.

'Maybe there are things we can't explain,' I say, realizing how much I want someone to believe me. 'Perhaps this life is more mysterious than we ever imagined?'

Over the next hour Joe and I talk at the bar, any awkwardness dissolving between us now that I've confided my secret. He is the only person I will tell. I don't want anyone doubting me or telling me this is a reaction to grieving, that it's all part of the process. As much as I love Kitty, she can be too black and white. Joe promises he won't say a word to anyone.

We talk about the past ten years. I describe my time in Florence. The art studio was in an old restored church. I stayed in a shabby apartment in the centre of Florence, close to the Ponte Vecchio. I made new friends and enjoyed walking from piazza to piazza at night. Hours slipped by in wine bars like minutes. I ask Joe if he still plays rugby. He tells me he hasn't had enough time since moving to Winchester, finding a flat to rent and starting his business. Moving on to his love life, 'I met someone out in Australia,' Joe confides. 'She was the daughter of one of Uncle Tom's friends, Camilla. She was beautiful and fun. We were together for a couple of years in London, but in the end she didn't want to settle over here for good, and I didn't want to live *down under*. I guess you have to really love someone to leave your world behind,' Joe reflects. 'We didn't love each other enough, but it hurt at the time.' He pauses. 'Anyway, I'm with Peta now. It's early days, but I'm happy.'

We talk about his father. Joe says the early warning signs of his dad's condition were when he kept on heading into Winchester but forgetting what he'd come in for, and not being able to find his way home. A few of his father's friends would call, saying they had found his Dad in Marks & Spencer, clutching a pair of maroon socks in a daze at the checkout, the staff patiently telling him that unless he had money to pay for them, he had to put the socks back where he'd found them. He became a danger behind the steering wheel too. Drove round a roundabout the wrong way.

'In his old age he's mellowed,' Joe admits. 'It sounds a strange thing to say, but we get on better now. Perhaps he's forgotten all the times I've failed him.' Joe confides that his father put money into Maison Joe. 'I didn't intend to stay here, but like I said, it just happened.'

I confess that being back in Winchester is both a good and a bad thing for me. When I'm walking in the meadows, by St Cross, I see Olly and me on our wedding day. I'm in my ivory dress with lace sleeves, approaching him at the altar. He turns to me, a proud look in his eye. The reception was held in Winchester College. My favourite part was when Olly played Bob Dylan's 'Make You Feel My Love' on the piano. Sometimes memories make me feel close to Olly; other times I wish I were as far away as possible.

Joe's mobile rings. He takes the call. 'That was Peta,' he says when he hangs up. 'She's on her way.'

'Great. I can't wait to meet her.'

'Becca, I hope you don't mind, but I told her about Olly.'

I nod. 'I'm glad you did. Sometimes it's easier when I don't have to explain.'

A tall slender woman strides towards the bar, carrying a stylish leather satchel over one shoulder.

Joe stands up, wraps his arms around her. 'Hi, darling,' he says. They kiss, before he introduces us.

She is one of the most striking women I have ever come across. She has black hair tied back with a leopard-print band, is wearing slim-fitting cropped trousers and high heels, but it's those eyes I can't stop looking at. They are a deep blue, the colour of sapphires.

'How are you getting on? What's Joe like as a boss?' she asks, sitting down on one of the bar stools. Joe laughs.

'Moody and bossy.' I smile.

'You're fired,' she points a finger at me, acting out Sir Alan on *The Apprentice*.

'Peta loves Sir Alan,' Joe says with affection.

'You shared a house at Bristol, didn't you? Joe mentioned you hadn't seen one another for a while.'

'That's right.'

'We've got a lot of catching up to do.' Joe looks at me intently. 'Ten years, to be precise.'

20

Kitty is visiting for the weekend and tonight we are meeting Peta, Annie and Annie's husband Richie, whom I haven't yet met, in Maison Joe.

But before our night out we are braving John Lewis in Southampton. I did go into Mothercare a week ago, but the moment I walked in I panicked and left empty-handed in a semi-trance.

While I am driving, Kitty reads out Annie's list as though it were a foreign language. 'Nursing bras with easy . . . what? Hang on . . . access, I think, winter blankets, waterproof sheets, bottles, bibs, baby whats . . .'

'Baby wipes.'

'Sterilizing kit, changing mat, Moses basket (you can have mine – it's in the attic) – car seat, this one's the best . . .' Kitty stops for breath and looks as if she's about to screw the list into a ball and chuck it out the window. 'Oh please, you don't need to buy nipple oil!' I laugh as she turns to me and says, 'This is going to cost a bomb! You need to win a premium bond.'

'Haven't got any.'

'Oh. The Lottery then.'

'Don't play.'

'Fine. You need to rob a fucking bank.'

The department store is packed and Kitty and I are tempted to run to the nearest coffee shop and eat chocolate cake when we are shown yet another model of a changing unit.

'You can put your towels and blankets here,' demonstrates the shop assistant, middle-aged with dyed blonde hair, 'and then . . .' She pulls out the wicker basket shelf, her bracelets jangling, 'you can put all your essentials here while you're changing baby, like the nappies and cotton wool for top-and-tailing.'

'Top-and-tailing?' asks Kitty, suppressing a yawn.

'Is this your first baby?' the assistant asks me.

I nod. 'I'm nearly twenty-five weeks.'

'Don't worry,' she reassures me. 'I understand there's a huge amount to take in, but you'll pick it up quickly. Honestly, it's very simple. I've got three little rascals.'

I smile, before asking her to explain top-and-tailing.

She begins, but stops when she hears a snort of laughter from Kitty. I apologize to the assistant.

'Shall I go on?' she asks frostily.

I drag Kitty away. We decide it's time for lunch. Kitty orders an extra-large glass of wine.

'Tell me more about Joe's place,' Kitty says. I've been working there for three weeks now, on a Tuesday and Thursday. We're coming up for the second lesson on the wine tasting course. 'It's fun. Why are you looking at me like that?'

'I can't get my head round it, that's all. Isn't it awkward?'

I wipe mayonnaise from the corner of my mouth. 'It was, to begin with, but we've got past that now.'

'Hmmm.'

'What? Come on, Kitty.'

'You don't feel anything for him now, do you? Sorry,' she says immediately when she sees my face. 'That was a stupid, insensitive thing to say.'

I push my plate aside, unable to finish my stodgy baguette. 'Joe was the last person I expected to meet again, but the strange thing is, it's good to be able to talk to him about Olly, just like I can talk to you. It helps.'

'I'm sorry,' she repeats, shuffling her chair in to allow an overweight couple to squeeze past our table, their trays laden with Danish pastries. 'Right, we need to carry on with that list. Let's just focus on one thing.'

'That's impossible!'

'I'm hardly an expert,' Kitty says, 'but I don't think you need to get everything Annie suggests. All your baby needs is you, Becca, you and love. Anything else is a bonus.'

The first car seat we are shown is an infant car seat, designed for newborns up to around fifteen months. 'But it's the weight and height of your child that is most important,' the assistant tells us firmly, 'not the age. As soon as your baby outgrows this seat, you'll need to buy the next model up immediately.' She's older, in her late fifties, plump with chestnut highlighted hair and glasses dangling from a beaded necklace. 'As you can see, it's rear-facing. Infant seats face the back of the car because in the event that there is an accident, God forbid,' she adds, touching my arm, 'rear-facing models are designed to spread the crash impact across the strongest part of their body, i.e. their back.' She takes in a deep breath. 'I have two golden rules about travelling with babies. Make sure you buy exactly the right model, and you can't go wrong with this one, and make sure your husband doesn't drive too fast!'

Kitty squeezes my hand.

As Kitty and I queue to pay for the infant car seat, I gaze at a couple standing at the end cashier desk. The woman looks about as pregnant as me. He takes the heavier bag from her, kisses her cheek. I watch them head out of the shop together.

'Becca?'

I turn to Kitty.

'Did I tell you what my mother said to me the other day when I asked her why she didn't go on a holiday this summer? Becca?'

'Sorry?'

Kitty repeats the question.

'What did she say?'

'"I can't afford to go on holiday, Catherine, I'm saving up for your wedding." So I say, "Oh, Mum, for God's sake, you could be waiting a long time." And she says, "Well, if you don't get married, you can use the money for my funeral."'

I find myself laughing as we approach the next free cashier.

Olly may not be here, but I am lucky to have Kitty by my side.

When Kitty and I return home we find Dad reading the weekend papers in the sitting room; Mum is in the kitchen with Oscar and Theo. Mum and Dad have been looking after them while Pippa's been working at the tennis club, coaching the Tiger Tims, a group of seven- to ten-year-olds. Normally Todd looks after the boys on a Saturday if she's working, but he's away. Again. 'Anyone would think that man had a second family,' Dad has said to me more than once.

I remind Oscar and Theo who Kitty is, but they're much more interested in their fish fingers and baked beans.

As Kitty is talking to the boys and I'm showing Mum the car seat, Pippa appears in her tracksuit and white fitted T-shirt that shows off her lean, toned arms. All hell breaks loose as Oscar and Theo get down from the table and run towards her, throwing their arms around her legs. 'Hello, my pumpkin pies! Have you been good for Granny?' She ruffles their hair. Oscar pulls away. He doesn't like that hair-ruffling business.

'Is it a free day tomorrow, Mummy?' asks Theo, with great concern.

'Yes, because it's Saturday today, isn't it? What day is it tomorrow, pumpkin pie?'

'Fun Day Sun Day!' Theo cries out happily.

Mum tells Pippa they walked Audrey to the playground, and then they went on the swings and the slide. 'You went on the swings and slide!' Pippa repeats in that hearty-hearty voice.

Oscar tugs at Pippa's dress, asks if he can watch TV. Pippa says yes. Mum says they haven't finished their fish fingers. But it's too late. They've gone. Mum runs after them with a cloth to wipe their mouths and fingers.

'How were the Tiger Tims?' I ask. Along with her summer holiday coaching, Pippa also runs weekend tennis camps in the autumn.

'Great! I reckon there's one, Digby, who could be amazing.' Pippa shows us what Digby's forehand looks like but stops mid-flow when she sees the bags. 'Oh? Have you been shopping?' She stares at the infant car seat, which isn't the one she recommended.

Kitty says, 'You should have seen Annie's list.'

'Annie's list?'

'I've used your list too,' I reassure her.

'She needs you, Mrs H.,' Kitty carries on obliviously when Mum returns to the kitchen. 'We didn't even know what top-and-tailing is!'

'I'd love to help,' Mum says.

'I was wondering if you were free next Friday?' I ask.

'Friday.' She walks towards the diary, over by the telephone. 'I'm sure that would be fine.'

'Hang on,' Pippa says. 'Aren't you taking the boys to Marwell Zoo?'

'Oh yes. So I am.'

There's an awkward silence.

'Look, you go with Becca,' Pippa says.

Kitty is quiet.

'We can go another time,' I offer, sensing Mum is torn. 'When I'm not working, Mum.'

'No, Becca,' Pippa intervenes. 'It's only right she should be with you at this difficult time.' Pippa doesn't mean a word of it. 'The boys will be disappointed, but . . .'

'Honestly, it's fine,' I insist, trying to disguise my irritation.

'Why don't you try to find someone else, Pippa?' Mum says, taking both me and Pippa by surprise. 'And if you can't . . .'

'It's fine. I'll take them.' Pippa gathers her racket bag and picks up her car keys from the table. For a moment I see the table all those years ago with my painting on it. I was thirteen. I'd drawn people sitting on the steps of the Buttercross, enjoying their ice creams; I'd laid it out to dry. Pippa had returned home with Mum and plonked her flashy racket bag right on top of my painting, ruining it. Hot tears ran down my eyes when Pippa asked me why I'd left it in such a stupid place. I longed for Mum to say it wasn't my fault. Instead she told me how much the bag had cost.

Pippa blows us all a kiss before leaving the kitchen, saying she needs to get home to put the boys to bed.

I notice she hasn't thanked Mum for having them. She expects too much all the time. I'm beginning to feel that resentment burning inside me again.

I don't think it ever went away.

21

'Wow! It's lovely,' Kitty says, and tonight, now that I'm not trying to operate the temperamental cappuccino machine, I can see how well Joe has designed this place. It's simple, with stripped floors and dark wooden tables. In one corner of the restaurant is a sofa next to a shelf filled with *Decanter* magazines and wine books. To the right of the bar, extending to the window that opens out on to The Square, is a library of wines on sale from different countries, though Joe specializes mainly in French and Australian.

'*Bella* Rebecca!' Edoardo greets us, and I introduce him to Kitty. He fixes me a ginger beer, heaping ice into the glass.

'Cute,' Kitty whispers.

'Gay.'

'Shame.'

'Used to work in film. Make-up artist. Switched jobs when he got bored of working in trailers.' I scan the crowded room and point out Peta, who's sitting at the corner table, typing on a laptop.

'Pretty,' Kitty says.

'Beautiful.'

'Bitch. I hate her already,' she laughs.

'Hi!' Peta beams. She crouches to kiss Kitty on the cheek. Since meeting Peta here a couple of weeks ago, we've been out for lunch once, when she wasn't needed on set. I found out she's in Winchester on location, filming a Jane Austen documentary. She met Joe during the first week of filming, when the cast and crew came to Maison Joe one evening to unwind.

'You must be Kate!'

'Kitty.'

'Lovely to meet you, Kate.'

Kitty and I exchange glances as we sit down to join her.

'You'll think me so rude, but I've just got to finish this blasted email to my agent, Derek. He wants me to audition for some television series . . .'

'Becca was telling me you're an actress?' Kitty says, picking up a menu.

'For my sins.'

'I hear you're playing Cassandra,' Kitty continues, 'Jane's sister.'

'Absolutely. Poor Cassandra! My fiancé dies of yellow fever in the Caribbean, so I end up an old spinster.' She flashes a white smile in our direction.

'Todd has competition in the teeth department,' says Olly.

Kitty's staring at her. 'Weren't you on that shampoo advert?'

'Yes!' Peta appears thrilled to be recognized. 'An organic apricot one.'

'It seems to work.' I gesture to her glossy hair.

'Fuck, no! Never used the product in my life!'

'I haven't met an actress before,' Kitty mentions. I'm nervous she's going to ask Peta for her autograph next. 'Is it as glamorous as it seems?'

She shakes her head. 'Ruins the old social life. The amount of times I arrange to go out, only to be told by Derek late afternoon that I need to be in Clerkenwell for an audition at nine the following morning so I have to learn my lines that night. Or this one time, right, I was about to go on my hols when I was told I'd been heavy-pencilled for an advert . . .'

'Heavy-pencilled?' I ask.

'Almost guaranteed.'

'Ah.'

'It was a sports car ad in LA. I cancelled my hols, and let me tell you, my boyfriend at the time was *not* impressed. We split up, I'm ready to go to LA, when Derek calls to say the job's fallen through.'

'Bastards!' Kitty exclaims.

She shrugs. 'If you can't take rejection, then step out of the lion's den.'

Kitty and I continue to grill Peta on her career. 'Most of the time my trailer is tiny, the TV doesn't work and it's so bloody cold that I have to warm myself up on the heater.' She's tells us she doesn't want her work here to end, gesturing to Joe, who's standing behind the bar with Luis. 'Thankfully filming has taken *a lot* longer than scheduled because we've had so many delays on set. We had to stop filming in the middle. Long story, won't go into it. Let's just say I've loved being here.' She gazes at Joe. 'I wish he'd move back to London. There was yet another drama today with his dad. I really think he should be in a nursing home, where he can get professional care. It drags Joe down.'

'What happened?' I ask.

'The old man escaped dressed in one of his suits. He didn't get very far, mind you, because he can't really walk.' She rolls her eyes. 'Joe found him slumped at the bus stop, muttering that he needed to be at the hospital.'

'He used to be a brilliant surgeon,' I tell her.

'I know. So sad,' Peta says, clasping a hand to her chest. 'Oh, look! Here's Annie! Let's get some more drinks!'

'Do you remember singing 'Bohemian Rhapsody' at school?' Annie asks Kitty and me, later on in the evening.

'Our class came bottom,' I tell Richie, who isn't what I expected at all, but then again I'm only going on what my own dentist, Cliff, looks like: short and balding, hums as he drills and is obsessed by military tanks. Richie is tall and slim and has soft dark hair that looks as if it's just been washed and tousled by one of his children.

Kitty laughs. 'We couldn't understand why we came last until we heard the tape recording.'

When Peta asks Luis for another prosecco, I turn to her, apologetic. 'This must be boring for you.'

'How long have you been going out with Joe?' Kitty asks her.

'Over three months now.' She crosses her slender fingers.

'Tell us more,' Annie urges.

'Yes, how did you meet?' Kitty demands. 'It's so hard meeting anyone single and decent these days.'

'Is it? Oh, poor you,' Peta sighs. 'Well, it was the end of a long day shooting, and *technically* we should have gone back to our hotel and read over our next day's lines, but our gang decided to come in here to relax.' She winks at Richie. 'Joe took one look at me, I him, and well . . . fireworks!' She swings her head back as if she's just had a shot of adrenalin in her arm. 'Anyway, we ended up talking till about four in the morning. I couldn't believe my luck. I'd just broken up from a long-term relationship, wasn't even looking to go out with anyone. Hey, honey,' she says, when Joe comes over. They kiss on the lips. 'How's your dear father?' she asks.

'OK for now.' He rubs her arm. I'm not used to seeing this open, affectionate side of Joe.

'I'm worried about you, sweetie,' she says.

'I'm sorry too, Joe,' I say.

'It's really nothing new,' he reassures us, before greeting everyone round the table, especially Kitty, whom he hasn't seen since the New Year's Eve party over ten years ago.

'I was just telling them how we met, honey,' Peta says to Joe, wiping away the lipstick imprint across his cheek.

Joe picks up the empty glasses. 'Richie,' he says, 'if it gets too girly, come over here.' He gestures to the bar.

'Why did you lose touch with Joe?' Peta asks me out of the blue.

'We just did. He moved to Australia, I went to Italy . . .'

Peta cuts me off. 'In my job, I move from pillar to post. One moment I'm in Shanghai, the next LA . . .'

'Then you're in Maison Joe,' I say.

'I'd love you to be away more,' Annie says across the table to Richie, though it's clear they are happy and it's all an act when he says he's sure arrangements can be made.

'When does shooting finish here?' I ask Peta.

'Well it *should* finish in a week or so, providing no more dramas.' She watches Joe talking to some diners near the bar area. 'He's different from the rest, isn't he? With other guys –' she touches Richie's shoulder flirtatiously – 'I can read them like a book, but Joe . . . I never quite know what he's thinking.'

I want to tell her that Olly was the only one who really knew him. All I end up saying is, 'He's always been reserved.'

'Tell me about it. I tease him, ask whether he's auditioning for the part of Mr Darcy.'

22

Janet marches up Stockbridge Down with her sturdy white stick as if commencing battle. I'm the one that has a job keeping up.

During our dog walks Janet tells me some history about the Downs. I have learnt that the Woolbury Ring was an Iron Age hill fort, used during the Second World War as a lookout post for enemy aircraft. Gregory had told her this, she explains. When they were married they used to visit her parents near Salisbury, and she and Gregory often walked on the Downs. She tells me there are over two hundred individual juniper trees, and the rarest insect I might see is the hornet robber fly, black and gold in colour. It makes me think of Olly's father, Victor. I haven't seen him, nor Carolyn, since the funeral, but we are in touch regularly and I am grateful to them both for all their support.

'We'd love to,' Carolyn had replied, when I'd asked if they could help towards a few things for the baby. 'I'm so glad you asked,' she continued, relief in her voice.

When we reach the top of a hill, an aeroplane soars above us. 'Do you ever wonder where they are, Janet?' I turn to her, but she's gazing ahead. Perhaps she didn't hear me.

'"He whom I have loved and lost",' she says, '"is no longer where he was. He is forever where I am."'

On the way home I describe to Janet how the chestnuts lining the road are just beginning to change colour. Janet tells me how much she loves autumn, that the cooler weather suits her, not that we have boiling summers. 'How's the wine tasting going?' she asks.

'It's fun. I had no idea about all the different grapes.'

'Gregory was in charge of that department at home, so I really don't know much about wine either, except that I enjoy drinking it. Ha! If I was a millionaire I'd drink champagne with scrambled eggs every day for breakfast.'

'In your silk kimono?'

She laughs at the thought.

An idea comes to me. 'What are you doing next Tuesday evening?'

'Probably twiddling my thumbs. Why?'

'We've got a spare place on the course. Someone pulled out.'

'Oh, Rebecca, I'm not sure I could afford it.'

'You wouldn't have to pay.'

'Joe's running a business, not a charity for the aged and blind.'

'Leave him to me. Would you like to come? You've missed the first two lessons, but I don't think that matters.'

'Well, I'll be jiggered! Fancy me going on a wine tasting course.'

'You'll love it. Interesting characters too. There are quite a few, er, how can I put it . . .' I'm trying to tell her about Adam and Henry in particular, but Janet's chuckling. 'A night out,' she ponders. 'Let me talk to my sofa and get back to you.'

Early evening I call Joe to ask him if Janet can come on the course.

'Yeah, why not,' he says. 'I was going to call you. Are you free tomorrow night?'

'Tomorrow night?'

'I've organized a small party for Peta before she heads back to London.'

My instinct is to say no.

Joe senses my hesitation. 'It'll be a few of her actor friends. They're a fun crowd.'

'Let me talk to my sofa, and get back to you.'

'I should think your sofa could do with a night off.'

23

Joe's flat is in the centre of town. 'You're the first one here!' Peta welcomes me inside, into an old-fashioned sitting room with heavy curtains and a Victorian fireplace. Joe had told me he was keen to buy his own place as soon as possible. I congratulate Peta on finishing filming the Jane Austen documentary.

'Thanks, but it's always nerve-racking because none of us know what's next.'

She then mentions Joe had to pop out to buy a jar of horseradish to make the sauce for his spicy crab cakes. 'He's a *demon* in the kitchen.'

'I know. He once helped me make a roulade. I was cooking for Olly.'

'Olly. Poor you,' she says quickly. 'He's a *demon* in bed too,' she goes on. 'Ouch! Too much detail?'

'Joe is thinking with his dick and not his head,' observes Olly.

Peta takes my jacket and stands back. 'Wow, you look incredible. Pregnancy suits you. And I love your hair! You should wear it up more often. Right, now this is our bedroom.' The flat is small, the bedroom bang next door to the sitting room. She places my jacket on the end of the double bed, quick to point out that the bottle-green velvet curtains make the space too dark. 'I tell you, Rebecca, he's such a bachelor, happy to live down a rabbit hole.' She rolls her eyes. 'What I want is for us to get our own place together in London. He could set up another Maison Joe in town. I know it's early days, but none of us are getting any younger. I'm thirty-three and you know what men are like . . . commitment-phobes!'

I hear a key in the door.

'Hi, Becca,' says Joe, entering the bedroom. He examines me, as if I've done something different. 'You look lovely.'

I blush. 'Thanks,' I say, looking down at the red dress that I bought from Annie's shop and touching the clip in my hair self-consciously.

'Hadn't you better finish off your crab cakes,' Peta says, pushing past him.

*

Soon Joe's flat is crowded and the sitting room has taken on the vibe of an office party, the volume level rising.

I talk to a couple of young actresses, who echo what Peta said about how terrifying it is finishing a project when nothing is lined up next. 'I'm glad to see the back of the catering van though,' one says, and the other agrees. 'They cram the salads with spring onions and garlic.'

'I hope you didn't have to do any kissing scenes,' I say.

'Not on screen, but there's been plenty of action off, if you know what I mean,' one claims, gesturing to a tall man with longish brown hair and piercing blue eyes standing by the window, chatting up a couple of women. 'That's Rupert, our director,' she whispers. 'We call him Mr Wickham behind his back. No one's safe when he's around.'

'Thanks for the warning,' I say, making my way towards Annie, who is helping herself to a second glass of wine. 'I tell you, by the end of the day I'm gasping,' she says.

We watch Peta introducing Joe to Rupert.

'Fuck, he's hot,' Annie says.

'Who?'

'That man! Well, Joe is too, we all know that, but the other one.'

'The gossip is he's a womanizer,' I say, feeling in the know.

'Joe's a wine specialist,' we overhear Peta saying. 'Joe, this is my director, Rupert Chambers.'

'I had a friend like that,' Annie says, '"This is Mike, he's a psychotherapist. This is Richard. He's a dentist." All I want to know is, are they a dickhead or not?'

'Shh,' I warn her.

'Hello, Annie.' I watch Peta air-kiss Annie's cheek, before offering us a plate of smoked salmon blinis.

Peta is dressed in a short skirt with ankle boots and an emerald-green top that highlights her black hair and kohl-rimmed eyes. When I tell her that she looks incredible and that I feel like a big fat sugar puff next to her, she says, 'No, you don't, and anyway sweetheart –' she gestures to my bump – 'you can't help it.'

Annie and I try not to laugh.

'Now, when I head back to London,' Peta says, 'do you *promise* to keep an eye on Joe for me?' She gazes at Joe talking to Rupert. 'Especially you, Rebecca.'

'Why me?' I almost choke on my blini.

'Well, you probably know him better than anyone else,' she says, before sauntering off to answer the buzzer.

'You look beautiful,' I overhear a male guest telling her at the front door.

'I think very few people are beautiful,' Annie says, turning to me.

'Audrey Hepburn.'

'Kristin Scott Thomas.'

'Stunning,' I agree, 'especially in *The English Patient*. What about Cate Blanchett?'

'What about her?' asks Joe, approaching us.

'I think she's beautiful.'

'I prefer Gywneth Paltrow.'

'No!' both Annie and I cry out.

'She's pretty,' I insist.

'And photogenic,' Annie adds.

'Angelina Jolie?' Joe asks.

'Oh no!' we both exclaim, more vehemently this time.

'And on that cheery note, I have to make a move.' Annie kisses us both goodbye.

'You're not heading off yet, are you?' Joe asks me, when she's gone.

I remind him I was the first to arrive. I tell Joe that Olly, like my father, became a stickler for punctuality, and regretably it's rubbed off on me. If due at an airport, wedding or party, he'd allow for every kind of eventuality that could go possibly wrong. 'I remember this one time, driving to the airport in our purple peanut–'

'In your *what*?'

'Purple peanut. It was our Peugeot,' I explain, aware he's smiling at me. 'We'd arrived at Gatwick at nine in the morning, for a one o'clock flight. Olly had wanted to leave plenty of time just in case there was a pile up on the motorway or we had a flat tyre.'

Joe laughs.

'So, what happened to the purple peanut?'

'It went to the scrapyard. God, I loved that car, but it was getting *a little* bit embarrassing parking it alongside Pippa's and Todd's BMW convertible.'

'What are you two laughing about?' Peta asks, joining us.

When I explain it was about my old car, I sense she feels excluded. 'Joe,' she says, 'I need you to open a couple more bottles.'

'In a minute, sweetheart. What did Olly–'

'Now my darling!' she interrupts him. 'People have empty glasses.'

Joe gets up, kisses her. 'You need to stop worrying. Everyone's having a great time.'

'I hope you're not going,' Rupert says to me, cornering me close to the bathroom door, 'since I haven't had the good fortune of meeting you yet.'

'Smooth,' grunts Olly.

'Hi. I'm Rebecca.'

'Rupert.' He smiles. 'Your face looks familiar. Are you an actress?'

'No.'

'I don't know why that's so funny,' he says, his blue eyes intense.

'The only part I've ever played is Friar Tuck.'

'Surely not! Hasn't anyone ever told you, you have beautiful eyes?'

I burst out laughing. 'Oh, please!' I say, catching Joe watching us from across the room. 'Listen, before you try another chat-up line, I'm a non-starter.'

'Why's that?' He looks amused, his eyes flirting now.

'Well, I know this dress hides it well, but I'm nearly six months pregnant.'

'Are you married?'

'Yes. No . . . I mean . . . I was. My husband, he . . . he died.'

Rupert's smile vanishes at once. 'I'm so sorry,' he says with genuine warmth.

I feel that tidal wave of grief inside me. 'He died in a motorbike accident.'

'I'm so sorry,' he repeats. 'If I'd known, I . . .'

I want to put him at his ease. 'It's OK. You weren't to know.'

'I can't imagine how you feel.'

He looks relieved when Peta joins us. 'Oh good, you two have met,' she says.

Rupert clears his throat. 'Rebecca was telling me about her husband.'

'I know. Poor thing. It's so sad, isn't it?' She strokes my back. 'But the thing is, Rebecca, as awful as it is, you're still young enough to meet someone else.'

Rupert excuses himself, looking deeply uncomfortable.

I walk past her and out of the room. Time to go home.

With a trembling hand I open the door to Joe's bedroom and stare at the bed, covered in jackets and handbags. Mine would be right at the bottom! I consider leaving without it. After all, it's just a fucking jacket.

'Becca,' Joe says, entering the room. 'Are you going? What's wrong?'

I'm shaking. 'Nothing,' I reply, tossing another jacket out of the way, and another . . .

'Here. Let me find yours.' I stand back and allow Joe to sort through the pile.

'That's mine,' I say when he reaches the bottom of the heap. My black jacket now looks as squashed as a dead bat. He places it round my shoulders. 'What's the matter?' he asks again, this time more gently.

'It was . . .' I swallow hard. 'It was just something someone said.'

'What did they say? Was it Rupert? I saw you talking to him.'

'Maybe I wasn't ready for tonight.' I can't tell him it was Peta. 'It's too soon.'

'What happened? What did Rupert say?' Joe persists, his arm placed protectively around my shoulder.

'It was me,' says Peta, standing at the doorway. She comes in and sits down on the bed, putting herself between Joe and me. She reaches for my hand. 'I'm so sorry, Rebecca, if I offended you. I really am. I wasn't thinking. The last thing I wanted to do was upset you.'

'It's OK.'

'Perhaps there was a misunderstanding,' Joe suggests.

I nod. 'Perhaps.'

'Forget what she said, Becca,' Olly tells me as I'm driving back to my parents.

I press my foot down hard on the accelerator and wind down the window, in desperate need of fresh air. 'I miss you, Olly.'

'I know. I don't know what to say.'

'That's a first.'

I hear him laugh, gently, before . . . 'Slow down,' he warns.

'I can't believe it. You're still side-seat driving.' I wait for him to make some quip, but hear nothing. 'Olly?'

'Sorry, I was thinking. I'm worried for Joe. He needs to get out of that relationship before she gets her claws well and truly stuck in.'

24

I sniff the milk and look at the best-before date. 'Where are my bloody glasses?' Dad is saying upstairs, as if someone has hidden them on purpose. He has an antique fair today, at the Guildhall in Winchester.

'Have you checked your pocket?' Mum suggests.

'Yes!'

I flush the milk down the sink and, while I'm at it, pick out some more dodgy-looking items in the fridge. Cottage cheese. Off. Hummus. Two weeks old. Chuck. Deeply suspicious-looking tartare sauce. Definitely bin. Soon I'm taking out everything in the fridge and examining the labels.

Mum comes downstairs as I'm about to chuck away a packet of ham. 'What are you doing?' She swipes it from my hand. 'It's perfectly all right. The twins can have it for lunch, with baked beans.'

'It's three days past its sell-by date.'

'They won't notice.'

'Fine,' I snap.

'What's wrong?'

'Nothing.'

We hear a howl from upstairs, as if Dad's just stepped into something nasty.

Mum takes a deep breath. 'How was the party last night?' she asks, looking towards Dad's jacket and scarf, hanging on the banister. She walks over, feels inside one of the pockets. 'They're here, you old fool!'

Dad emerges at the top of the stairs. 'But I checked there!'

The telephone rings. Mum picks up. 'No, I don't want a new kitchen.' She slams the phone down.

'I'm going out.' I edge my way past her.

'Could you help tidy up first?' she demands. Dad comes downstairs, takes his coat sheepishly. He informs us the fair ends at four o'clock. He's hoping to sell his Davenport inkwell.

Ignoring Dad, Mum continues barking, 'And bring down any washing that needs doing, will you. I'm putting on a dark load in a minute.'

Dad leaves, dressed in his smart trousers, shirt and pink cardigan.

'I've got so much to do!' Mum hurls breakfast mugs and cereal bowls into the sink. 'Pippa will be here any second, and everywhere I look, there's mess!'

'Why the hell doesn't she get some proper help then? It's ridiculous, Mum! Todd can afford it!'

'That's not the point,' Mum says coolly. 'I enjoy it.'

'Do you? It seems way too much. They're here all the time. I love the boys, but . . .'

'Todd's a control freak. He doesn't even like Pippa working, let alone a stranger looking after their children.'

'Well, that's his problem.'

'Rebecca!'

'You've looked after Pippa and me. Why are you doing it all over again?' I glance out of the kitchen window, see Pippa's Volvo estate pulling up outside. She opens the passenger door, unbuckles the seat belts. Theo jumps out first, dressed as Batman, waving his Happy Hopper cow in the air. I know I should stay. Tidy up, bring down my washing and offer to help Mum with the twins. I think of the party last night, what Peta said . . .

I need to walk. Anywhere. I don't care.

I make for the back door.

I march through the water meadows. The view of the river, the swans in the distance and the beauty of St

Cross Church should make me feel at peace, but my mind is still spinning. I decide to walk up St Catherine's Hill. When I reach the top I scream. Then I turn round and walk down again.

When I return home, the washing is hanging neatly on the line outside, my maternity knickers next to Dad's old-fashioned pants. I open the back door and walk into the kitchen to find Oscar and Theo enjoying their baked beans, cheese and three-day-old ham, in between pulling faces at each other. I encourage them by sticking out my tongue and wiggling my fingers on my head to make bunny ears. They giggle. I catch Theo secretly feeding Audrey a chunk of ham under the table.

'I was worried,' Mum says, when I hand her some flowers, bought from the market. 'Where have you been?'

'Walking. I'm sorry, Mum.' When I attempt to explain she says, 'Not now,' gesturing to Oscar and Theo. I can see how tired she is, close to tears. I've hurt her. 'Sit down and finish your lunch,' Mum orders, when Oscar slides off his chair and runs towards the door. She rushes over to the table, drags him back. 'Sit down! Lunch isn't over. I've made strawberry jelly.'

'Here, Mum, let me do that,' I say, taking the cloth

from her and wiping the sticky tomato sauce off Oscar's podgy little fingers, telling him he must be good for Granny.

When lunch is over I tell Mum to have a rest. I'll entertain the boys. She looks grateful, saying she wouldn't mind going upstairs for an hour.

Oscar, Theo and I play Grandmother's Footsteps in the garden. I'm always the Granny. They laugh when I turn my back to them and wiggle my bottom. I can hear their feet thudding towards me. When I turn . . . 'I saw you move, Theo! Back you go!'

After twenty games, I lie down on the grass, and they crash down beside me. Theo touches my tummy. 'When will it be ready?' he asks, as if my baby will pop out of the oven when it's cooked.

'Well, it's September now, and my baby's due in late December.'

'How many sleeps is that?' Oscar asks.

'I tell you what. It will be ready around Christmas time.'

'Wow. Will Father Christmas bring it down the chimney?' Theo asks, wide-eyed.

'Not exactly.'

'Is it a real baby?' Oscar continues.

'Very real. It's a boy.'

'Will Olly be back at Christmas to see it?'

I look away. 'No.'

'Why not? If it's real, he'll want to see it.'

'Mum says Uncle Olly's gone away, but where's he gone?'

I catch my mother standing at the garden door, listening. 'Why don't we watch a film until your mummy gets here?' she says.

Alone in the kitchen, Mum arranges the flowers into a vase. Her blonde hair is held back loosely with two clips, accentuating her blue eyes, and she's wearing a soft cream jumper with jeans.

'I'm sorry about earlier,' I say. 'I really am grateful for all you and Dad are doing for me, and I promise – *promise* – never to take you for granted again. Look at what you do for Pippa and for me, and those lucky boys.'

'Maybe you have a point,' she reasons, confiding that she and Dad have got into such a routine looking after the twins that it's hard to unravel it. 'Your father thinks the same. I do enjoy them, but I am tired. I might have a word with her.'

Relieved to have cleared the air, we hug. 'I wonder

how Dad's doing?' I ask, picturing him standing poised behind his trestle table, ever hopeful.

'He called while you were in the garden,' she tells me, a sparkle in her eye now. 'A couple of Japanese collectors came in with a wad of cash and bought virtually all his stock. He's over the moon, said he's taking us out on the town tonight.'

'Oh, Mum, I'm working,' I say, mildly relieved. 'But it'll be nice for you and Dad to go on your own. When was the last time you did that, went on a date?'

'Rebecca, we're too old for dates.'

I laugh, and tell her I'd better get ready for the wine course. 'You know you're not, Mum. We only live once. Wear that silver dress I love,' I call over my shoulder.

25

Adam is the first to arrive at the wine tasting, modelling a bright purple sweatshirt with jeans. Janet follows closely behind, on the arm of her chauffeur for the evening, Michel. Michel is in his seventies and has known and worked for Joe's father for many years.

Janet's wearing a royal-blue wool dress with pearls, her hair has been washed and set and puffs out like a peacock's feathers, and pinned to her dress is her precious regimental brooch. Michel tells Janet her carriage will await on the dot of ten.

'What a charming man,' she sighs, watching him leave. I kiss her on the cheek, inhaling the smell of lily of the valley. 'Most interesting too. He comes from Syria, but only lived there for three weeks.'

I lead her over to Adam's table and introduce them. 'Wow, you look like the Queen,' he says.

Henry is the next to arrive. Tonight he's wearing a tweed jacket with an antique silver watch chain dangling from the breast pocket. I point him in the direction of Janet. Luckily she won't be able to see his unfortunate nasal hair.

Monica is the last to arrive, slipping in discreetly at the back and sitting next to handsome Australian, Scott.

'Chardonnay is a misunderstood wine,' Joe says, as I hand round glasses containing either vanilla pods, knobs of butter, honey or melon, all key characteristics of chardonnay. The students sniff before passing on to their next-door neighbour. This exercise is encouraging them to identify flavours in wine. When Janet smells the honey she lets out a blissful sigh. 'It reminds me of my childhood.'

A couple of the students laugh mockingly, so I could hug Joe when he says, 'Janet's made an excellent point. Wine is evocative and can remind us of a childhood memory. Who in this room likes Chardonnay?'

'No, I don't think I do,' says Janet, matter-of-fact.

'Not all Chardonnays,' Adam replies. 'You have to pick and choose carefully.'

'Good, Adam, that's right, because there are so many varieties. OK, Rebecca is going to hand round some smoked salmon. Just take two pieces,' he gestures towards Henry.

'Oh, how delicious!' Janet cries.

'Now, we talked earlier about how dishes with a high acidity and lots of spices, like Thai food, work really well with a Sauvignon Blanc. What I want you to tell me now is which wine, out of the Sauvignon and Chardonnay, is a better accompaniment to the smoked salmon. One is going to really complement the fish, cut through it and refresh the palate. So, pick up glass number three.'

'Glass number three,' Janet repeats, and Joe's about to help her, but Henry and Adam beat him to it. 'I'm blind, you see,' she's apologizing to them.

'It doesn't matter,' Adam shrugs. 'My mum Mavis says I'm different, but it doesn't matter either.'

'Here we go,' says Henry, carefully handing her the right glass. Nasal hair or not, Henry is a kind man.

'Now for a bit of blind tasting.' Joe claps his hands, to stop the group from talking. 'Pick up glass number ten.'

'Now, which is that,' I hear Janet saying in a muddled voice, accompanied by a chiming of glasses.

Henry discovers he's in a muddle too.

Adam, remarkably cool, helps both of them out.

'Splendid. This is such fun.'

Janet is holding her glass upside down. Oh dear. Janet doesn't do spitting.

'Right, so you're in a restaurant and the menu has a "Pouilly-Fumé". What's it going to be?' Joe asks, wrapping the evening up with a quiz.

'Sauvignon Blanc!' Adam calls out with confidence.

'And where's the spiritual homeland of Sauvignon Blanc?'

'The Loire,' chorus Adam and Henry. Scott and Monica are whispering together at the back.

'La la la la Loire,' says Janet, who's been drinking steadily for an hour.

By the end of the evening she's fallen asleep on Henry's broad shoulder, every glass empty and an ecstatic smile spread over her face.

Janet thanks Joe and me again, her skin aglow from the evening. 'My taste buds haven't had as much fun in a long time.' I watch her totter towards the stairs on the arm of Michel.

'Take care of her, Michel!' I call out. 'She's precious cargo.'

*

At the end of the night Joe walks me home. I tell him about Dad needing the car to take Mum out on the town, courtesy of a couple of Japanese buying his porcelain. Joe finds this funny. His father's passion was fishing.

It's a chilly evening and I think of Janet, back at home, alone in the darkness. I admire how she has coped all these years without her sight and without Gregory. Hopefully she's fast asleep, dreaming of vineyards in the south of France.

'Janet likes Michel,' I say. 'I think she's made a new friend.'

'He's wonderful. "There is nothing I won't do for my customers," Joe imitates Michel. "I go to bed with my mobile, and if a customer calls in the middle of the night I come! *Ring-a-ding-ding*. Twenty-four/seven I'm there.'

I smile, unused to this light-hearted side of Joe. We walk past a group of scantily clad teenagers on a night out.

'Makes you feel old, doesn't it?'

'And fat. The funny thing is, their night is about to begin as we're heading home to our beds.'

'That's not funny.' Joe shakes his head. 'It's tragic. I'm taking the day off tomorrow. I should be out partying right now.'

'How about a nice cup of herbal tea at mine?' I propose.

'Perfect.'

We walk on, in comfortable silence, until Joe asks, 'How have you been today? After the party.'

'Fine, honestly. Thanks for asking.'

We walk into my parents' drive. 'Becca,' he sounds nervous, 'Peta told me what she'd said to you. Sometimes she doesn't think before she speaks. She's dramatic, flamboyant, but not necessarily . . . oh, look, I'm not excusing it, but I don't think she set out to hurt you.'

I open the front door; place my keys on the hall table.

'I know,' I say. 'The thing is, I won't meet anyone else, Joe. I don't want to.'

We walk into the kitchen. 'I understand.' He watches me turn on the kettle.

'Some people think you can just switch off and move on, as easy as that.'

'I don't think she meant it that way.'

'I'm not just talking about Peta.'

'Peta hasn't lost anyone. Until you have, it's harder to understand. But she is very sorry.'

'Thanks, Joe. And honestly, it's fine,' I say, not wanting him to worry any more.

'Do you think . . . well, do you think you could tell her that? Could you call her?'

'OK.' I nod. 'Of course.' But I know I'd be doing it more for him than for her.

'Thanks.' Joe hesitates. 'Perhaps you can't imagine meeting anyone else now, but maybe in a few years' time –'

'No, Joe,' I insist, grabbing a couple of mugs. 'I won't. It's unimaginable.'

26

I press the buzzer one more time, am about to turn round and head home, telling myself it was a bad idea, when . . .

'Hello,' he says through the intercom.

'Joe, it's me, Becca.'

He opens the door in his pyjamas. 'Oh no, have I woken you? I should have called.'

'My fault.' He glances at his watch. It's ten o'clock. 'I fell asleep on the sofa,' he says, massaging his neck as if it's sore. When he asks me in, I can sense he's wondering why I'm here.

Standing in front of the fireplace I tell him, 'I bought us some croissants and . . .' I peer into the next brown paper bag as if I've forgotten what's inside, 'blueberry muffins. These are really good warmed up. Oh, and some coffee.' I thrust the tray of cappuccinos at him.

'I thought, seeing as it's your day off, I could treat you to breakfast.'

He looks surprised, before telling me he'd better have a quick shower and get changed. 'I should take the day off more often,' he calls over his shoulder.

Joe enters the kitchen with a fresh face and damp hair, a towel wrapped round his neck. 'I'm starving,' he says. 'What's this in aid of?'

'To say thank you.'

'What for?'

'For giving me a job. Being a good friend.' I manoeuvre myself on to one of the kitchen stools next to him and dip a croissant into my coffee. 'I called Peta this morning –' I take a bite '– and it's all sorted.'

'Great, thank you.' He sounds relieved.

I take a second croissant and stop mid-mouthful, aware Joe is watching me. 'What?'

'You've got quite an appetite.'

'You *have* to have two, Joe. It's compulsory. One croissant is never enough.'

'What else is compulsory in life?'

'Oh, I don't know. Sunshine. Holidays. Sleep. Beautiful paintings.'

'Champagne on a dark day. Cold beer in the summer.'

'Friends. Laughter.'

'Facing your fears. Doing what you love. Never holding on to regret.'

'Olly would have said writing. Writing and having fun.'

Joe thinks about this. 'Why don't we just go out and have some fun today?' He puts the plates into the sink in a way that says he has no intention of washing them up.

'Now?'

'Why not? I rarely take the day off so I refuse to look at the accounts or feel guilty that I'm not visiting Dad. In fact, I could do with some help later on, looking round a couple of flats. Are you free?'

Joe and I are shown into a flat in the centre of Winchester, which on paper boasts a modern kitchen, but in reality is wallpapered in an ivy-trellis pattern, and when Joe opens a cupboard the door dangles from one hinge. 'You could easily fit a cot in here,' suggests oily-haired estate agent Shane when we walk into the minuscule master bedroom. Joe and I exchange a look before deciding not to explain.

Flats two and three are no more promising, so Joe and I decide to cut our losses and head towards the nearest cafe, where we order bacon sandwiches for lunch, plus a portion of hot salty chips to share. As we wait for our food to arrive, I glance at a couple of teenage girls at the next table. One looks as if she could be Spanish or Italian, the other has chestnut-coloured hair like mine and pale freckled skin. 'What we've got to do is write down the things we'll be doing in ten years' time,' says the fairer of the two, handing her friend a piece of paper. 'You know, stuff like where we'll be working, who we'll marry, how many kids . . .'

'I reckon you'll marry someone artistic,' suggests the dark-haired one. 'A painter or something.'

'Oh, I'd like that! You'll be with a doctor,' she states with certainty. 'I'm going to work in fashion.'

I catch Joe watching them too.

Olly had said he'd be a famous writer.

'I was going to rule the world,' Joe murmurs.

'My work was going to be auctioned at Sotheby's for millions, yet I haven't painted for years.'

'I run a wine bar. I'm bound to end up an alcoholic.' Joe raises his glass to mine and pulls a goggle-eyed face.

'I'll marry at twenty-seven,' the fairer one continues, ''cos my mum did, and I reckon I'll have three kids, two boys, one girl, in that order.'

I lean across the table, unable to carry on listening.

'Excuse me,' I say, 'I'm so sorry but I *have* to say something . . .'

They both stop writing, pens poised. They stare at me as if I'm mad.

'Stop writing now, because nothing – I mean *nothing* – works out the way you think.'

'What do you mean?' the fairer one asks, blushing.

'What we're trying to say is, enjoy today,' Joe tells them reassuringly, 'because we never know what's going to happen tomorrow, let alone in ten years' time.'

'None of us live in the moment, do we?' I say to Joe when we leave the cafe. 'Maybe I shouldn't have interrupted them. I think I terrified those poor girls! What next? Shall we barge over to that couple on the bench?' I point to an elderly couple sitting outside the bank. 'Tell them to go bungee jumping while they're still young enough and have their own teeth?'

I wait for Joe to answer, but he seems a world away. 'Becca, I didn't go to Olly's funeral.'

'I know. If I could have done things differently, I–'

'I don't want you to feel guilty anymore. But I have an idea. I'd like to say goodbye, in my own way. Will you help me do that?'

*

Joe and I stand at the edge of St Catherine's Hill and admire the view. 'This was Olly's favourite walk,' I tell him. 'We used to come up here at Christmas, to get away from Pippa and Todd, the twins, the board games, the smell of turkey in the house. We'd stand here and scream and then, after that, we'd dance.'

'Olly loved to dance. He used to drag me on to the floor, do you remember? Stuffed shirt, he called me.'

'He still does.'

Joe turns to me, his face breaking into that smile that lights up a room. I'm surprised and relieved by how unfazed he is by the voices. 'Did he have a favourite spot up here?' he asks.

I lead Joe to the maze at the top of the hill, dark lines cut out of the turf. 'Olly was fascinated by the myth behind it,' I recall. 'I think one legend was that it was dug out in the seventeenth or eighteenth century by a Winchester College boy who had been condemned for doing something wrong, no one knows what exactly, but it must have been pretty bad, and as part of his punishment he was kept behind in college during the holidays. He was said to have roamed on the hill and was going out of his mind with boredom so he devised and cut out the maze. I think I remember my dad saying he'd done it with a spoon.'

Joe stands in the middle. 'I want to do it here,' he decides, holding the strings of the three blue balloons that we bought from the toyshop, after lunch.

'Olly,' he begins, 'I'm going to keep this short. You know I was never a man of many words. I'm sorry I let you down, and I'm so sorry I didn't see you again. Please forgive me for hurting you.' He lets a balloon go. I watch as it takes off into the sky, wondering where its flight will end.

'I'm here with Becca, and I want you to know that I will help look after and support her and your son as best I can. I know you'll be with them in spirit, guiding them, but if you'd like me to, I'll encourage your boy to get into music and writing and to enjoy rugby and football, not just weevils. If I'm lucky enough, I'll kick a ball around with him too and tell him about all the adventures we used to get up to at Bristol.' The second balloon follows the first skyward.

Tears come to my eyes.

'You were a light in everyone's life. Of course you weren't perfect,' he adds with a smile, 'but what I loved most about you was your sense of fun. I *am* a stuffed shirt at times. You brought out the best in me, and I won't ever forget you.' He lets go of the third and final balloon.

*

'This is where Kitty, Annie and I played "Mr Froggy, may we cross your golden river?"' I tell Joe as we're standing on the edge of the maze, about to leave. Then I have an idea. 'Wait there.' I walk to the other end and face Joe, thinking about what he'd just said about Olly and his sense of fun. 'Say it!'

'Say what?

'Mr Froggy, may I cross your golden river?'

'Mr Froggy . . .' He stops, looks around . . .

'No one's here!'

He relaxes, turns back to face me. 'Mr Froggy, may I cross your golden river?'

'Only if you're wearing something blue!'

Joe examines his clothes. His jumper's grey. 'I'm not, so what happens next?'

'You have to cross my river without me catching you. I can't believe you've never played this.'

Joe jumps from one bit of the maze to another, dodges to the left, moves forward. He makes a run for it and I chase him, but he reaches the other side safely. 'One more go, and I'm going to get you this time,' I warn him, as he asks if he can cross my golden river again.

'Only if you're wearing something red!'

He makes a run for it, me charging towards him.

'Come on, fatty! Hang on!' He stops dead. 'My boxers are red.'

'Doesn't count! Can't see them.'

Before I know it, he's pulling down his jeans. We are both soon out of breath from laughing so much, until we stop, realizing we're not the only ones here any more. Tentatively we turn to see a class of children wearing grey blazers and bottle-green trousers, pointing their textbooks at us, giggling as they're told by their teacher to move swiftly on.

We're back in Joe's flat, drinking tea. On the way home it started to pour with rain, so Joe has lit the fire to warm us up.

'Are you happy living here?' I ask, clutching my mug of tea in both hands.

'Yes. I didn't think I'd ever want to return to my childhood home. People think it's unimaginative – you should experience something new, not go back to where your parents lived.'

This is what Olly and I had thought about Pippa, but I don't tell him that.

'But it feels natural being here, coming back to my roots. I feel proud it's my home. I enjoy running my own business, and ironically I have a much better relationship with my father now. I've made a few new friends down here too. It *is* new to me. I still miss London, of course I do. I miss the pace . . .'

'If Olly and I went away for a weekend, maybe visiting his parents in Northumberland, I'd get butterflies in my stomach when the train pulled into Euston,' I say. 'Everything quickened the moment we stepped on to that platform.'

'London. I liked being at the heart of England.'

'Winchester used to be the capital once.'

'True. I miss the coffee bar culture,' he carries on, 'the pubs, the West End.'

'The parks are beautiful too. Olly and I used to love visiting the Serpentine Gallery on a Sunday afternoon.'

'Hyde Park in the early hours of the morning, when no one is around except for a few joggers and dog walkers. Most of all I miss the anonymity,' Joe confides. 'That only comes with big cities. Living and working here, it can feel like I'm in a goldfish bowl, and the thing is, *everyone* knows my father.'

'But you're happier now, aren't you?'

'Much.'

'You're not the great doctor's son anymore. You're Joe, and you're good at what you do.'

He smiles. 'Thanks.'

'What about Peta?'

'What about her?'

'How's it going?'

'Well,' he replies elusively. 'She's got this audition coming up, for a six-part thriller. She's trying for the lead role. It could be her big break.'

'I hope she gets it.'

'I think she will, or if she doesn't, she'll get something else soon. She's determined. She told me she'd wanted to be an actress since the age of two, told her mother, who was peeling potatoes at the kitchen sink, that that's what she wanted to do. She paid her way through drama school. I admire that.'

'Will you miss her when she's in London?'

Joe tenses his shoulders. 'Yes, I probably will. I've enjoyed the last few months, I like being with her. She takes me away from the problems with my dad. When you're alone, you can tend to dwell. What about you?'

'Me?'

'Tell me more about your life with Olly.'

'We were happy, but we went through tough times too. Olly could be the life and soul of the party – you remember what he was like.'

Joe nods.

'But behind closed doors he'd have these dark spells.

He'd stop playing the piano, wouldn't want to see friends, didn't want to talk . . .'

'I remember he could be moody, want things his way.'

I explain about the writing and the rejections.

'What did he write?'

'Historical novels to begin with, lots of research, his second home was the library. Then he switched to comedy. He wanted to write something contemporary.'

I confide how unhappy Olly had become teaching, but I don't tell him how he'd packed in his job without telling me; I'd feel disloyal. 'He was always funny, warm, lovely to be around, when he wasn't driving me insane,' I add with a smile.

'And you? Do you still paint? I loved your lemon tree. It was hung over your fireplace at Bristol.'

I'm touched he remembers.

I take a sip of tea. 'I gave up my freelance illustrating to work for Glitz. Olly felt guilty about it, and I did resent him for a while, but one of us had to change careers. We needed to earn more, especially if we wanted to have children and buy a house. It all seems fairly pointless now.'

'Becca, do you think you could live here again?' he asks, as if the idea has just come into his head.

'I don't know.' Until this moment, I hadn't even given it any thought.

I'm chopping tomatoes, while Joe is adding various ingredients to the bubbling mince. 'A pinch of paprika,' he says, 'a slosh each of Worcester sauce and balsamic vinegar . . .'

I hover over Joe. 'Vinegar in mince?' I say, before realizing with panic that I sound like my mother. Fuck.

'Has to be balsamic. Gives it a kick and a punch. What are you smiling at?'

'I don't know.' I'm now thinking of the schoolchildren gaping at his red boxer shorts.

'Come on. Tell me.'

'I can't believe you stripped down to your boxers.'

'I'm competitive.'

'Actually, I don't know why I'm surprised. You did whip your towel off in front of me the first time we met.'

He slips past me to get the cheese grater, his arm brushing against mine. 'Thank you,' he now says to me.

'What for?'

'For breakfast. Going to St Catherine's Hill. Today . . .' He pauses, runs a hand through his hair. 'It meant a lot to me.'

I think of Joe letting go of the balloons and the things he'd said. 'What you said, it was lovely, and I know it would have meant a lot to Olly too.'

27

It's early October, week six of the wine course, and tonight Joe has prepared a lesson on Riesling, Gewürztraminer and Chenin Blanc. 'Riesling smells like petrol, citrus fruits and beeswax,' Joe claims.

Adam raises his hand to talk, something Joe has been encouraging him to do. 'Wasn't Riesling a favourite of Queen Victoria's?'

'Spot on. There's a small vineyard in Hochheim called Königin Victoriaberg, which means Queen Victoria's Hill. She and Prince Albert visited it, and it was duly named after her and her love of Hoch wine.'

I sit down, exhausted, my feet swollen like puff pastry. Mum is concerned I'm overdoing it now. I have my twenty-eight week scan tomorrow and my tiredness is increasing. I have reassured Mum that when the course finishes in two weeks, I will slow down, and focus on the baby and my forthcoming antenatal classes. I have asked Kitty to be my birthing partner. 'Great, so long as I don't have to watch,' she'd said.

'OK, you know the rules,' Joe says. 'Everyone on their feet. Let the competition begin! Is this wine a Chardonnay or Sauvignon? Sit down if you think Chardonnay.'

There is a lot of muttering, which Joe discourages.

Everyone sits down except for Henry. 'Well done, everyone; bad luck Henry, you're out. It *is* a Chardonnay.'

I continue to watch Joe. Since our walk up St Catherine's Hill we have become closer, and I'm selfishly relieved Peta secured that role in the thriller as it keeps her in London.

Joe has talked to me a lot about his father. When he first moved down, his dad was still able to teach him how to fish and they spent many happy hours on the river. 'He talked to me about Mum and how he'd taken her to *Swan Lake* on their first date. For the first time, Becca, he asked me about my break in Australia with Uncle Tom. He regretted losing touch, said he'd been a stupid old fool. He described his childhood, how he'd spent a lot of time abroad because his father was an ambassador. I hadn't even known that! Some of his memories of the Second World War were incredible,' Joe continued, and I could see how much this time with his father had meant to him. 'His family had to flee France, which had fallen to Germany by then. They caught the last ship out of Bordeaux. The boat was meant to carry two hundred people, but seventeen hundred were shipped across to England. Dad would have been a little boy back then.'

'Next question,' Joe says, 'is this wine New or Old World? No conferring!'

Some evenings, after work, Joe and I have headed back to his flat to eat toasted sandwiches. He makes me a mug of hot chocolate and occasionally we watch television. Sometimes we talk about Olly and the old days. When I think of what lies ahead I'm excited, but I'm scared too. Joe listens, doesn't spout clichés or tell me everything will be all right, because deep down, who knows what the future holds?

Joe scans the room. 'Just three of you left in the game now.' It's between Janet, Scott and Adam.

Gallant Henry helps a tired and tipsy Janet to her feet once again. 'Final question – and this is a toughie, Scott,' Joe does a poor imitation of the Australian's accent – 'is this wine made in the northern or southern hemisphere? Sit down if it's the south.'

Come on, Janet!

She collapses into her seat. Scott and Adam stay on their feet.

Joe makes the sound of a pretend drum roll. 'It's the south. We have a winner!'

'Well, I'll be jiggered. I've never won a damn thing in my life!'

Adam and Scott clap graciously.

'Never mind all that. What do I win?' she asks.

'Didn't have the foggiest,' Janet whispers to me when the lesson is over, 'but my knee was giving me jip.'

'I love this,' I gesture to her red coat, helping her put it on.

'Bought it at a charity shop. Oh look, Michel's here.' Am I imagining it, or does her face light up?

Joe and I watch Janet being escorted from the room on the arm of Michel. They are chattering like teenagers, Janet telling him about her winning a bottle of nice wine, which she will keep for Christmas and drink with mince pies when her sister comes to stay.

'I think they're in love, don't you?'

I turn to him, incredulous. 'She's eighty-four, Joe.'

I'm waiting for Olly to say something funny, but he has been quiet for a while.

'So? He's seventy-six, but what are numbers?' Joe continues. 'Michel would drive her to the moon if he could.'

Janet turns to me, waves her stick in the air to say goodbye. She's a picture of happiness, her cheeks glowing. Or maybe that's just the wine.

28

Twelve weeks to go. I sit in the waiting room ready to see the midwife, who is going to measure me and do routine blood tests.

I'm not sleeping well. The closer I am to having our baby, the more I think about Olly. Maybe it's because I'm apprehensive about returning to London. I've been with my parents for four months now, and once I've had the baby, I need to think about our future. I have also been thinking about Glitz and whether I want my old job back after the baby is born. Can I afford not to work? In many ways I need to make a new start, but where do I begin?

Olly, tell me what should I do, talk to me. I close my eyes, trying to conjure him up, craving the sound of his voice. Has he stopped communicating because I've been busier working at Maison Joe, and happier these past few weeks? Or is it because I'm spending more time with Joe? *Are you jealous? You don't need to be, I promise.*

'Rebecca Sullivan.' I open my eyes. 'Rebecca Sullivan?' the midwife repeats. 'How are you today?' she asks as she leads me into her office.

When I return home, I put my car keys on the hall table. Oscar and Theo are lying on the sitting-room floor, watching *Kung Fu Panda*. I kiss them both, their skin soft and I'm touched when Oscar hugs me, even if he promptly pushes me out of the way so he can see the screen again.

Walking down the hallway, I hear Mum and Pippa talking in the kitchen.

'You know what Todd's like,' I overhear Pippa say. I remain outside the closed door, listening. 'He hates the idea of a stranger looking after the boys.'

'I know, but I think it's time,' Mum says. 'I'm not getting any younger, darling.'

'Has Becca said something to you?'

'Of course not. Now, I've got chicken drumsticks for their tea.'

'Has she talked to you and Dad about what's going to happen next?'

'No.'

'You look tired, Mum. It's too much for you, isn't it? Having her around.'

I hold my breath, lean closer towards the door.

'What can we do?' Mum raises her voice. 'We have no choice. We can't chuck her out on to the street. She's our daughter, and if you were in her position, we'd do the same for you.'

'I know,' she agrees huffily, 'but Todd and I get the impression Becca thinks she can just stay here forever.'

'It's hard . . .'

'I know it's hard for her, but what about you and Dad?'

'I do a lot for you and the boys,' Mum points out. 'Rebecca needs me now.'

'I know, but we still have to be realistic. There's no way Dad can cope with a screaming baby for months on end . . .'

Anger rises in my chest. I want to shout at her, 'But he can cope with Oscar and Theo anytime?'

'I think you need to tell her where you stand. Otherwise she'll think she can stay here indefinitely.'

I hear drawers being opened. 'She doesn't have a Todd.' Knives and forks slam against the table. 'She's just lost her husband . . .'

'Yes, but–'

'I'll be honest, it's not always easy having her here, this is far from an ideal situation but . . .'

'Well, tell her to go then!'

I push open the door and face them.

'Sorry, I didn't mean that.' Pippa apologizes quickly, colour draining from her face. 'I've had a tough day and . . . I really didn't mean that,' she repeats, coming towards me.

I step back, holding up my hands to ward her off.

Mum looks from Pippa to me and then back to Pippa, who clears her throat. 'All I was saying to Mum was–'

'I heard everything,' I say, choked with emotion. 'Ever since I came back, you've been jealous.'

'Jealous?'

'All your life you've been spoilt, Pippa.'

'I have not!'

Mum steps towards us. 'You two, please calm down. Let's talk about–'

'Do you know what it's like to lose someone, Pippa? To go to bed and cry yourself to sleep every night?'

She stares at me. 'I know what you're going through –'

'No. No, you don't. I will never see Olly again. My baby has no father, but all you can think about is how it's affecting *you*!'

Mum shuts the kitchen door. 'That's enough. The boys will hear.'

I turn to Mum, determined now to ask the question that's haunted me for most of my childhood. 'Why don't you *ever* stand up for me? When Pippa wrecked my painting, all you could say was it was *my* fault for leaving it in the kitchen!'

'That was years ago,' Mum replies, but I can see she's shocked that I've harboured this resentment for so long.

'I've never felt good enough, Mum.'

'Oh, Rebecca,' Mum says, searching for the right thing to say. 'Listen, we're all tired . . .'

'I'm not tired!' I compose myself. 'But you're right. This isn't ideal. I'll leave. Go back to London.'

'Rebecca,' Mum pleads. 'I don't want you to go.'

'Now you're just being over the top,' Pippa claims, when I open the door. 'I didn't mean for you to go right now, all I was *trying* to say was you need to make plans, you need to–'

'Pippa!' I turn to face her. 'Keep quiet, before I say something I will truly regret.'

As I'm walking up the stairs, I hear Mum talking to Pippa, and to my amazement it sounds like she's giving her a bollocking.

29

The taxi driver turns into a smart crescent in Notting Hill, pulling up outside a stylish white building with steep steps leading up to the front door.

'Can I take you up on your offer to stay?' I'd asked Glitz, calling him from the train platform at Winchester.

The house was in turmoil when I left. Mum was in tears; Pippa was gathering Oscar and Theo, both of them protesting because *Kung Fu Panda* hadn't finished.

'I need some space,' I'd insisted to Dad, who had returned from his buying trip with Mr Pullen, the antiques dealer.

'But where will you go?' Dad objected. 'You need to look after yourself. Please stay – sort this mess out.'

But I had to get away.

'You are coming back, aren't you?' Mum had asked, fear in her eyes.

'Crikey, Rebecca, how long are you moving in for?' Glitz asks as he heaves my luggage up the stone staircase. I tell him I was in such a rush I just hurled everything in.

There are flowers in my room, a flat-screen television with a selection of DVDs, and glossy magazines lie on the bedside table. In my ensuite bathroom are lavender bath oils and rose and geranium shower creams. I tell Glitz I might move in permanently. He raises an eyebrow at that, before telling me that Marty's in America visiting family, so it's just the two of us rattling around.

'Lovely,' I say, fighting the urge to cry.

'Are you going to tell me what happened?' He sits down on the bed next to me. 'Marty always says we Brits are too buttoned up, it's better to let it all out.'

'When I'm angry, Glitz, I walk to the top of St Catherine's Hill and scream. I used to do it with Olly.' I stare out of the bedroom window. When I turn back to him there is a pillow held in front of me. 'Go on,' he says.

Unsure, I hit the pillow.

He shrugs. 'Not bad.'

I hit it harder.

'Better.'

I thump it now. *Punch!*

I picture Olly's face the morning he died. 'I'm so proud of you,' he'd said. I miss not hearing his voice. *Talk to me, Olly. Please come back.*

I punch the pillow repeatedly, until I have no strength left.

Later that night, after I've unpacked and had a bath, I find Glitz in the kitchen on the basement floor, listening to opera music as he throws together a pasta dish with garlic and herbs.

'I'm sorry to dump this on you. You're my boss and here I am telling you all my dramas.'

'You're my friend,' he puts me straight. 'I hope you're hungry. You must have burned a lot of calories tonight.'

'Who needs the gym, eh?'

Glitz laughs as he drains the pasta.

A black cat jumps on to my lap. Glitz tells me he's called Bond.

'Bond, James Bond.' I stroke him.

As we talk about the business and Marty's family, I

find it therapeutic listening to the sound of Bond's contented purring.

'Glitz, it won't always feel like this, will it?' I ask him over supper.

'No. You'll get better at it.'

'Better at it?'

He puts his fork down. 'You never get over it; you get better at dealing with it.'

'Have you lost someone?'

He pushes his plate aside now. 'Rose. My daughter.'

'I'm so sorry. All this time, I had no idea.'

He refills his glass with white wine. 'How were you to know? I blamed myself for years,' he confides. 'She was in a deeply unhappy marriage. She called late one night, asked if I could go over. I'd had one too many gins, was in no fit state to get in the car, so I told her I'd be with her first thing in the morning.' He pauses. '"Everything's all right," I said to Diana, my wife back then. Rose took an overdose. I'll never know if she meant to or not.'

Glitz takes off his black-rimmed glasses and rubs his eyes. 'Diana left me, and I lost my job in the City, though it is true to say I never liked the job anyway. All I wanted was to be miserable and blame myself.'

'But it wasn't your fault. It wasn't.' I look at him then, thinking how we never know people, not truly, until we show them our own vulnerability.

'I should have heard the distress in her voice and jumped into a cab.'

'Oh, Glitz. How did you get through it?'

'Marty. She was an old friend back then. She broke down the door of my apartment – I was living in squalor, Rebecca – and she told me she was taking me away, whether I liked it or not. Brave girl . . . or very stupid,' he adds with a wry smile.

I fold my napkin in half, and then in half again. 'I don't know what to say.'

But he doesn't hear me. He's back with Rose. 'In my sleep I still see her,' he says, 'I'm pushing her on the swing and she's saying, "Daddy! Higher!" She used to wear her flowery knickers on her head, pretend they were scarves like her mother's.' We laugh at that. 'She loved jewels too, would dress up in Diana's pearls and heels and take the dog out for walks. She was my ray of sunshine. In many ways you remind me of her.'

Late that evening I call home. Dad picks up after the first ring. 'I'm fine,' I reassure him. 'Is that Becca?' I hear Mum calling in the background. She comes on to the line. 'I'm so sorry.'

'Me too,' I reply tearfully.

'I've been thinking about what you said.'

'I was angry.'

'I can see I was taken up with Pippa. Growing up, I was passionate about sport, but my parents couldn't afford lessons . . .'

'Mum, it's OK.'

'No, it's not. I wanted Pippa to have the chances I'd never had, but I should have encouraged you more too, especially with your art. I should have given you more time. I'm so sorry. Where are you?'

I tell Mum I'm with Glitz. I'm safe. I won't do anything stupid to harm the baby.

'What a day,' I whisper to Olly, before telling him about Mum and Pippa. 'You always said there was too much unsaid between us all. Well, it's all out there now, like on *The Jerry Springer Show*.'

I still don't hear his voice. If I return to Winchester, I will find Jim and Noodle and ask why Olly has stopped talking to me.

30

'Why don't you stay here while I'm in America?' Glitz proposes over a scrambled-egg breakfast. 'You can water the plants and look after Bond. Fend off any burglars. I've spoken to Marty – she's more than happy. Invite a friend for the week. Don't be alone right now. Have some fun.'

'OH MY GOD!' Kitty jumps up and down from room to room exclaiming that her entire flat could fit into Glitz's dining room. The sitting room has a grand piano and a bar! She gazes at a brightly coloured still life painted by someone called Alberto Morrocco. The kitchen houses a fridge that competes in size with Todd and Pippa's, but whereas theirs was stocked with ominous fruit kebabs, inside Glitz and Marty's fridge is food you'd eat in heaven; smoked salmon, crème brûlée, passion-fruit cheesecake and Belgian chocolate.

Kitty and I sing, 'Who Wants to Be a Millionaire?' as we make our way upstairs. We go into Glitz and Marty's bedroom. It's large, painted soft yellow with white wooden shutters. Kitty opens the wardrobe, peeps inside. 'Stop it!' I drag her away. But I can't help asking: 'Did you see anything interesting?'

'Fuck me, there's a games room!' she cries out, picking up a ping-pong bat.

I clap my hands. 'It's all ours, for a week.'

That evening, after Kitty and I have helped ourselves to a drink from the bar (I have a small glass of champagne, before reluctantly moving on to something soft), we decide how to make the most of the next seven days. When I'd called Kitty and told her about Pippa and Mum, she volunteered to take time off. 'I know I don't have to,' she said. The only commitment I had had to cancel was my work. I called Maison Joe. Joe was out, so I left a message for him with Edoardo, explaining something had come up and I needed time away. I also called Janet, to explain why I wouldn't be at the next wine-tasting session, though reassuring her I'd be back soon.

My best friend is in her element organizing. 'I don't want to schedule our week to death, but I think tomorrow we should go to the Tate Modern and then we've *got* to have afternoon tea somewhere and oh, I know! I was thinking we should blow our budget and have a facial or something.' Kitty reaches for her glass of champagne. 'This is much more fun than any holiday. A week of unadulterated pleasure without the airport or hiring a car! We can be tourists in our own city.'

'And no mention of home, of Pippa, Mum . . .'

'Agreed. Amen to that.'

Over the next week Kitty and I tick off all the major galleries until we feel so drunk on art that we have to turn our attention to more important matters: pampering and food. We go to a tea shop in Bloomsbury where we indulge in pink and yellow cupcakes and scones with clotted cream. We have a pedicure in a fancy Notting Hill salon. I opt for my toenails to be painted ruby red; Kitty goes for silver.

To work off the cupcakes and clotted cream, we go for a long walk in Richmond Park and get caught in the rain. We brave Westfield (it's my first time) and shop, mainly for Kitty since I am six and a half months pregnant now, but I can't resist a pair of brown leather boots that are on sale. We browse Borough Market on Saturday and get hotdogs for lunch with lashings of fried onion. One evening we stay in and eat crème brûlée in bed, watching episode after episode of *Mad Men*. What I realize I enjoy most, however, is walking the streets among people I don't know and not having to hide from Mum's friends in the supermarket. 'I like being anonymous in London,' Joe had said. I realize I have missed the noise and buzz of London and the randomness of people. A man on the tube sits opposite Kitty and me and sings to us, reggae style, 'Hey, beautiful *laydee*, long time no see. Won't you come and spend the night with me?' He bursts into happy laughter and wishes us 'a lovely day', as we step off the train.

'He was singing that to me,' Kitty says, as we follow the exit signs.

'No, I think you'll find he was looking at me,' I beg to differ.

A violinist plays in a Covent Garden wine bar as we sit surrounded by couples sipping cocktails. Sylvie joins us one evening to go to the cinema; we opt for the latest feel-good romantic comedy. 'That's life in a sugar-coating,' Olly always used to complain. Yet sometimes, it's exactly what you need.

*

On our last night, Sylvie and Jamie meet us in an Italian restaurant just round the corner from Glitz's place. In many ways it reminds me of Maison Joe, with its stripped wooden floors, modern paintings, wine served in carafes and jazz music playing in the background. It's also busy, waiters balancing plates of food as they hurry from one table to another.

'So what's he like now?' Sylvie asks, referring to Joe. When I'd left for Florence, Sylvie moved into another house for her third year. She'd kept in touch with Olly and Jamie, but not Joe.

'He's bigger, isn't he?' Kitty says. 'Fuller-faced.'

'What? Fat?' Sylvie sounds appalled.

'No. He's just filled out a bit,' I say.

'Is he as fat as Jamie?'

'Fuck off,' Jamie says with a generous smile.

'He's still good-looking,' Kitty remarks. 'I'm going to have the fried squid and then the spaghetti carbonara . . .'

'Because you haven't eaten quite enough this week,' I suggest.

'Who's he dating now?' Sylvie dips some crusty bread into olive oil.

'Peta. The actress I told you about.'

'Still? Wow, that must be a world record.'

'He's grown up, Sylvie!' I explain that he'd had a long-term relationship with an Australian.

'Peta's beautiful, but a bit *actressy*,' Kitty says. 'Only likes to talk about herself.'

'That's because you didn't stop asking her questions,' I defend Peta. 'But I know what you mean.'

'Joe was hot, in a Heathcliff kind of way,' Sylvie continues. 'Funny thing is, he was the one guy I couldn't get.'

'Hilarious,' mutters Jamie.

'Even if I'd thrown myself on to the bed, naked, he wouldn't have been up for it.'

'Literally?' Jamie raises an eyebrow.

'I couldn't work him out,' Sylvie sighs, circling the rim of her wine glass with her finger. 'I guess that's why he was so attractive. Still, I didn't expect him to just quit Bristol without telling anyone, especially Olly. That was weird, even for Joe.'

I remind them that his mother had died. He'd travelled to Australia to see his uncle. 'He was in a mess.'

'I know, but why didn't he tell Olly?' she says, still refusing to accept this as explanation enough.

'Grief does strange things to you,' I say.

'He never wanted to be a doctor.' Jamie comes to his

defence too. 'There was a nice side to him, you know. When you left, Becca, for Florence, Joe supported Olly more than anyone else. Olly played the field a bit, you know that,' Jamie continues, 'but it was obvious nothing was going to last because he was so in love with you. He was terrified that you were falling for that chef guy. The relief I felt when Joe put him out of his misery and booked Olly on to that flight.'

'Joe did that?'

'Yep. He bought Olly the ticket, even drove him to the airport. "Stop moping and do something about it," he said. I thought you knew this.'

I shake my head. I'd had no idea. A waiter bustles over, asks if we're ready to order.

Towards the end of the meal the mood sobers. 'What are you going to do next?' Jamie asks me, a question we have all been putting off.

'Go home.' I explain that I can't be anywhere else. It's where I'm having the baby. I'm registered at the maternity unit in Winchester. I can't find a new place, move in and settle down before the baby's born. There's no way. 'I need my mum,' I admit.

They all mutter in agreement.

'I'll move back after Christmas.'

'I wish I was loaded,' Jamie says. 'Then I could set you up in a nice home with a nanny.'

'Oh, Jamie,' I say, my heart melting. 'A full-time cook would be great too.'

'And a chauffeur?' he suggests.

I think of devoted Michel. 'Perfect. One that looks like George Clooney.'

Sylvie asks for the bill. 'Did you ever send Olly's script to an agent?'

I tell her I haven't.

'You've got nothing to lose,' Jamie says.

Except one final rejection. Maybe Olly was right. I had lost faith in him.

'What about Pippa?' Kitty brings up her name finally. During the past week we stuck to our promise, but often Pippa crept into my mind. So did Oscar and Theo, but in a good way. I'm surprised by how much I miss home: talking to Dad in his hut, cooking supper with Mum in the evenings, even when she says, 'Oh, you do it like that, do you?' in that way she has.

I enjoy my walks with Janet, Woody and Audrey. I'm also surprised by how much I've missed Maison Joe, and the man who owns it.

'Are you nervous about facing her?' Sylvie asks.

I nod, but I'm still thinking about Joe.

'I would be too,' Sylvie continues. 'She was out of line. That girl needs a giant kick up the arse.'

'Becca?' Kitty nudges me. 'Something else is worrying you. Is it your mum?'

'It's Joe.' I'm surprised not to have heard a word from him.

'Maybe he's been busy at work,' Kitty suggests. 'Or it could be something to do with his dad.'

'You're right. It could be anything.'

'Face it, us guys are no good at calling up for a chat,' Jamie concludes, as we leave the restaurant.

31

Pippa doesn't hear her doorbell ring, but the door's unlocked so I let myself in. I find her in the sitting room, the carpet littered with toys, felt-tip pens and a train set. 'I told you not to play in here.' She looks on the verge of tears. 'Look at the mess you've made!'

'Auntie Becca!' Theo charges towards me.

'OUT!' she orders the boys, pushing them away. 'Go and sit in the kitchen and don't you dare move until I tell you.'

I touch her shoulder. 'Let me help,' I say, slowly bending down to pick toys off the floor.

'They've marked the sofa.' She gestures to red felt-tip pen. She still won't meet my eye. 'God, I'm exhausted.'

'Why don't we leave it now, tidy up later?' I suggest. 'I thought we could take them to the indoor play place . . .'

'Not that they deserve it.'

'Yes, but at least they can burn off some energy while we sit and eat cake.'

'I could murder a piece of cake. I'll get changed.' Pippa is dressed in a grey tracksuit and white T-shirt stained with what looks like strawberry jam. 'Then we need to talk,' she says nervously, leaving the room.

'How was London?' Pippa asks, as the twins cavort around the play centre, jumping on bouncy castles and careering down snakes-and-ladders slides with an army of other mad screaming children.

'Mummy! Auntie Becca!' Oscar waves to us as he's about to plunge into a pool of plastic balls.

I take a sip of tea; burn the roof of my mouth. 'Great.' I tell Pippa about Jamie, Sylvie, Kitty, and Glitz's house, all the time thinking, when are we going to say sorry?

'Pippa,' I begin, 'about the other week . . .'

'Mummy!' Theo flies down the slide, lands in a heap at the bottom, before picking himself up and starting all over again.

Her face reddens. 'I should go first. I said things I regret and I was wrong to talk to Mum about you behind your back. I'm sorry.'

I can see how much this admission has cost her; her sense of blame makes me feel more generous than I'd expected. 'You were right,' I acknowledge. 'I do need to make plans. I know I can't stay at home forever. I don't want to, and I'm sure Mum and Dad don't want me to either.'

Pippa nods.

'But it's difficult to see the right way forward. It's terrifying,' I confess, wanting her to understand.

She stares ahead. 'I am spoilt, and I've always been jealous of you.'

'Jealous of me?' I look at her, stunned.

'Oh, Becca, you might think I have everything – the house, the flashy car, the rich husband – but the truth is Todd's always away, and even when he's at home he's so irritable with the children. We haven't had sex in months. Sorry, too much information?' she asks, when she clocks my face.

'It's fine.'

'That day, before I talked to Mum, I accused him of having an affair. Don't tell her.'

I gasp. 'Is he?'

'I was in a foul mood because he'd just told me he had to go away on business again, and then when Mum said she couldn't help with the twins on such a regular basis, it was the last straw. I'm not excusing what I said,' she's quick to add.

'Back to Todd,' I insist.

'I accused him of putting his work before his children and me. Then I asked if there was another woman. You should have seen his face, Becca, so shocked. I don't think he is – there's no evidence, no lipstick on his shirt. '"Everything I do, I do it for you, for our family," he said. Blah blah blah.'

'Not much good if you never get to see him.'

'Exactly. He has a relationship with his BA gold card, not with me.' She turns away, searches for Oscar and Theo.

'They're over there,' I reassure her, pointing to the slide.

'I don't think he's having an affair –I'm sure he's not – but that doesn't change the fact he's always working and I'm alone. I don't have a close network of friends, not like you. Even when we were kids, you were the popular one. I was always playing tennis so had no social life. Not that I'm complaining, I loved it, but . . .' She flicks a hand through her hair. 'If I didn't have my work at the tennis club, I'd go mad. They want me to do more coaching. Todd says we shouldn't have had children if I wasn't prepared to look after them.'

'That's ridiculous and outdated.'

She waves at Oscar, who's shouting at her through the netting. 'But you were right. What with Todd's family being in America, I do depend on Mum too much and she's right to put her foot down now. When your little one comes along, she'll need to be there for you too. And I am sorry about Olly.' She shrugs helplessly. 'I have no excuse. What you're going through, I wouldn't inflict it on my worst enemy . . . but you're coping so well. You've always had strength, Becca. I've always been needy and craved approval or praise. I used to get that from Todd. But I'm on my own, Becca. I'm lonely, really lonely. Not in the same way that you are, but sometimes . . .' She digs into her handbag to find a tissue.

I wasn't expecting this.

'I've found someone to look after the twins part-time. She's called May. She's gentle, maybe too much so, because you know what Oscar's like!'

I confide what happened with the fruit kebabs. Pippa finds this funny, and for the first time in years we're laughing together.

'I'm quite excited about her starting next week, and Todd's just going to have to get on with it. You're right. Why shouldn't I work?'

'Me caveman, you woman!' I beat my chest and we

both laugh again. 'Pippa,' I have to ask, 'do you still love Todd?'

She nods. 'But if our marriage is going to survive, something has got to change. You've made me see that.'

'Look, Mummy!' Oscar says, as he's about to tackle the climbing frame.

'They adore you,' I say.

'Good mother, bad sister.'

'I haven't exactly excelled in that area either. I had no idea, until moving home, how hard it is to raise twins. I haven't given you any credit or support these past three years. Olly and I didn't visit you much after the birth, and I regret that so much now. I didn't really think about how wonderful but *scary* it must have been to have two of these at once,' I gesture to my ever-growing bump. 'Until these past few months, I barely knew Oscar and Theo. You're a great mum, Pippa.'

'Despite the felt-tip on the sofa.'

'Just cover it up with a cushion,' I suggest. I reach out, take her hand. 'I'm enjoying getting to know them. Talk to Todd. Don't put it off. Tell him how you feel. Don't let secrets or bad communication come between you.'

She nods. 'I will. I'll talk to him.'

'Perhaps it's time we supported one another too, rather than competed?'

'Please, I'd like that,' she says.

32

I find Jim sitting outside the bakery, with Noodle curled up by his side. I knew he'd be here today, just knew it. He's grown a beard and is wearing an old shabby coat. He smiles, as though he expected to see me too.

'I've been looking for you,' I say.

'Noodle and I have been out and about, haven't we, boy? We had places to go, people to see.'

I crouch down. 'It's Olly's birthday today.'

'I know.'

'He's stopped talking to me. I need him now more than ever.'

'Why?'

'Why?' I repeat, taken aback. 'I miss his voice, him telling me funny things. I miss him so much.' Tears well up in my eyes.

'Olly can't stay with you forever,' he says softly.

'But . . .'

'At his funeral, you weren't ready to say goodbye, were you?'

I shake my head.

'Nor was he.'

'I'm still not ready.'

I fear what Jim is going to say next. 'You need to move on now, and so does Olly.'

I inhale deeply. 'Can I sit with you, for just a minute?'

He nods. I stroke Noodle. 'Thank you, Jim,' I say.

'Well, thank you too, for the sandwiches and coffee.' He gestures to the food I brought with me. 'I'm glad I came here. He always said you were a top girl.'

'Goodbye.' I kiss his cheek. 'So long, Noodle.'

It's the last wine tasting session. Joe holds up a wine menu in front of the class. I typed and printed it off earlier. 'So, you want to impress your hot date.'

Scott and Monica sit at the back of the class. I'll wager they're holding hands under the table. There's no doubt they're in a relationship now. As for the rest of the class . . .

'I'm too old for dates, let alone hot ones,' Janet cackles.

'I've never been on a date,' Adam says, dressed in a maroon shirt and plum-coloured cardigan.

'My husband doesn't do dates,' calls out Felicity, sitting next to her friend Diana.

Joe glances at Henry, with his hair sticking out in all directions, and reassesses. 'OK, you're not on a hot date, you're out with friends, but you want it to be one humdinger of a night. This is your chance to engage with the sommelier, and if they're good they will want to interact with you too. So, you see Chablis *premier cru*, Fourchaume, J. C. Bessin – what are you going to think?'

'Chardonnay,' calls Henry.

'Good. And Chablis? Come on. Where is Chablis?'

'Burgundy,' says Scott.

'North,' adds Joe. 'Could you order the Chablis with the smoked haddock?'

'Yes,' they shout.

'It's buttery, high acidity,' says Henry, reading from his notes.

'Excellent. Can you all see that before the wine is even put in front of you, you're beginning to taste it? Pinot Noir?'

'A diva!' Janet calls.

'That's right,' says Joe. 'Pinot Noir is without a doubt the diva of grapes because it's temperamental, obstinate and needs constant attention and care. It can't just grow anywhere . . .'

'If the vine's too cold it gets the flu,' Adam says, 'and if it's too hot the grape makes jam,' he concludes.

'I don't think I need to teach you any more,' Joe concludes, scrunching the menu up and throwing it in the bin.

'Are you sure you're all right?' Joe asks again, helping me pick up the pieces of glass on the floor. This is the second one I've dropped tonight. He urges me to sit down. 'What's wrong?'

'It's Olly's birthday.'

Back at his flat, when Joe is in the kitchen making us a cup of tea, I think back to this time last year. Olly and I had discussed booking ourselves into a fancy hotel in London. We'd looked at the website and dreamed of room service in bed, saying that ten years earlier we'd never have thought about food before sex. Then we talked about the cost and decided to keep on putting any savings into our house account.

'I'm only thirty-one,' Olly had said. 'It's no big deal. When I'm thirty-five we can throw a big party or, if we've saved up enough, we'll go to America.' We had always wanted to go on a six-week road trip to the States. We loved the idea of going to Mexico. Why didn't we just go? Blow our cash and just do it. Get on with life, instead of saving up for it?

Joe's telephone rings. 'Sorry, Peta. I was going to call you. It's been a long day,' I hear him saying.

I get up to stretch, stubbing my foot against the coffee table. 'Fuck! Ouch . . .' I hop from one foot to the other.

'It's Becca. She's here.'

There's a pause.

'Darling, you have nothing to worry about,' he says in that quiet controlled tone. 'It's Olly's birthday and understandably she's feeling low.'

Joe hands me my mug of tea. 'I hope I haven't made things awkward,' I say. I wonder if we're spending too much time together.

'It's fine. I explained,' he says, clearly wanting to draw a line under that conversation.

'I don't want Peta to think–'

'Becca, Olly was my friend too,' he says. 'I'd like to be with you tonight. Remember him with you.'

'"Don't feel sorrow that he's gone, but celebrate his life." That was the message in most of the cards and letters people sent,' I say, curled up on one end of the sofa. 'It's fine to say that about somebody who's old, but not Olly. Of course I feel sorrow.'

He asks me about my time in London. Did I need to get away because Olly's birthday was approaching? 'My mother's first anniversary was very difficult,' Joe says. 'I wouldn't have got through it without Uncle Tom.'

I find myself telling him about my row with Pippa and Mum. Joe doesn't say a word, doesn't even express shock. I used to think he was bored or didn't care, but I see things differently now. He's listening, and he does feel things, deeply.

I find myself telling him about Olly's job too. Everything tumbles out of my mouth. When Joe says Olly should have told me, I stop him by saying, 'So what? He resigned! It's just a job.' The truth is, Olly was right. That's how I feel now, since I've been injected with a whole new sense of perspective, but before this happened I would have felt differently. It's such a rat race in London, everyone wanting more, including me. Bigger house, faster car, more money, the latest gadget. More, more, more. 'If only we'd talked, we'd have worked it out,' I say. 'We were a team. That's the thing, Joe. I'm not part of a team any more.' I confide that I don't hear Olly's voice anymore. 'I know he's telling me to move on. I just wish I knew how.'

'When Mum died, I was lost. If it hadn't been for Uncle Tom I'd have probably carried on at Bristol and become a doctor . . . no doubt a very bad one,' he adds. 'The best piece of advice Uncle Tom gave me was that in order to be happy, you have to find yourself.'

'Find yourself?'

Joe detects my cynicism. 'I told him he made it sound as easy as heading off to the lost-property office, picking yourself up and taking yourself home, but what he meant was, don't live your life according to what others expect or want. Find something that makes *you* happy.'

I twist my wedding ring round and round.

'What do you want, Rebecca?'

I stare up to the ceiling. 'That's the trouble. I don't know any more.'

I watch Joe light a candle and place it on the glass coffee table. 'I do it every year, on Mum's birthday. Here, take one.' He hands me a tea light with a box of matches. I light the small white candle and place it next to Joe's.

'I think about heaven,' I reflect. 'Whether it's real. Do you?'

'Sometimes. More so since Mum died,' he admits. 'I hope she's surrounded by flowers. Her favourite place was Kew Gardens.'

I readjust my position on the sofa. 'Olly and me, we used to play this game. If you weren't you, who would you like to be? After Chopin or Bob Dylan, he said Gauguin.'

Joe laughs quietly. 'I wonder why.'

'Maybe Olly is lying on a beach with exotic women.'

'I don't think so.'

'Where do you think he is then?'

He shrugs. 'Tahiti's all very well – I wouldn't mind going there myself – but my guess is . . .' Joe stops, looks at me.

'What?'

'He's with you.'

My head hits the pillow. When he slides off my shoes I feel the weight of the world slipping away, like sand running through my fingers. He sits at the edge of the bed, strokes my hair. I like it. Being touched. He turns off the bedside light and I hear him walking away, gently shutting the door.

33

There's a knocking sound. I think it's in my dream but then the sound is tugging at me and soon I'm awake and can hear things sliding about on what sounds like a tray. 'Come in.' Disorientated, I feel for the light switch on the bedside table.

Joe enters the room armed with breakfast. 'Room service,' he announces in a French accent. '*Le café et les croissants*.' He reverts to English as he says, 'And I thought you might like this rather delicious-looking –' he picks up the jar, studies the label – 'Bonne Maman apricot jam that my father is rather partial to.' I shift myself into a sitting position. 'Here,' he says, grabbing a cushion and placing it behind my back. His care makes me think he'd be an amazing doctor. 'Did you sleep well?' He puts the tray on the empty side of the bed and laughs, saying it could almost balance on my tummy now.

To my surprise I did sleep well.

'Anything else you need?'

'For you, monsieur, to sit down.' I pat the bed and pick up a warm croissant. 'Eat one with me.'

He picks up a couple. 'Didn't you say you *have* to eat two?'

'What are you doing today?' Joe asks me over breakfast, lying down on the other side of the bed.

'I might see if Mum can come shopping.' Pippa's old bedroom now looks like a baby department, but the one thing I've yet to buy is a buggy. 'Oh my God,' I say mid-mouthful. 'She'll be frantic! She'll think I've driven into a ditch or . . .'

'Calm down, I've spoken to her. Last night, when you were asleep, she called on your mobile. I told her you were here.'

Relieved, I thank him.

'Becca?'

'What?'

'You've got . . .' He gestures to the side of my mouth, looks as if he is about to touch my face, but before he can, I wipe away the small blob of apricot jam. 'Aren't you working today?' I ask.

He shakes his head. 'I'm looking after Dad. While you were in London he had a nasty fall.'

'Oh no. What happened?'

'He fell out of bed. Mavis found him. He's home from hospital now, but she's got something she needs to do today.'

'Why didn't you say anything before? You could have called me.'

'You were away, Becca. Anyway, he was fine. Just bruised.'

'I wish you'd called me.'

'I wanted to, I did, but . . .' He runs a hand through his hair. 'Edoardo said you'd sounded anxious. The last thing you wanted was me telling you about the dramas going on down here.'

'We're friends,' I tell him. 'Ring me next time, promise?'

He nods.

I put my cup of coffee on the bedside table. 'Right. I'd better get going. Thanks so much for last night, for . . .'

'Hang on . . .'

'What?'

'Why don't you spend the day with me? Meet my father?'

'Meet him?' I repeat inanely.

'Why not? He's a tricky old thing, but if you're up for a challenge . . .'

34

When Joe introduces me to his father, sitting in his straight-backed chair, I try to disguise my shock. It's not the sight of the deep bruise on his forehead or his pale face that startles me. It's his weight. His jumper hangs off him; his trousers gape at the knee.

'All morning he's been wanting to go to the Lobster Pot, wherever that is,' Mavis is saying. 'Now, Joe, there's a lasagne in the fridge and I've put clean sheets on the bed, so everything's dandy.' Adam's mother is a busty, generously built woman in her sixties, and I can tell she has a can-do attitude. Immediately I like her, and I can see why Joe worships the ground she walks on. 'Mavis, this is Rebecca.'

'*The* Rebecca?' she asks, beaming. She touches my arm with a podgy freckled hand. 'Adam has told me all about you. He thinks you're as pretty as a princess, which you are.'

'He thinks she has hair like Julia Roberts,' comments Joe.

I feel myself blush. 'I'll get a big head if you carry on. Carry on,' I add, laughing.

'The wine course meant the world to him, Joe,' Mavis says.

'Adam was top of the class,' I say.

'He's talented, picks things up quickly,' Joe continues.

'He's a very good cook too.' There's pride in her voice. 'Always has been, that boy.'

'Excuse me, I am here,' Joe's father reminds us.

She and Joe stand on either side of his father, encouraging him to shuffle forward in his chair, before placing an arm under each shoulder to help him up and into the wheelchair, a professional team now. Though he looks slight and frail, I can see how heavy he is to move. 'Well done, Mr Lawson!' Mavis applauds. On the way over here Joe told me that Mavis refuses to call him by his first name, Francis. 'She's old-fashioned like that,' he'd said.

'Now it's not too warm, but at least it's not raining,' Mavis comments merrily, as she and Joe help Francis put on a coat. She also places a rug over his knees. 'Mr Lawson, keep still, please.'

She looks at me, asks when the baby is due.

'Just after Christmas. About ten weeks to go.' I tell her my antenatal classes start soon, in the next ten days or so.

'Are we going to the Lobster Pot?' Francis says, eyeing me.

'Dad, the Lobster Pot's in London. He used to take Mum and me there,' Joe explains. 'Lovely French bistro place.'

'Why can't we go there now?' he demands, struggling to get out of his wheelchair. 'Who's taken my scarf!'

Mavis rests a strong hand on his arm, sits him back in his chair and tells him to relax, his scarf is right here. No one's taken it.

'Oh.' He stares at me. 'Who's this, Joe? Is she your wife?'

'No, Dad.'

'I'm a friend,' I say awkwardly.

'Dad, this is Rebecca, a friend from university,' he says.

The old man's watery grey eyes rest on mine for a moment.

'Right. Are we ready to rock 'n' roll?' Mavis unlocks the brakes. 'Now, Joe, don't you forget about the quiz this weekend, will you?' She explains to Mr Lawson that the Black Dog is holding a charity evening to raise money for Parkinson's, 'and your son has kindly taken a table. Isn't that grand!'

'Rebecca's coming too,' Joe reminds me.

'Wonderful. Adam will be chuffed.'

Francis hits both arms of the wheelchair again, impatient. 'Are we off to the Lobster Pot?'

Joe wonders if he should explain once more. 'You'll see,' he replies, as if he's just had a better idea.

Joe pushes his father in the wheelchair, along College Street, past Wells bookshop. We stop for a moment, watch a couple being photographed outside the front door of a small Georgian town house. It looks like a ghost house now, only darkness behind the windows. I read the plaque: 'In this house Jane Austen lived her last days and died 18 July 1817.'

'Forty-one years old,' Francis says, taking me by surprise, 'and buried in Winchester Cathedral, but not a single mention on her tombstone of her being a writer,' he chuckles. We walk on, until Francis orders us to stop. 'Beautiful,' he says, gazing up at a delicately carved statue of the Virgin Mary. She's graceful, serene. I feel ashamed and daren't tell Francis that I have walked past this building so many times and not once have I noticed her.

'Somehow she didn't get smashed up,' Joe reflects. 'Isn't that right, Dad, that a lot of Winchester's medieval works were smashed up by Cromwell's bastards? The cathedral's west window was trashed, all the statues in the great screen were destroyed.'

'I hope Cromwell's down there,' I say, gesturing, 'and not up there.' I point to the clear blue sky.

'Are we going to the Lobster Pot?'

Joe parks the wheelchair outside the porter's lodge, asking the porter in charge if his father can revisit Chamber Court and show us round the grounds of Winchester College. 'He lives in the past,' Joe whispers to the grey-haired man. 'I think he'll enjoy revisiting old haunts.'

'Tell Rebecca about your time here,' Joe suggests, as we walk down a cobbled pathway, past the warden's lodgings on the left.

'Who's Rebecca?'

Joe looks over to me helplessly. 'Me!' I say with a jolly smile. 'I'm Joe's friend!' When I realize I am talking in the same tone that I use with Oscar and Theo, I tell myself to snap out of it at once.

*

We stand inside Chamber Court, a large square that houses the scholars. 'I lived here, in the sixth chamber,' Francis says, as Joe and I peer through a narrow cobwebbed window into a dark musty space. 'In my day there were four hundred and seventy boys. Ten houses with forty, and seventy scholars. My parents paid a hundred and five pounds a year for me to be here.'

Finally I understand the pressure Joe must have been under, to become a scholar and excel here too.

'And he can't remember what he ate for breakfast this morning,' Joe says to me, but I can tell he's pleased by how well this is going.

'Chamber Court was where any important VIP guests came,' Joe continues. 'Dad had to line up on ceremony.'

'George VI came once,' Francis remembers.

The college chapel is ahead of us. 'The outside's been repainted, hasn't it, Dad?'

'Don't like it.'

'The colour doesn't work,' I agree. 'It looks like Wensleydale cheese.'

'Becca's an artist,' Joe tells his father.

Francis swivels round in his wheelchair, stares at me with his beady grey eyes. 'Who *are* you?'

Joe and I laugh. We can't help it.

*

After lunch in the Wykeham Arms, we stroll through the water meadows. This is what's special about Winchester, I decide, what I didn't appreciate when I was growing up. You have the water meadows, a national treasure, the fishing on the River Itchen, rowing, bird-watching (if you're into that), and then on the other side is the cathedral, the coffee shops, wine bars, art galleries, boutiques and the general bustle of the city centre.

We reach a sticky point when we come to the small white wooden gate close to the entrance of St Cross Church. Oscar and Theo's kissing gate. How do we get through? It's too narrow for Francis's wheelchair.

Joe takes charge, lifting his frail father into his arms, and thankfully a couple of passers-by take pity on us, picking up the wheelchair and handing it over the gate for us.

When we return to the house, I watch Joe settle his father back in the sitting room. It is possibly the worst house Francis could live in, since it's on many different levels. There are steps going down into the kitchen, more steps up into the sitting room. Luckily he has a stairlift that takes him up to his bedroom.

Francis's cheeks look a warmer colour, his eyes brighter, and he's still on a roll about his old school.

'Winchester College has produced scientists, lawyers, doctors, politicians – mostly Labour ones,' he contemplates. 'Probably the most famous soldier was Wavell.'

Joe kneels down in front of his father. 'Now, Dad, would you like a cup of tea? Or maybe something stronger? A brandy? Sherry?' I watch Joe smiling at his father and I feel a wave of affection towards him.

'Who was the most famous? Anthony Trollope, the writer, now he went to Winchester. There aren't many businessmen though.'

'Hang on,' I step in, 'don't forget, Mr Lawson, it produced a great wine connoisseur.'

Joe gets up, says he's going to put the kettle on.

'Joe!' Francis calls out to his son.

'And I think Mavis has made you a fruitcake.'

'You're a fine man. I'm proud of you.'

'Oh, Dad,' Joe says, standing at the door looking like a bashful schoolboy.

'I'm proud of him, Rebecca.'

When Francis falls asleep in front of the television, Joe and I leave the room and head into the kitchen.

I tell him what a good idea it was to take him round his old school. I enjoyed his father's stories of eating snoek and powdered egg in the dining hall, along with his football disaster. Francis had hooted with laughter as he'd recalled letting in eight goals in twenty minutes during a match against Southampton.

Joe smiles sadly. 'He'll have forgotten about it tomorrow.'

'Yes, but it made him happy today.'

'I'm going to have to think about a nursing home soon,' Joe confides. 'I hate it, but I don't know how much longer we can cope alone, in this house.' He clears up the plates and mugs.

'I think it's amazing the way you look after him.'

'He's my father,' he says simply. 'What else can I do? Let him rot in a home?'

I think of what Peta said. 'No, of course not. I didn't mean it that way.'

'I wouldn't have Maison Joe without Dad.'

'I still think it's–'

He cuts me off. 'I have help. Lots of help.'

I put my mug down. 'Why can't you accept a compliment?'

'It'll be great to see Jamie again at this quiz. Peta's coming down too. Did I tell you that the series she's been working on has been put on hold, the male lead has tonsillitis . . .'

'Shut up, Joe! Sometimes I wish you'd . . .'

'What?'

'Let me finish a sentence.'

Finally he looks me in the eye, smiles. 'The great wine connoisseur.'

'Well, you are.'

'Thanks for saying that.'

'He is proud of you. You know that, don't you?'

'It's the first time he's said it to me.' He breathes deeply. 'Dad and I, we're quite similar like that, find it hard to show our feelings.' He looks at me, and for a brief moment I picture Joe and me all those years ago at Bristol. I can see him placing a hand over my mouth and saying, 'You know I have feelings, you know I care, Rebecca.' I see us in my bedroom and remember his touch against my skin.

35

The Black Dog is holding a quiz tonight in aid of Parkinson's. Mavis's brother lives with this condition. It's a cosy pub, with a log fire and colourful kilim rugs. Kitty, Annie, Peta and I grab one of the corner tables, while Joe and Jamie are at the bar, ordering drinks. Peta asks me how I am, her tone sympathetic. I haven't seen her since the party at Joe's flat. 'I know you were upset about Olly's birthday,' she continues.

'Who's that?' Kitty asks, noticing someone waving at me. 'Another of your perky pensioner friends?' Earlier today, we visited Janet and Woody for tea.

I smile. 'It's Mavis. She looks after Joe's dad.'

'And that person?' asks Peta, when Adam sticks his thumbs up at me. He's wearing a cap and a brown leather jacket.

'Adam, Mavis's son.'

'What a weirdo.'

I want to say something, but Mavis is approaching us, dressed in a woollen skirt and frilly shirt. She places her hands around mine. 'Mr Lawson liked you, Rebecca. I could see he had a lovely time with you and Joe.'

'You've met his dad?' Peta asks, the moment Mavis bustles back to her table to join her team.

'The other day, it was last-minute.'

'What did you think? I couldn't believe the state of him. When we wheeled him out,' Peta says, as if Francis were a sack of potatoes, 'he fell asleep over his lunch.'

'He's old, Peta, and unwell,' I say quietly, making sure Joe can't hear.

'Can't do illness. In sickness and in health? I don't think so. I'd pack my bags first thing!' She laughs, and I find I have to give her credit for her honesty, if nothing else.

Joe and Jamie head over to our table with drinks.

'Becca was saying she met your father,' Peta says, when Joe hands her a glass of wine. 'How is he, darling?' she asks.

'Not too good at the moment.'

'I do worry, Becca, such a lovely man. But honestly, Joe, you should think about a home,' she says, stroking his back. I'm shocked by how two-faced she is. I'd be nervous of what she'd say about me behind my back.

'Let's not talk about it now,' Joe replies, as supper is served. 'This is my night off.'

After lasagne and a hefty slice of cheesecake, untouched by Peta, the atmosphere heats up as the organizer, Jackie, in her late fifties, hands each team the question papers assembled into different categories.

Over the microphone she thanks us for being here tonight and tells us that so far The Black Dog has raised over three hundred pounds. Everyone cheers, especially Adam, who waves at me again from across the room. 'You have thirty minutes, and make sure you put your team's name at the top, please.'

Joe is assigned the task of writing down our answers.

First category is general knowledge. This is where I need my father.

'That's the one,' I say, when Jamie whispers, 'José Luis Rodriguez Zapatero.'

'Spell it right!' Kitty screeches. 'We get penalty points if it's wrong!'

'God, she hasn't changed at all, has she?' Annie rolls her eyes at me.

When it comes to soap operas and scandal, I'm on a roll. Joe says I should be ashamed. 'I've had months of being at home,' I remind him. 'It's great to know my time hasn't been entirely wasted.'

Joe is in his element in the booze category.

'Federer's won Wimbledon four times,' I say, certain Dad told me Federer's record when he was watching the tennis last summer. 'Or was it five?'

'Is that your final answer?' asks Joe.

'Or do you want to phone a friend?' Annie suggests, laughing.

'Put four,' I say, causing Peta to stir in her seat.

'Federer? It's six,' she overrules me. 'Keith loves tennis. She's wrong.'

'Who's Keith?' asks Annie.

'My father.'

'My sister loves tennis too,' I say, not meaning to sound quite so spiky.

'Why not compromise?' Jamie proposes. 'Plump for five.'

Peta dismisses him in a flash. She'd eat him alive if they were going out.

If only Pippa were here . . .

'That's cheating!' Joe attempts to stop me sending her a text message under the table.

I clutch my phone tightly. 'Stop it, let go,' he's saying teasingly, his hand still on mine.

'It's six.' Peta glares at us.

'Put six,' everyone urges, including me.

'It's only a quiz.' Jamie attempts to thaw the atmosphere.

Joe is either brave or stupid when he says he's going to stick with four.

The bell rings. Time's up. Everyone has to swap answer sheets with a neighbouring table. We are marking 'The Nitwits'. The grey-haired leader of the Nitwits smiles at me; he's missing one of his front teeth, I notice.

'We got that.' Kitty nods when it's announced Zapatero is the Spanish prime minister.

'*Come Dine with Me!*'

'*Salad Days.*' Annie points out that she knew that one.

'Botticelli.'

'Beaujolais.'

'Cheryl Cole.'

'Cherie Blair.'

When it comes to Jackie telling us how many times Roger Federer has won Wimbledon, my heart is beating like a drum. Peta sits poised. Kitty, Annie, Joe and Jamie wait with baited breath.

'Six times.'

Fuck.

'I'm so sorry, Peta,' I concede.

'I knew I was right.' She fans her face with one of the question papers.

Jackie, the team organizer, reads out the results. Our team, 'The Silly Billies', has come second. 'Only one point in it,' she says.

Annie and I do a celebratory high-five. Peta turns to Joe. 'If you'd listened to *me*, we would have come joint first.'

Joe seems tense. 'Fine. I'm sorry, but it's only a game, Peta, for *charity*.' As he heads over to Jackie to thank her for the evening, Adam bounds over to our table and introduces himself to everyone. 'We came third!' he announces. 'First the worst, second the best, third the one with the hairy chest!' I tell him his leather jacket makes him look like Tom Cruise in *Top Gun*.

'For God's sake,' says Peta under her breath, watching Joe talking to Jackie.

Adam sticks his thumbs up. 'Got to go! Mum's calling me.'

'Oddball. What's wrong with him?' Peta asks, when he's out of earshot.

'He's a lovely man,' I say.

'Is he stupid or something?'

'He's not stupid.' I defend Adam. 'Actually, he was one of the best students on Joe's course.'

'*He* was on Joe's course?'

'Adam's a kind, funny, big-hearted soul,' I say with feeling. 'Life probably hasn't turned out quite the way he'd hoped, but he doesn't deserve your scorn.'

Joe returns. 'Right, are we ready to . . . ?' He stops, sensing the atmosphere. 'Everything OK?'

'Absolutely.' Peta smiles. 'I just met Adam. Sweet boy.'

I stare at her. She's an excellent actress, I'll say that for her. Part of me wants to tell Joe what she has just said, but I force myself to keep quiet.

'And I'm sorry about snapping about the Federer thing, but I'm not feeling too good. Faint, a little sick.' She fans her face again. 'Maybe I'm pregnant too! Wouldn't that be funny?'

A silence descends. I notice Joe's face turn grey.

'Do you mind if we go home, darling?' she says.

36

I'm in the loft, drawn up there by something Joe said. I scan the shelves for my old wooden paintbox, finally seeing it next to a case filled with Pippa's tennis trophies and medals. It's covered in dust.

I remember Joe taking me down to his father's cellar that day we visited Winchester College. 'Can I show you something?' he had asked after tea.

'Of course.'

I took his hand as he helped me down the steps. 'You know that thing I said about finding yourself? How when Mum died, I felt I had to start over again?'

'Yes.'

'I'd always been interested in wine, since I was about ten. I was mystified and fascinated by all the different names on the bottles and what they could tell me.

Careful here. Your mother would never forgive me if you fell.'

When I open my paintbox and look inside, I feel as if I have been reunited with a friend. I pick up a tube of red oil paint. When I was a child, Dad used to take me to my favourite craft shop at the weekends, where I'd spend all my pocket money on these tubes of oil paints – sweeties I called them. I unscrew the top, try to squeeze a little on to one finger. It's impossible. The paint is dry, hardened by age.

My mind wanders back to Joe and me in the wine cellar. It was a dark room, with a wooden table in the centre, and on top of the table were a couple of wine glasses and a claret decanter. Racks of wine stood against the walls, displayed in order of vintage and region. 'I used to spend all my time down here,' he said.

'Drinking?'

'No. I'd have been hung, drawn and quartered! Dad was saving his wine. It was an investment. I'd just read the labels.' Joe pulled out a bottle of red. '1982 Chateau Lynch-Bages, Pauillac. Grand Cru Classé.'

Impressed, I said, 'Not the kind of wine you'd drink with spaghetti bolognese then?'

'Not the kind of wine you drink at all.'

I shook my head. 'Your dad should share it with you now, while he still can.'

I search for my A-level art portfolio. It's tucked away on one of the bottom shelves, lying underneath some of my old art books. I slide it out and carefully sit myself down, before unfastening the ribbon that binds the folder together. As I flick through my work, I come to one of my charcoal drawings of San Miniato al Monte, the church that my Great-Aunt Cecily painted, close to the centre of Florence. It came to be my sanctuary, a place I visited when I needed time alone, away from the studio. I took Olly there when he came to see me in Florence. We revisited it on our honeymoon. We had promised ourselves we'd return one year, maybe for our tenth anniversary.

'Where is she?' I overhear Mum asking my father.

They spot the ladder.

'Are you all right, darling?' Dad calls up into the roof. 'What are you looking for up there? You should have let me get it for you.'

I stagger to my feet. 'Dad, you're over seventy!'

'And you're pregnant!'

'What's going on?' Mum sounds cross. 'For God's sake, Rebecca, why didn't you just wait for us to help you?'

'You used to be passionate about your art,' Joe had

said, 'ever since you were a little girl. Go back to the beginning, Becca.'

'I am being careful,' I promise, handing my portfolio down to Dad. 'I'm going to start painting again.'

'No, you're not. You're coming down here at once,' Mum says. 'Darling, you help her. I'll hold on to the ladder.'

37

The following morning, I am sketching Woody from a photograph. When it's finished, I'm going to give it to Janet as a present for her eighty-fifth birthday. As I work, she asks me to tell her about my time in Florence.

'I was there for a year and met some lovely people.' I describe my flamboyant American teacher, Vivian Rogers. I tell her about my brief romance with Luca.

'What about Olly?' Janet asks, jutting out her chin.

Before I'd left for Florence, Olly had accompanied me to the airport. There was an emotional goodbye. At the time I was still struggling with guilt about Joe, but I don't tell Janet that. Olly and I promised to give *us* a chance, to see if we could make a long-distance relationship work. To begin with, we wrote cards and telephoned regularly. However, after a couple of months our communication started to dwindle, like a fire going out. I was beginning to make friends, and other things were getting in the way, like study, wine bars, parties, late nights and romantic walks with Luca, a chef I'd met in a nightclub. When I discovered he worked at my favourite restaurant, close to the Ponte Vecchio, he seemed too good to be true. He was handsome, in a dark, Italian way. I remember mad rides on the back of his bottle-green scooter, me clinging on when he took a bend too quickly. When I plucked up the courage to tell Olly, he also confessed he'd slept with someone else. We were being unrealistic, we decided. There was hurt on both sides, neither one of us wanting to let go completely. I missed his friendship almost more than anything else.

'When he did visit, for the first time, I hadn't seen him for six months, Janet.'

We'd arranged to meet inside the Duomo. My heart lifted when I saw him. He was standing, his back to me, wearing his old cord jacket and jeans. We hugged, before Olly tentatively suggested we go and have a coffee. As we walked to the nearest cafe, to fill the silence we talked about the weather. After ordering drinks, Olly asked about my course and I wanted to hear about Bristol, and how he was feeling, especially since finals were looming. Our conversation felt awkward, too polite. I wondered if Olly were here to tell me he had met someone else.

Finally, Olly said, 'I haven't come all the way here to talk to you about your course or my finals. I've tried hard to forget about you, Becca, but I'm not interested in anyone else.'

'Oh Olly.' I took his hand, the relief overwhelming.

'I can't serenade you in a gondola, not in Florence . . .'

We both smiled, the tension disappearing.

'And I'm not a very good cook,' he admitted, 'but I love you. I want us to go back to how we were. Of course you need to finish the course, I understand that, but I'll fly out again, after finals. I mean, wow, look at this place! Who wouldn't want to be here? I'm so proud of you, Becca.'

I called Luca that night, broke it off. He met someone shortly afterwards. I'd wounded his pride, but I didn't break his heart.

Olly stayed with me for three weeks. Another thing I don't tell Janet is that we barely left the bedroom for the first ten days.

'Olly did visit again, after finals, and then we flew home, for good, at the end of my course. We shared a flat with Kitty and Jamie in Balham.'

'I remember your wedding,' Janet sighs. 'Olly sang

and played the piano. There was lots of dancing too. I remember your father boogying on the dance floor!'

I smile at the word 'boogying'. 'We rented a flat in Ealing after that and I set up my illustrating company.'

'Oh, how wonderful,' she says, putting the kettle on. 'Come to think of it, I do remember your mother mentioning that.'

'It worked well for a while,' I say, without looking up from my drawing. 'I did some illustrations for magazines, a few restaurants, travel brochures. I worked with a writer on a couple of gardening books.' But my income was as precarious as balancing on a tightrope, and I didn't have time to do my own work. 'I'd get nervous when I didn't have a single commission. It kept me awake at night.'

'Oh, darling, how awful. Tea?'

'Yes, please.'

'Builders OK?'

'Perfect.' I watch Janet reaching a shaky hand for a mug. I want to help, but she gets cross if I try to do too much for her.

Finally, stick in one hand and tea in the other, she puts a mug on my side of the table. She squints at my drawing, telling me I've got Woody's eyes just right, though I don't think she can really see.

'You must have missed painting when you worked for that Glitzy man.'

I laugh. 'I love Glitz. I enjoyed working for him, but you're right, I did miss it. I want to paint again,' I confide. 'Even if it's just a hobby. This is me. It's what I love doing.'

She nods knowingly. 'Gregory was an asthmatic, so we could never have dogs. I always told myself that when I was on my own I'd have a dog. I started up a pet nanny business too. You remember all the dogs, don't you?'

'Oh yes.'

'You see, I was only sixty at the time, so I had to earn a crust. They were the children I'd never had. When Gregory died, I had to find myself again, and the basic me was the girl brought up by her parents, the girl who loved animals, who would have dreamed of being a vet given half the chance. That's why I returned to Winchester, to be close to my childhood home.'

'I didn't know your family lived here.'

'They lived out towards Stockbridge, close to Pippa. I needed to return to my roots. It helps, you know, thinking of the things that you won't miss about that person when they're gone, things you can do on your own. I found it liberating.'

She must sense my shock as she goes on to say, 'People can idolize their loved ones after they die. I didn't know your Olly well. I liked him very much of course – he was charming and funny – but there must be one or two things you don't miss about him.'

I grip my pencil hard, thinking about the way he'd flush the coffee grounds down the sink. How he'd play computer games at the weekend when I wanted him to talk to me.

'Oh, lots of things,' I say. 'Olly was bad at calling his mum and dad. I always had to remind him. And I wish we hadn't cut ourselves off from my own family, and I hate him for not telling me about his job, for keeping secrets from me. I'm so angry with myself too. I should have taken that motorbike down to our local garage and sold it. He would have been angry with me, sure, but that would have been a whole lot better than him losing his fucking life! Oh, Janet, sorry about that.'

'It's fine. I've heard the "f" word many a time. Might even have used it myself a few times.'

'Oh, Janet, I love you.' I feel a flood of affection for her.

'I love you too, my girl, as if you were my own.'

Later that morning I tell Janet about my recent outing with Joe's father. She enjoys the Lobster Pot story.

'He's vulnerable, that boy.'

'Vulnerable? Joe?'

She plays with her wedding ring, twisting it round her slender finger. 'There's something missing. I may not see, but I hear it in his voice. It's something Michel said too. He's loyal to the family, won't tell me their troubles, but I sense there have been many. I'm probably wrong, but . . .'

'No, you're not wrong. You see more than anyone, Janet.'

'He likes you, Rebecca, very much, that I do know. You seem to have been able to put the past behind you.'

I had told Janet on one of our walks that we'd lost touch at Bristol. He'd hurt Olly and it was my fault too. I didn't go into the graphic details, and she'd sensed not to push me. All I said was how I hadn't seen him in over ten years. Talking to her, I realize how much has healed between us. 'I like him too,' I say to Janet. 'He's become a good friend again.'

At that moment, the doorbell rings. 'Oh! That'll be Michel,' she says. I remember how long it took Janet to reach the door that very first time I knocked, when I was delivering a cottage pie. Now she positively skips towards it. Michel strides in, dressed in a smart overcoat, his hair combed, shoes polished, bearing flowers, and I can smell spicy aftershave.

She sniffs the flowers, lets out a deep sigh, as if she wants to eat them. 'How delicious, thank you.'

'Hello, Rebecca.' Michel shakes my hand. I tell Janet I'll pop the flowers into a vase.

'Where are you going?' I call from the kitchen.

'I'm taking her to a French brasserie. Thought we could put her new wine tasting skills into practice.'

'I miss the course,' Janet says nostalgically. 'I'm quite lost on a Tuesday night, but thank goodness I still have you, Michel!'

As I'm leaving, I happen to see on the front seat of Michel's car a small black jewellery box. Perhaps Joe was right after all? Have they fallen in love?

38

It's early November, and it's cold. Mum told me we had our first frost last night. I'm on my way to Maison Joe to meet Annie for lunch, when Kitty calls me on the mobile. I sense something is wrong since she never rings me at this time; we stick to our morning call, before work. She's supposed to be driving down this evening, to stay the weekend. I'm thirty-two weeks pregnant and tomorrow is my first antenatal class. I don't want to turn up without my birthing partner.

'I could have killed the bastard,' she says, after explaining that as the automatic doors had opened she'd felt someone crash into her from behind, and the next thing she knew, she had been catapulted out of the bus and into the street. 'I was lying face down on the road, smack, Becca.'

'Oh God, how awful. That must have hurt.'

'I'm really sorry,' she continues, and I dread what is coming next. 'But I'm not going to be able to make it this weekend. I've sprained my ankle, I can't drive. I feel terrible letting you down . . .'

'I understand,' I say, trying to hide my disappointment. 'I'm so sorry, Kitty.'

Kitty tells me that to add insult to injury, most of the passengers getting off at Green Park simply stepped around her, as though she were a minor inconvenience en route to their office. 'Except for this one guy, Steven.'

I manoeuvre myself out of the way for a woman pushing twins in a buggy the size of a spaceship. We give one another a supporting nod, as if we're in this baby business together.

'He's asked me out,' Kitty goes on. 'He's a doctor. An anaesthetist.'

'Wow, how exciting,' I exclaim, though my mind is still fixed on how I don't much fancy going to my first antenatal class alone. Week one is specifically for couples. Kitty must sense my worry as she says, 'I wish I could come. I feel dreadful, but . . .'

'It's OK. It's not your fault,' I reassure her, almost outside Maison Joe now, though wishing I was at the top of St Catherine's Hill. I could do with a good scream.

*

Briefly I explain the dilemma to Annie over lunch, aware of Peta eavesdropping at the bar. Since our spat over Adam and the tennis question, I've found myself hoping not to see her again, even wishing Joe might break up with her. She's not good enough for him.

'I'm away this weekend,' Annie sighs, 'with the in-laws. Oh, Becca, I wish I could help.'

I blow on my piping-hot pumpkin soup.

'Listen, you're strong,' Annie continues. 'You'll be fine on your own. The teacher knows about Olly, doesn't she?'

I nod.

'I'll come,' says Peta, to my total amazement.

She pulls up a chair and joins us. 'You can't go on your own, Becca, not if it's for couples. I won't let you.'

'Oh, don't worry,' I exclaim with false jollity. 'That's really kind, but I'll be fine. I'm a big girl, no pun intended!'

Joe laughs behind the bar.

''Tis no trouble. Joe's working all weekend.'

'Not *all* weekend,' he says.

She rolls her eyes. 'Practically all weekend, and I'm busy doing nothing.' She asks me where it is and at what time. 'Right, I really do have to fly now, but pick me up tomorrow?'

I look over to Annie, unable to disguise my discomfort. 'Thanks,' I call out to her as she's about to leave, 'though you really don't have to,' I find myself adding, catching Joe's eye.

Peta blows Annie and me a kiss. 'What are friends for?'

39

Little Angels antenatal classes take place in a private house in Chandlers Ford, not far from Winchester. Peta and I walk into a crowded room scattered with bright orange and pink birthing balls. Among the pregnant women, Peta stands out in a pale-grey woollen dress that shows off her figure, and black leather knee-high boots. We find seats next to a couple and I introduce myself. Their names are Keisha and Paul, who are having their first baby too. I discover Keisha is from Jamaica. She has beautiful dark skin and deep brown eyes. Paul is fair with freckles. I catch him glancing at his watch and then vaguely remember Dad mentioning something about a rugby match after lunch.

For the next five minutes we all introduce ourselves. I overhear chat about breast pumps, fatigue and ankles the size of balloons.

Keisha works for British Airways. She met Paul on a flight to New York. She has been a flight attendant for five years, but wants to take a year off after the baby is born. She glances at Peta and asks if I have a partner, a question I have prepared myself for, but however much I prepare, I'm never ready. 'Was he clever enough to get out of it?' Paul asks, winking at his wife. 'Fake a headache so he could watch the game?'

'He died,' I say, a conversation-stopper if ever there was one. I had planned to say it more gently, explain that it was a motorbike accident.

'Welcome!' Our teacher strides into the middle of the circle. Keisha is staring at me, unable to say a word, but I can see pity in her eyes. If Paul hadn't wanted to be here before, he wants it even less now.

Our teacher is called Augusta Reid. She's in her early forties, heavily made up and wearing a low-cut stretchy scarlet top that shows off her cleavage.

'So, here we all are!' Augusta claps her hands. 'Waiting for "Baby" to arrive! No pregnancy is the same, otherwise we'd know exactly what to expect, so my role over the next six weeks is to talk you through all the different approaches to birth. I don't know about you, but who here finds choice overwhelming?'

Everyone mutters in agreement.

'In a cafe, you can't just buy coffee with milk, can you? You have a whole blackboard of choices. Well, it's the same with birth.' She turns to the whiteboard, bends down to find one of her thick-nib coloured pens.

'Do we have a home or hospital birth? What pain treatment do we opt for?' She scribbles down the various options on the board. 'Do we go down the natural path or choose medical pain relief? But first things first . . .'

Augusta makes each one of us say what we do so we can get to know the group.

We have a surveyor, an electrician, a teacher, a clinical psychologist, a young woman on her third marriage but this is her first baby, single girl Chloe is here with her best friend. I smile at her, wanting her to know she's not the only one on her own. Keisha is having a baby girl.

'And I'm here to support Rebecca,' Peta addresses the group, the last person to speak, and I can tell all the men fancy her. 'She lost her husband in a tragic accident . . .'

Oh good grief! I should have brought Mum. She was hinting she was free. In fact, I think she would have been touched. Come to think of it, why didn't I ask Pippa? Things have been steadily improving between us. Todd's at home this weekend . . . oh, bugger.

'. . . and it's at times like this that you need friends.' She rubs my arm. 'Oh, and by the way, I'm an actress. Some of you might recognize me?' She stops rubbing my arm. 'I'm about to star in a Jane Austen documentary, Sunday night, 9 p.m.'

For our first exercise, Augusta wants us to write down three things that are concerning us about having a baby. 'Try not to consult with your partner. This is what *you* are preoccupied with . . .'

'So, what are you writing?' Peta asks, leaning across to see. 'Oh yes, pain. Some people just spit 'em out, *pop*, and then others go through a twenty-four-hour labour only to go and have a bloody emergency Caesarean.'

I agree. Annie had to have an emergency Caesarean after thirty hours of contractions.

'I'd just book myself in for a C-section straight away,' Peta continues.

My second concern is, what if I can't breastfeed? Mum couldn't. Out of the corner of my eye I see Peta holding in her stomach.

'I'd be worried about my figure too. I don't like not being in control.'

I can't concentrate.

'It's my job to look good. I'd be axed.' She make-believe cuts off her head. 'But you're lucky, you don't have to worry about that.'

I can just let myself go, I think to myself. Let my boobs droop to the ground and put on tons of weight and wobble down the street like blancmange. No one will care, or notice for that matter. I smile at this new image of myself.

She leans across me to see what else I'm writing. 'Premature?'

'Pippa's twins were.'

'I wouldn't give that a second's thought, Becca,' she steamrolls over me. 'The hospital's used to dealing with all kinds of problems. Tell you what I'd be concerned about. Sex.'

'I hardly have to worry about that,' I say sharply, but she doesn't seem aware of the point I am making.

'How's everyone doing?' calls out Augusta, circulating through the group.

'Should I be writing anything?' Peta asks when she approaches us.

Why didn't I just come alone? What's so frightening about it? I've got to stop acting like that insecure person who doesn't want to push open the restaurant door first, preferring to shuffle in behind the leader. I need to be the person who can look the waiter in the eye and say with confidence, 'A table for one, please,' and taste the wine with confidence. I glance at Peta, studying her own stomach again, as if imagining a baby inside. It's clear she has no interest in supporting me, but what I can't work out is why she is sacrificing a Saturday afternoon to be here?

After the class I offer Peta a lift to Maison Joe, and in the car we laugh about some of the men's concerns: parking meter money, where can they buy a Chinese takeaway, changing nappies, will they feel excluded, can they bring wine or champagne into the hospital to celebrate?

'I want to be pregnant before I'm thirty-five,' Peta reflects. 'I don't want to be an old mum at the school gates.'

'Lots of women don't have children until much later now though. I mean, look at the class today. I'm considered young at thirty-one. How old are you?'

'Thirty-three and a half, so Joe had better hurry up!' Her laughter stops as abruptly as a power cut when she asks, 'He hasn't said anything to you, has he?'

'About what?'

'Me? How he feels?'

'No, nothing.'

'Really? You've been spending a lot of time with him recently, haven't you?'

'Not much,' I reply, trying not to be intimidated by the accusation in her tone.

'Joe's so *private*.' She gazes out of the window. 'It's hard to know what the hell he's thinking. Of all people, I thought he might have talked to you.' She turns to me. 'You seem close.'

'We're old friends, but he doesn't talk to me about that stuff.'

'It's frustrating. Joe's down here, I'm up in London. How are we ever going to have a serious relationship if I only get to see him the odd weekend? He won't take any time off work, and when he does, he spends it with his dad. I don't sense I'm anywhere near the top of his priority list. Oh, I just wish his father would kick the bucket . . .'

'Peta!'

'Well, he can barely remember his own name, Becca. It's very hard for Joe.'

Shocked, I park outside Maison Joe, the engine still running. 'Peta, that's a terrible thing to say. It is hard for Joe, but he still loves his father.'

She shrugs. 'I'd hate to be a burden on my family, I wouldn't allow it.'

'I'd better go,' I say, when I notice a traffic warden coming towards the car. 'Thanks for coming with me today.'

Peta makes no attempt to unbuckle her seat belt. 'Have you two ever gone out?'

'Gone out?'

'Yes. Had a fling, relationship, call it whatever you like.'

The warden is getting even closer.

Peta carries on. 'You must have found him attractive. *Do* you find him attractive?'

The traffic warden is way too close for comfort now. 'Peta, go!' I point to the man in uniform, now studying the car behind us, circling the Honda like a shark, tapping something into his machine.

'You haven't answered–'

'Peta, you need to know where you stand, I get that, but I'm not the one you should be talking to. If Joe isn't committed–'

She turns to me, fire in her eyes. 'He *has* said something to you, hasn't he?'

'No! He hasn't said a word. Not one. Now GO.'

I feel nothing but relief when she gets out of my car and I drive away from an imminent parking fine.

Now I understand exactly why she sacrificed her Saturday to be with me. She wanted to quiz me.

Why can't Joe see through her?

40

I open my wardrobe, wondering what to wear tonight. Options are limited when you're eight and a half months pregnant. All I feel like putting on is my baggy track-suit and furry slippers. I'm going out for supper with Annie and Pippa this evening, at Maison Joe.

Pippa looks stunning in a slim-fitting black polo-neck dress, her long blonde hair scooped into a simple pony-tail. Annie's frizzy hair is restrained by a clip, and she's wearing pink suede heels that came from a charity shop, she shows off. I laugh, telling them my navy dress looks more like a tent, and look at my squishy shoes. They're flat and roomy, just the kind of shoes you'd wear if you were suffering from chronic bunions. Annie laughs too, telling me I'm exaggerating, but when she glances at them again she says, 'Maybe.'

Joe shows us to our table, says he hopes to join us later, when it's less busy.

Pippa can't help staring at him. 'You didn't tell me how handsome he was.'

'He's the most sought-after bachelor in town,' Annie fills her in. 'Peta, that's his girlfriend, is one lucky girl.'

After Luis has taken our order, Pippa is incredulous that she hasn't visited Maison Joe before. 'I've walked past, but the thing is, I hardly ever go out during the week. I'm pretty antisocial these days.'

'Me too,' agrees Annie. 'This is a serious treat. I just thought we should have a last supper with Becca before the baby arrives.'

They both ask me how I am. I recall my sleepless nights. 'Just as I'm about to nod off, pillows all in the right place, I get . . .'

'Leg cramp?' Pippa guesses. 'And you have to heave yourself out of bed . . .'

'Pillows flying everywhere?' Annie finishes.

'Exactly.' I realize I am talking to a couple of experts.

'Not long to go now,' Annie says.

'The twins are excited,' Pippa tells her. 'Honestly, it's all they can talk about.'

'How about you, Becca? How do you feel?' Annie asks.

'Do you want the honest answer?'

'Sock it to me.' Annie leans back in her chair as if ready for the punch.

'Like a beginner skier at the top of a black run.'

'You're not alone.' Pippa touches my hand. 'You're bound to have a few falls, but you'll be fine.'

Over supper I tell them about the antenatal classes. They were useful, on the whole. Weeks two and three were for women only, and I became good friends with Keisha. 'I now have a first-class knowledge of both male and female genitalia,' I boast to my sister and Annie. 'Test me. I can tell you all about them and lots more besides.'

Annie pulls a face. 'No, thanks. I didn't bother going to classes for my second, so I've forgotten it all now. D'you think you'll have any more children, Pippa?'

'No,' comes the answer at lightning speed.

'Anyone who tells you giving birth isn't painful is talking bullshit,' Annie continues. 'Sorry, Becca, I ain't gonna pretend.'

I tell them I'm under no false illusions. We watched a birthing video (hell). I tell them how Keisha was the first in the group to give birth. Little Freya came into this world at a healthy seven pounds and two ounces. 'When Keisha came into our final class to tell us about the birth, we had to know exactly how it had happened and how painful it was on a scale of one to ten. She said TEN!' I break out into nervous laughter.

'Don't be brave. Have the drugs – take whatever they offer you,' Pippa advises, explaining she'd wanted to go without, but bugger that. I remember being on holiday when the twins were born. I'd called home to find out the news. Mum had said the births had been difficult, but it hadn't meant much to me at the time, or to Olly. I realize now how much we both missed out on our families. Olly didn't see his parents, nor his brother and nephews, nearly enough either.

'Do you know what you're going to do after the baby is born?' Annie asks. 'Have you thought about staying down here?'

When I tell her I want to return to London she pulls a sad face. I'm going to look for a flat to rent. I've worked out my finances, and Olly's parents, Victor and Carolyn, are helping. 'Mum's worried about you being on your own,' confesses Pippa, when I tell her I've been in touch with estate agents.

Deep down I am nervous that the longer I stay at home, the harder it will be to leave. I'll miss everyone. Mum, Dad, Pippa, Oscar and Theo, Annie, Janet . . . 'Oh, and I'll miss Joe,' I say, when he approaches us.

'What's that?' he asks, when I know he heard loud and clear.

He pulls up a chair and I introduce him to Pippa.

'Joe, help me persuade Becca to stay in Winchester,' Annie urges.

'Stay. London's filthy and there are no decent wine bars.'

I laugh before changing the subject by telling Joe about Michel. He hadn't proposed to Janet. She'd found the idea funny. 'I'm in the departure lounge, Rebecca!' Michel had given her a silver bracelet, with her initials engraved on the inside.

'How's Peta?' Annie asks.

His smile fades.

'What?' she pushes. 'Are things not great?'

I fold my napkin in half.

'Joe!' Edoardo calls.

'Excuse me. I'm needed at the bar,' he says.

41

The following afternoon Mum sends me into town to run a couple of errands. Winchester High Street is adorned with Christmas decorations. According to Mum's list, I need to buy a tin of dog food, a pint of double cream, petits pois, some Christmas wrapping paper and a jar of mincemeat. I see a number of my parents' friends in the supermarket, but this time I don't hide in the frozen foods section. 'It must be any moment now!' Mum's tennis friend Marjorie says, before wishing me, '*Bonne chance*, my dear! And keep warm!'

'Just ten more days to go before I meet you,' I say to my boy as we leave Sainsbury's, 'providing you behave and stick to the programme.' I smile, thinking that's what Olly might have said. *Olly?* Deep down I know he's gone. *I miss you talking to me. I think about you all the time.*

I walk on. 'But we'll be fine, won't we?' I say quietly

to my boy. 'It might not be perfect, but it's going to be an adventure, and we'll have each other.'

On my way home, I walk past the Buttercross. My friends Jim and Noodle have gone. I don't expect I shall see them again. I wonder where they are now, and if Jim is delivering a message to somebody else like me?

I walk through The Square, decorated with fairy lights, and decide to walk home via the Cathedral Close to watch the ice skating.

As I approach Maison Joe, I stop, glance through the window and see Joe sitting alone at the bar.

'Joe,' I say, walking inside.

He mouths, 'Not now,' at me.

'What?'

'Go,' he urges.

I hear someone coming upstairs. Finally I understand and retreat towards the door.

'Oh, look who it is!' Peta says, scorn in her voice.

As she approaches me, I take a few steps back.

'So, you've heard the news?' she asks.

'News? What news?'

'You were about to ask Joe how it went, were you?'

'Sorry?'

'Comfort Joe in his time of need?' Peta continues.

'I don't know what you're talking about.'

'Peta, enough. I think you should leave,' Joe says in that quiet but forceful tone.

'Why? This is getting interesting. You finish with me, and then *voila*! Here's Becca. She's always here Joe, getting in the way.'

'Peta, I'm sorry. I was just passing . . . I had some shopping to do.' I gesture to my bags. 'I had no idea.'

She turns on him. 'Did you ask her to come here?'

'Come on.' Joe hands Peta her coat. 'You're upset. I think you should go now.'

'What's going on between you two?'

'Nothing!' I exclaim. 'Nothing at all.'

'Us breaking up has nothing to do with Becca,' Joe reinforces what I've said. 'This is between you and me alone.'

'I used to think he felt sorry for you, because you lost whatshisname,' she says. 'But now . . .'

Joe catches hold of her arm and steers her towards the door. 'How dare you talk to Becca so insensitively. Go. I've had enough!'

She wrestles herself free. 'Don't worry!' she screeches. 'I'm going.' But before she leaves, she turns to me and says, 'No one has ever dumped me before. I have *never* been treated like this, and it's all because of you!'

42

Returning home, I can't concentrate on painting, and for once I don't feel like eating. Mum is out. I find Dad in his hut, writing at his desk. I collapse on to the sofa, next to his shelf of porcelain.

His mouth twitches from one side to another. 'I'm fed up with our broadband service so I'm writing one of my stinky letters.'

I sit steaming in the corner. There were so many things I should have said to Peta. How dare she accuse me of having an affair! And then she couldn't even remember Olly's name.

He seals the envelope and turns to me. 'What are you up to?'

'Nothing.'

'Nothing always means something. Rebecca? What's wrong?'

I decide to tell him the whole story.

He looks aggrieved.

'Who is this nasty girl? I'm coming after her.'

The determined expression on my father's face makes me smile. 'It was like a scene on *Dynasty*,' I confess.

After Peta's outburst I'd left immediately. I had to get home. *Whatshisname?* I needed to be alone.

'If Joe wasn't already sure he was doing the right thing ending this relationship, he must be now,' says Dad.

Early that evening I leave another message for Kitty, saying it's urgent, but adding, 'Don't worry, I'm not in labour.'

Later that night, lying in the bath, I'm replaying the conversation with Peta. I know I had nothing to do with the break-up, so why do I feel like the villain?

With a towel wrapped round me, I look at my watch. It's seven o'clock. '"She's always getting in the way,"' I mimic. 'Pah! Oh, Olly, you should have seen her.' I reach for my soft stretchy pyjamas underneath my pillow and slide my fat feet into furry slippers, sighing with relief. 'My clubbing days are well and truly over,' I tell him. 'From now on it's pyjamas and slippers all the way to the birthing pool.'

As I make my way downstairs I wonder if there's anything decent to watch on television. Mum and Dad are out for supper and bridge tonight. Mum suggested I decorate the Christmas tree Dad bought from the garden centre today. In hope, she's left the baubles and tinsel out. Halfway through my journey downstairs my mobile rings. I waddle back to my bedroom.

'It's me,' Kitty says. 'Sorry I missed your ten-thousandth call. What's up?'

I tell her, without drawing breath.

'Slow down.'

I breathe.

'Perhaps you and Joe have been seeing one another a bit too much?' Kitty dares to suggest, before making sure to say she's not defending Peta in any way.

'But how can she think I'm the reason it went wrong? We're just friends.'

'You know that, I know that, but she's insecure. She needed someone to blame, she found you.'

'I hope Joe's OK. Maybe I should call him?'

'No. All you need to do is relax, stop stressing.'

I take a deep breath. 'God, this baby needs to come out soon.'

'Stick a DVD on and eat something hot and spicy.

Forget about Peta and try to get a decent night's sleep. I'll talk to you tomorrow.'

I make a desultory start on the tree, then fall asleep watching *Breakfast at Tiffany's*, only to be awakened by the sound of knocking against the back door.

It's pitch black and pouring with rain. I head to the door. Joe isn't wearing a coat, and his hair is dripping wet. I usher him inside, out of the freezing cold. 'Were you about to go to bed?' he asks when he sees me in my pyjamas and the zebra-striped furry slippers that Olly gave me last Christmas.

'I wanted to find out how you are,' Joe says, sitting down at the kitchen table. 'I'm so sorry. I had no idea she was going to take it *that* badly.'

'I'm OK.'

'She's used to getting her way all the time – that's what it was about. She was hurt, but that doesn't excuse her behaviour.'

Joe reaches for the bowl of sugar in the middle of the kitchen table, heaps sugar into the spoon, pours it back into the bowl repeatedly.

'If anyone's to blame, it's me,' he confesses. 'We had a great time the first few months. It was mainly lust,' he admits. 'I was bowled over by her looks. I'm shallow. There you are.' He holds up his hands, guilty as charged.

'You're a bloke. If I were a man, I'd have fancied her too.'

'I knew I had to end it though. When she asked me to meet her parents, I didn't want to. I realized I had no deep feelings for her and I never would. I tried to let her down gently today. I didn't want to do it over the phone.'

I reach for his hand to stop him from playing with the sugar. 'I'm so sorry she forgot Olly's name,' he says, 'and for the way she spoke to you.'

'Don't worry. I'm a big girl. Especially now.' I place both hands either side of my bump.

Joe doesn't smile. 'She should have taken it out on me. After everything you've been through, the last person I wanted her to hurt was you.'

I've persuaded Joe to stay and help me decorate the Christmas tree. He finds a lonely branch and hangs a smiling Santa on it. 'No more talk about Peta,' he says. 'How are *you*?'

I tell him I have a mouth ulcer from eating too many pineapples.

'Why are you eating pineapples?'

I hang a bright-red glass heart on the branch above Santa and our arms touch. I tell him pineapples supposedly help bring on the baby.

Joe laughs as he bends down to put a glittery gold bauble on a lower branch. He glances at an envelope wrapped in ribbon under the tree. 'For my parents,' I say. 'I bought them tickets to Siena next spring.' I tell Joe it's a thank-you for everything they have done for me.

'There's something here for you too.' I pick up a flat package wrapped in brown parcel paper and finished off with a red velvet ribbon.

'For me? Wow.'

'Open it.'

'I haven't got anything for you.'

'Good. You don't need to. Open it,' I demand again.

Inside is an oil painting of a lemon tree, just like the one he'd loved at Bristol.

He looks at me, warmth in his eyes.

'Thank you, Joe. You were the one who encouraged me to paint again.'

'I love it.'

'It won't sell for millions at Sotheby's, but . . .'

'It's priceless to me.'

We continue decorating the tree, me unwrapping a

second chocolate reindeer and laughing as I say in between mouthfuls that it's for the baby, who happens to have a very sweet tooth.

'How convenient of him. How many days to go?'

'Ten.'

'Fuck.'

'Thanks.' I take the silver angel and stick her on top of the tree. 'Now I feel *so* much better.'

Over eggs on toast Joe asks about my plans after the baby is born.

'I'm moving back to London as soon as I can.'

'You won't miss your family?'

'London's only an hour and a half up the M3.'

'Do you want to go back?' I notice he has barely touched his food.

'Yes and no.'

'You haven't thought about living down here?' he asks, tentatively adding, 'Permanently? It could be a new start.'

'Joe, I'll miss you too.'

'I'm thinking practically . . .' He stops, checks himself. 'I will miss you too, Becca.'

I smile. 'These last six months, they've been hard, but what's largely got me through is my family's support, meeting Annie again, this baby . . .' I look down to my enormous stomach. 'Losing your mind isn't a luxury you have when you're pregnant. And the other thing that's got me through is working at Maison Joe. Well, not just that, it's you.'

'Me?'

'I'm glad you came back into my life, and I'm so happy we've put the past behind us. Despite everything, it's what Olly would have wanted too. I won't forget this time we've had together.'

'Nor will I. But we're going to stay in touch, aren't we? You're talking as if we won't see each other for another ten years!'

We start to recount the wine course, Adam's pride at receiving his Maison Joe certificate at the end, which he told me he was going to frame. We think about Janet's gutsy laugh and her getting tipsy, and Monica avoiding wild-haired Henry before falling for the lovely Scott. I remember Joe helping me get through Olly's birthday and spending time with his father, Francis. 'Can we go to the Lobster Pot?' I ask Joe, before we both laugh.

'If we didn't laugh, we'd cry,' Joe adds.

We sit and listen to the rain outside. 'You've helped me too, Becca,' he says, finally breaking the silence.

'There was always this gap, this void after losing touch with you and Olly.'

'Wait there.'

'Becca? What are you doing?'

'You'll see. I've got something else for you.'

I go up to my bedroom and slide out the box of Olly's things from underneath my bed. I return with an envelope, hand it to Joe.

He opens it. Inside are the passport photographs Olly had kept in the bottom drawer of his desk. Tears come to Joe's eyes. 'I remember that day. We were pretty bored so we walked into town. You were in Florence.'

'Well, it would be boring without me there,' I joke.

He picks up the other photograph. 'This was taken at Kitty's New Year's Eve party, wasn't it? It's a great shot. Look how *young* we are! Can I really keep these?'

I nod, touched by how much they mean to him.

We continue to reminisce, recalling our day trekking up St Catherine's Hill, Joe letting go of the balloons to say goodbye to Olly. I see us playing Mr Froggy in the maze and the school children laughing at him in his red boxer shorts.

'After the day we've had, I could do with a good scream. Shall we go now?' he suggests.

'I don't think I could climb one step.'

'I could carry you.'

'And break your back?'

'Ten days until he's due,' he says, thinking out loud, 'and then everything will change.'

'I know. I've been lucky, cushioned down here. It's terrifying moving on, but I think I've found a possible place to rent and . . .'

'I don't want you to go.'

'You can come and visit us, plus I'll be down here all the time. You'll hardly notice I've gone.'

'I don't want you to go.'

'Joe?'

He takes in a deep breath. 'Peta was right to be jealous.'

'What?'

'Oh God, I can't believe I'm going to say this now.' He gets up, paces the room. 'The thing is, Becca, she had a point. Partly the reason we split up was, well, I'm not in love with her. I don't think I've ever been in love, not properly.'

I get up from the table, take my mug to the sink.

'Becca, look at me.'

He's standing by my side now. He takes my arm, turns me towards him. 'I fell for you back at Bristol, you know that. We had that one night together, but I could never have you. You were with my best friend. Do you *know* how that felt? You meant everything to me, you still do, and the idea of not seeing you again, not having you around, it breaks my heart, and–'

I pull away from him. 'Joe! Stop. Don't say it.'

'I can't help the way I feel.'

'Joe, please . . .'

'I love you.'

'No! It's wrong, this is all wrong.'

'Becca . . .'

'You can't replace Olly. No one can!'

'Right. Right, I understand.'

He walks out of the kitchen.

I hear the back door close.

I squeeze my eyes shut, wanting to block the pain out.

I hear footsteps along the gravelled driveway. What am I going to do? What have I just done? 'Joe! I'm sorry!' I call, running towards the back door. I fling it open and stagger out into the pouring rain. I rush back into the kitchen and grab my telephone, deciding to call him and tell him to come back, but then I feel a dull pain right across my swollen stomach. Then my waters break. I wad some kitchen towels between my legs and clutching my belly I head for the back door, but he's too far away. 'Joe!' I shout. He doesn't hear me. 'Joe!'

He's gone.

I dial his number. 'You have reached Joe Lawson . . .'

I hang up and try once more, stabbing at the buttons.

The pain comes again, only stronger this time.

43

West London, Eighteen Months Later

'No more!' I take the packet of ginger snaps away from my son. His face wrinkles like a prune, so to prevent tears I take his hand and pull him towards our favourite red swing. 'You'll feel like Superman,' I say, when I promise to push him high, 'and Superman never cries, does he? He's a superhero!' I lift him into the seat just as it starts to drizzle. 'Why do we live in London, hey? It always rains, *drip, drop,* even in the summer.'

'Jip, jop,' he repeats, wriggling about.

'Here we go, my poppet. Are you ready to fly!'

He giggles, hits the sides of the swing in eager anticipation, biscuits forgotten.

I push him with a 'Whoosh!'

He laughs again.

I love it when he laughs, because in that moment he reminds me of Olly. I see that light shining in his big brown eyes.

Alfie came into my life in a fairly traumatic way: a labour that lasted over twenty hours, and I can still remember Kitty fainting when she saw the pool of red water. Birth is magical, but it's blood, guts and toil too. After my waters broke, Mum and Dad rushed home from their bridge evening. I called Kitty too, and she said she'd jump in the car straightaway.

My father was muttering like an old man and walking with a dramatic limp. 'Why are you walking like that all of a sudden?' Mum snapped, cleaning up the mess I'd made on the kitchen floor. It wasn't just a trickle; more like a burst pipe. 'Go and get the bag!'

'The bag?' Dad was flustered. Audrey was barking and chasing her tail.

'That we packed for hospital! It's in Becca's room. Quick.'

Dad limped out of the room.

'Why's he walking like that?' Mum repeated, mopping the floor with a vengeance. She was like a gale-force wind that needed to calm down.

'Mum, I've only had a few contractions, so please, *please* relax.'

'I'm so excited,' she then said, clutching my hands.

My mind returned to Joe. I felt terrible; guilty – he'd been so supportive, such a good friend – but I couldn't deal with what he'd said.

Close to one o'clock in the morning the four of us drove to the hospital. Dad was driving cautiously in the darkness, Mum frustrated by our progress. 'There's nobody on the road, Harvey!'

Poor Dad. 'I have precious cargo on board,' he argued. 'Stop harassing me.'

To ease the tension he complained that I'd called him just when he had a demon hand of cards. 'I was about to make a grand slam.'

Kitty was squeezing the life out of my hand, encouraging me to concentrate on Augusta's breathing exercises. Later, when the contractions became more intense, I remember screaming Olly's name.

'More, Mama,' Alfie demands. I realize I'd lost my concentration. 'Off we go, high in the sky!' I say with renewed energy.

My head midwife was a man called Willy. 'Only you would have a midwife called Willy,' Kitty had whispered, making me laugh in spite of everything.

I remember the first few minutes of holding my baby

in my arms and feeling his warm and tiny body nestled against my chest. I loved him gripping my fingers. I stroked his hair, breathed in his smell. He made me feel close to Olly.

All my friends sent cards, chocolates and baby clothes, turning my room into a gift shop. When Pippa, Todd and the twins entered the ward, they looked as if they'd brought with them the entire toy department of Hamleys.

Kitty joined me, perching on my bed. 'You've possibly put me off giving birth for life,' she said, 'but well done – you did it.'

I took her hand. 'We did it. Will you be his guardian, if anything happens to me?'

'Nothing will happen to you.' Kitty tried to calm me down, told me I was tired.

'It's not morbid. I just need to know.'

'And then you'll stop worrying?'

I nodded. 'My parents are old, it's too much responsibility. Pippa has the twins and she'll always be his aunt, but you're my best friend.'

Kitty smiled, touched. 'I promise I'll look after him.' We hugged. 'Any ideas for names?'

I looked down at my boy.

'Alfred Oliver Sullivan. Alfie for short.'

Most of all, I shall never forget my mother saying she was proud of me. It made me think of Olly and Joe and how, in a way, that's what the three of us have always craved: approval in our parents' eyes. 'I love you, and I'm so proud of you,' she said, rocking Alfie in her arms.

As we make our way home from the park, I think about Mum and Dad and how much I miss them.

After Alfie was born, I spent a month at home over Christmas and New Year, my mother and I establishing a routine and my father often being sent out on errands to the supermarket or newsagents. Mum taught me everything I needed to know about looking after Alfie, including how to swaddle him in the old Shetland knitted shawl that she had used for me and had kept so carefully for her own grandchildren.

On a daily basis I received further blue-coloured congratulatory cards from friends, but I didn't hear from Joe, which was understandable. I had made it clear how I felt; we couldn't just turn around and resume a normal friendship, pretend nothing had happened.

Since leaving home, Alfie and I have built a new life in west London. I didn't go back to work for Glitz. Alfie is my one piece of Olly, and maybe it's an unhealthy attachment, but the idea of handing him over to a stranger is impossible right now. I talked this over with Victor and Carolyn. 'We'd like to support you,' Carolyn had reinforced, 'to make sure you can stay at home and not worry too much about money.'

I felt guilty when Carolyn told me that they had sold a couple of paintings to help funds. 'Please say yes,' she'd insisted, handing me a cheque. 'We want to help.'

'I should have given Oliver a lot more support when he was alive,' Victor had added. 'Let me do it for you and for Alfie. He needs his mother. But most of all, let me do it for my son.'

Another reason I haven't returned to Glitz is I'm painting again, and it feels wonderful, as if a small part of myself is returning. I'm not doing it on any serious scale, as I haven't had enough time, but I have been in touch with a local art dealer who runs private exhibitions in central London. She liked my Italian landscapes and has said she will commission me in the future. When Alfie goes to nursery and on to school, I shall work hard to see if I can make a living out of my art full-time again. One thing I have learned, however, since Olly's death, is not to agonize over decisions, but take each day as it comes. Right now I want to enjoy being Alfie's mother. It is hard work being a single mum, and I realize now how worn out Pippa must have been, having twins and a husband abroad half the time. I wish we'd been closer when they were tiny. I would have supported her. I can also understand why she needed Mum so much.

Alfie loves seeing his grandparents. When I take him to Winchester we also meet up with Keisha from the antenatal class, or we visit Annie in her shop, which is hanging on in there in the recession. Oscar and Theo love their baby cousin, although every now and then I have to make sure they're not about to pinch him, or poke him with their fork just to see if that will make him wake up. In London, Godmother Kitty often visits, and sometimes she brings Steven. Steven is short, chubby in the face with intelligent blue eyes, and lots of fun. He's also more than a match for Kitty; there's no way he's going to allow her to boss him around. She and Steven enjoy telling Alfie the story of how she'd been pushed off a double-decker bus by a big monster man and Superman Steven had flown to her rescue. They act it out with great drama, making Alfie laugh. Sometimes I see Kitty recognizing that twinkle in his eye when he giggles. 'He looked just like Olly then,' she says, catching her breath.

Jamie often visits with Sylvie, whom I can tell isn't interested in babies or baby talk, but she does her best not to show it.

Victor and Carolyn also visit regularly, staying in a local bed and breakfast close to my flat. I have told them about Olly's script. Finally I read it, and wished I'd done so sooner. I might be biased, but I couldn't put Olly's novel down. 'It's a comedy,' I told them. 'At times I laughed out loud, but it's also moving. There are these two characters who should be together, but–'

'Don't tell me,' Carolyn had said. 'I'd like to read it too.'

Losing a son has aged both of them, but I can see how much Alfie is helping them fill a void. Victor promises Alfie that when he's bigger he must come and stay in Northumberland. They have a lovely garden with a vegetable patch. He's looking forward to showing him how caterpillars turn into butterflies.

Every so often Alfie and I meet Glitz for a cup of hot chocolate in our favourite cafe close to New Bond Street. But it's Janet's visits my boy enjoys most. He loves seeing her and playing with Woody. When he hears the toot of a car horn he runs towards the window in a flap of excitement. Michel drives her up to see us once every month, before discreetly slipping away to see a film or exhibition. Over the months I have noticed how she now leans heavily on Michel's arm and is much slower on her feet. 'My old ticker isn't so strong these days,' she jokes, though I know it is more serious than she lets on.

When she was last here finally I plucked up the courage to talk to her about Joe. If anyone had any significant news about him, it would be Janet, because Michel knows the family inside out. 'How's Joe's father?' was the warm-up question.

'In Cherry Trees nursing home. Oh dear lord, I hope I don't end up there. But Joe thought it was for the best. It was becoming too much for him.'

'Right. And Joe?' I offered her a biscuit with her cup of tea. 'How is he?'

'Michel says Maison Joe is booming! A bright spark, that man.' She felt the biscuit in her hands.

'Custard creams. Your favourite.'

'Oh, how delicious.' She took a large bite and half of it fell on to the carpet. It was Woody's lucky day. 'I'm sure Joe would love to hear from you,' Janet said, picking her words carefully. She knew why we hadn't been in touch since Alfie was born, that he had said he loved me. 'I do miss him, a lot,' I'd told her months ago, 'but it could never work between us, Janet.'

I reminded her how much I'd hurt him.

'Was he *trying* to replace Olly?' she asked.

'No,' I muttered, not wanting to think about what

I'd said. 'I did write to him, about six or so months after Alfie was born. I asked him to visit us and sent photographs. I didn't hear back.' I paused. 'I often think of him. Anyway . . .'

'Do you love him?'

'Janet!'

'It's a simple question.'

'Do I like chocolate? That's a simple question.'

'Fine, but if you can't talk to an old fuddy-duddy like me, who can you talk to?'

I relaxed my shoulders. 'Since things have settled with Alfie and I've had more time, well, yes, I miss him, but does that mean I love him?'

'Do you think you *could* love him?' she asked, more gently this time.

'I feel guilty.'

'Guilty?'

'He was Olly's best friend.' I decided then to tell Janet the whole story this time, starting from the very beginning, going right back to our university days. She listened, transfixed, didn't even eat her biscuit. I censored some parts, but Janet very much got the gist. 'He's probably met someone else anyway.' I crammed a custard cream into my mouth. 'Oh, Janet, I'm scared of falling for anyone again. It's easier being on my own.

In fact, I'm not on my own. I'm with Alfie. He's my man.'

'When I was growing up, Rebecca, I didn't want a dog.' I noticed her hands were shaking, causing her cup to rattle against its saucer. 'Why get a dog when it will die? So I asked Mum if we could train guide dogs instead. That way they'd leave us when they were still young. I was terrified of death, you see, I don't know where this fear came from, but it was there.'

I nodded, curious to know where this was heading.

'So this is what we did. We trained Billy the Labrador for a year before, handing him back and taking on Maisy the golden retriever, and so on . . . until Mum finally persuaded me that we should get our own dog. Pepper was our first, a grey-and-white miniature schnauzer. He died ten years later, when I was twenty-two. I cried for days. Days, Rebecca! It was my first real experience of grief, but it taught me a lesson. To love you have to lose. Grief is the price you pay for love.'

I felt tearful.

'Life is essentially wonderful, Rebecca, but you know, as much as I know, it does have the ability to kick you in the teeth when you're least expecting it. So many people rail against the injustice, the unfairness, they don't move on. We are not entitled to anything in this life, we are not as in control as we'd like to be, but we do have choices. All I'm saying is, make the best choice you can and don't feel guilt. It's a waste. You can't help who you fall in love with, and Olly would not want you to be unhappy.'

As I turn the corner into our street I see Kitty hovering outside my front door. She's babysitting tonight, with Steven. She helps me get Alfie and all our belongings inside, before grilling me on what I am going to wear for my date. 'Don't tell me you've forgotten!' Kitty has been persuading me to 'get out there' again.

'You could go on a few dates,' she'd suggested, 'nothing serious, just see how it goes.'

All of my friends have been encouraging me to do the same. Even Mum asked if I was meeting new people, and I could tell from her tone that she didn't mean the mums at the toddler group.

'I haven't forgotten,' I assure her. 'Come on Alfie, let's get you some supper.'

'Are you OK?'

'Nervous. I can't remember how to talk to men, let alone flirt.'

'You'll be fine.' She follows me into the kitchen.

'You used to have disastrous dates,' I remind her.

'Remember peanut head and *Sister Act* man?'

She laughs. 'Yeah, but at least this guy has come highly recommended from Steven. Andrew and he are good friends. They trained together, and I promise you his favourite film won't be *Sister Act* or *Mrs Doubtfire*.'

'I love *Mrs Doubtfire*,' I say.

'I've got a good feeling about tonight.'

'We can't both go out with anaesthetists.'

'Why not? It'll be fun, I promise.'

'We'll see.'

44

I am late for my date, but it looks like he is too. I grab the last free table in the corner of the crowded bar. I sit down, rummage through my handbag to make sure I've brought my phone in case Kitty needs to call. A party are enjoying cocktails at the next table. I look out of the window, at the sweeping view over London towards Big Ben, telling myself I am going to enjoy tonight.

Five minutes later I pretend to be absorbed in the drinks menu before glancing over to the bar again. Relax, I tell myself. It's a date, not an exam.

My telephone vibrates, alerting me to a text message. For a second I'm hoping my evening is cancelled so I can kick off my high heels and get back into my cosy jumper and jeans. It's Kitty.

'Alfie's asleep. Remember, you look *hot*. Good luck x'

Earlier tonight I'd opened my wardrobe. Alfie was playing with some toy wooden bricks, though he was far more interested in a shoehorn found at the bottom of the wardrobe.

Kitty picked out one of my red dresses – casual but sexy, she described it. 'I remember you wearing it to that film premiere thing.'

'That was years ago. I can't wear it tonight. It's a bit over the top, isn't it?'

'No!' She'd swiped my jeans and safe black top away from me and thrust the dress into my hands. 'I won't fit into it,' I protested, gesturing at my wobbly tummy before tripping over one of Alfie's bricks and cursing. I'm trying to find substitutes for the 'f' word these days, but nothing works quite as well.

I look at my watch. It's seven fifteen. We did say seven, didn't we?

Why am I so nervous?

Probably because the last date I went on was with Luca, in Florence, well over ten years ago. Since Olly's death I haven't wanted to be with anyone. Only recently have I begun to re-examine my life, especially after what Janet said to me. When I saw Kitty and Steven kissing on my sofa (they didn't think they had an audience, but I was on my way downstairs, having just put Alfie to bed) I noticed for the first time a flicker of longing, a desire to have what they had.

'Andrew Matthews,' says a man, standing at my table and taking off his jacket. 'You must be Rebecca. I'm so sorry I'm late.'

'Oh, don't worry. I've only just arrived,' I lie through my teeth.

Steven told me Andrew divorced over a year ago. I'm guessing he's in his late forties and his handshake is firm, always a good sign, but my eyes are drawn to his pine-needle hair, like shark's teeth.

'So,' we both start.

'Would you like a drink?' he asks at the same time as I say, 'You're an anaesthetist, like Steven?'

'Yes,' we both say again, before laughing. I can see he is nervous too.

Over drinks, Andrew tells me about his work.

As he's talking, my mind wanders to Olly. I remember us buying this red dress together many years ago. Olly called it my 'banker's bonus' dress. 'How much is it?' he'd asked.

'Don't!' I shielded his eyes from the price tag. 'It's nasty.'

'How nasty? Minor injury on the credit card or . . .'

'A & E. Cardiac arrest. The card might never recover.'

'Oh, go on, try it on,' he said, pushing me towards the changing room.

Inside the cubicle I whipped off my jumper.

'New bra?' His fingers slid under one of the straps.

'Not here,' I laughed, before peeping my head out of the cubicle and pulling the curtains shut.

'Let your hair down,' he said, when the dress was finally on.

I let my hair down.

'You're beautiful, Becca.'

'Oh, Olly, you old romantic.'

'Almost as stunning as the new iPod,' he said with that mischievous smile that Alfie has inherited.

I long to see his face opposite mine. What I'd give to kiss him again, feel his touch, his arms wrapped round me. Despite all our ups and downs, what we had was true. What I'd do to walk Alfie to the park with Olly and me on either side of our son, holding his hand. I even miss our arguments about all the silly stuff. I'm terrified that I am forgetting the sound of his voice. I never imagined I'd be dating again, always believed we'd grow old together. We talked about how we'd live in a retirement place by the sea. We'd play cards and amble along the beach, watching the waves.

As Andrew carries on I try to listen, but instead I'm

wondering who to send Olly's script to. This script *is* good. Even if it doesn't get accepted, I wish I'd told him I was proud of him. I see him writing in our flat, one of his records playing in the background. I sneak up on him, glance towards the screen. He snaps his laptop shut. 'Oh, Ol, can't I read just a teeny-weeny bit?'

'When it's finished.'

'I'll be an old lady by then.'

He pulls me on to his lap. 'Right, missy, you deserve a smack for that!'

Next moment we're kissing, laughing, his hand creeping up my skirt and I'm unbuttoning his shirt, kicking my heels off . . .

Suddenly I feel angry. Why can't I enjoy this evening? Am I always going to hang on to the past? Isn't it about as useless as hanging on to an old pair of shoes that don't fit any more?

The waiter brings a bottle of wine to our table. I hadn't even noticed Andrew ordering it. He presents the bottle in front of us, expertly pours a small amount into Andrew's glass.

'May I?' I find myself saying.

Andrew hands me the glass. I sniff the wine and swirl it around. It's like a wine helicopter.

I take a sip. The wine throws a punch, as Joe would say. It's crisp, smells of lime or maybe gooseberry. I think it's a Sauvignon. 'It's lovely, thank you,' I say, before the waiter proceeds to fill my glass.

As Andrew and I talk about our day-to-day lives, I see Joe's confidence when he stands in front of his wine students. I see his vulnerability when he's talking about his father. When we were showing Francis around Winchester College I saw kindness.

'Was he *trying* to replace Olly?' Janet had asked.

'I'm sorry, have I put you to sleep?' Andrew asks. 'Rebecca?'

'I'm so sorry,' I gasp when I realize I have no idea what he has just been saying to me.

'I'm boring you. I haven't been on a date in some time,' he says. 'But who am I fooling? I was never very good at this at the best of times,' he admits with self-deprecating humour.

'It's not you, Andrew, I promise. I have a little boy, Alfie, and I haven't slept properly for weeks. In fact I'd *love* you to put me to sleep.'

He laughs with me.

'I haven't been on a date in months, years either,' I confess.

'Steven mentioned your husband died. I'm so sorry.'

'Thank you,' I say, touched. So what if he has pine-needle hair? Make an effort.

We talk about my art, his work again, his first marriage (briefly), my son (almost as briefly).

He has no children. As we talk, Joe continues to gate-crash my date. 'I fell for you back at Bristol, you know that. We had that one night together, but I could never have you.' Only last night I woke up after a deep dream where I saw him with someone else. He was in love with another woman. I couldn't breathe. I felt that sense of loss all over again, that I'd let him go. 'You meant everything to me. You still do.' I'm going to call him, I decide, realizing how much I want to see him again. I need to see him. I don't want to look back in regret.

My mobile rings, sending a shiver down my spine. Why do I think it might be Joe, after all this time?

'Please, go ahead,' says Andrew, knowing he's defeated by my tiredness this evening, that my mind is far away from him.

'I'm so sorry,' I say, excusing myself.

I look at the screen, and am overwhelmed with disappointment. Mum knows I'm on a date. Immediately I think of Dad. Has something awful happened?

*

Outside, Andrew hails a cab for me on St James's Street. He mutters something to the taxi driver, before opening the passenger door. I step inside and sit down.

Andrew waves goodbye and I turn to watch him walk away, down the busy street, a solitary figure carrying his briefcase. No doubt he's heading back to an empty house. There is too much loneliness in this world.

As the taxi drives on, I stare out of the window, replaying the conversation with my mother, tears in my eyes.

45

St Cross Church, Winchester

'Well, I'll be jiggered,' the vicar begins.

There's laughter from the congregation. 'Janet would be amazed by how many people are here today.' Although I'm not. I turn to see many people standing at the back, including Henry from the wine class, wearing a suit with his antique watch chain. Tentatively he waves and I wave back. There is still no sign of Joe. I'd called him to let him know, telling myself not to get too emotional when I heard his voice. He didn't answer and I was both relieved and disappointed. I know he would have heard about Janet from Michel, but I still left a message on his voicemail, telling him the time and date of the service. At the end I said I hoped he was well. I wanted to say how much I missed him,

that I'd love to see him again, and that Jan
had put so much into perspective, but why is i
say how we feel? 'I hope you are well' is overused and lame. What does it really mean tagged on to the end of a message?

'We have come here today to remember before God Janet Grace Morris, and to give thanks for her long and varied life,' the vicar continues. 'We come to honour a remarkable woman, someone of great courage and uncomplaining in adversity. Right up to her final days she took a huge interest in life and in people . . .'

I think of how I saw Janet only a fortnight ago, how she listened so patiently to me talking about Joe when no doubt she was feeling fragile and unwell, though to be fair she managed to put away three custard creams.

I look down to the service sheet and the photograph of Janet as a younger woman, with Gregory, a river in the background. Underneath the photograph is the inscription I recognize. I remember her saying it to me when we were out on the Stockbridge Downs:

He whom I have loved and lost
is no longer where he was
he is forever where I am.

Janet's death was sudden. Michel was with her at the time, which is comforting to know. She had mentioned to him that she felt unwell, a huge admission on Janet's part as she was loath to complain or talk about her health. She didn't want to eat out, nor did she feel up to going for a walk. Michel had popped out of the sitting room to pour her a glass of sherry and make them both a cheese-and-pickle sandwich, only to return to find her asleep. Then he'd realized she wasn't asleep.

I look over to him, his face etched with pain. No matter how much you say someone is old or they have had a good innings, she was our great friend and she will be missed.

'We remember with affection the devoted love of Gregory and Janet,' the vicar says, and I hold back more tears.

I sense Janet telling me to stop looking so sad. 'What a wonderful way to go, Rebecca! I didn't have to suffer years in Cherry Trees nursing home.' I can hear her gutsy laugh. 'I shall miss you, but now I can be with him.'

'Many of you may not know everything about Janet,' the vicar says halfway through his address. 'During the Second World War she was a Wren and carried out highly classified work plotting the movement of convoys and enemy submarines.'

I hadn't known that. I wish now that I'd asked her more questions about her life.

'She would have been taught never to mention or discuss her work, and I think anyone here today will know that Janet was the kind of person to keep her word. She suffered in her life. During wartime she lost her fiancé, a naval officer. She was very young at the time, but she went on to meet many years later her beloved Gregory, who had also fought in the Second World War, in the Coldstream Guards. They met well into their forties and a great regret was they were never able to have children.'

I reach across to Mum, grip her hand. Pippa sits on my other side, but she didn't bring Oscar and Theo. They're having tea with friends after school today. Alfie is being looked after by Mum's tennis friend, Marjorie. She will drop him back at my parents' home this afternoon.

'During her last few years,' the vicar continues, 'she found great comfort and happiness in her friendship with Michel.' I hear steps across the stone floor, someone entering at the back of the church. I turn and, when I see his face, swing back, knocking my handbag on to the stone floor.

*

Mum and Dad have organized tea and cakes at home, after the service.

As we leave the church Joe grabs my hand, pulls me away from the crowd. Without thinking we hug, forcing people to swerve around us. He thanks me for letting him know about Janet. He digs into his pocket for a handkerchief, hands one to me. I'm crying for Janet, for Olly, and now for Joe.

'How are you?' we both say, before answering, 'Fine', and then smiling.

Where do you start when there is so much to say?

'Rebecca?' I hear my mother call, searching for me.

'Are you coming back for tea?' I ask him.

'Alfie, come and meet my friend,' I say, out on the lawn. Mum and Dad have inherited Woody, who's playing with Alfie, in the hopes that he'll be fed biscuits. It's a warm summer's day, the sky a Wedgwood blue. Alfie rushes towards me and I scoop him into my arms. Joe ruffles his hair, says, 'How do you do, Alfie?'

Joe admires my son's T-shirt with a crocodile on it. Alfie runs off to see Granny and the plate of shortbread.

'He has your hair,' Joe says.

I gaze over to my son and watch him grab a biscuit

in his podgy hands. Alfie's hair is chestnut brown, with a hint of red, and it's thick with angelic curls.

'And Olly's eyes,' he says quietly.

'How are you, Joe?'

He loosens his tie. 'Good. It's lovely to see you.'

I take his hand and hold it for a second too long before losing my nerve and letting it go, but he reaches out and takes my hand again.

'I was sorry to hear about Janet.' His grip tightens. 'I know you two were close. She used to pop into the wine bar every now and then with Michel. I could hear her laughing from downstairs. She was a special person. A wise old owl.'

I smile, agreeing that's exactly what she was.

'Alfie loved her too. How do I tell him he'll never see her again?'

We're both silent, pretending to be absorbed in watching Alfie playing with Woody. 'How's your father?' I ask at the same time that he says, 'Are you enjoying being back in London?'

'Not great, but he's happy in the new place. It's distressing – he doesn't really know who I am now.'

'Oh, Joe, I'm so sorry.'

Glass hangs between our words, both of us too scared to mention what happened the last time we were together. 'How's Mavis? And Adam?'

'Becca, I'm sorry . . .'

'No, *I'm* sorry.' From the corner of my eye I can see Alfie running towards the back gate. 'Hang on, Joe. Don't move.'

When I come back he isn't in the garden any more. I search inside the house. Maybe he went to the loo. Is he in the sitting room? Not there. I run into the kitchen where Michel is talking to Janet's sister. He's not there either. 'Rebecca?' Michel says, sensing my panic.

'Have you seen Joe?'

'I think he left. Is everything all right?'

Without answering I rush out of the room and into Mum's conservatory to ring him on my mobile, but thankfully I don't have to. He's standing by the pine dresser. When he turns to me I am overwhelmed by relief, as if I have managed to catch something valuable that was about to slip through my fingers. I notice now how smart he looks, dressed in a shirt and black tie, and his thick dark hair is swept away from his face, highlighting those grey eyes. There's no trace of arrogance left in Joe; all I see is a friend I have missed.

'Maybe Joe came along too soon after Olly,' Kitty had said to me, when I'd dared to explain my feelings after hearing about Janet, and when recounting my date with

Andrew. 'The truth is, I think you've been in denial about Joe for some time,' she said. 'You've been scared to admit it to yourself, worried you'd be betraying Olly again.'

'I thought you'd gone,' I say.

'I had to take a call. Is Alfie OK?'

'Oh yes, he's fine. He's with Pippa. What were we saying?'

Say it again, Rebecca. Say how sorry you are too and that you want to be friends. Maybe more than friends. Say *something*.

'Mama!'

Pippa holds his hand, his knee bleeding. 'He fell off the swing, it's nothing serious,' she explains. 'I have to run, pick up the boys.' She senses the atmosphere. 'I'm sorry. I'll call later.'

'Mama!' he wails again.

'That looks nasty, Alfie,' Joe says, 'but I'm sure you'll be brave for your mum.'

'Mummy, hurts.'

'I know, sweetheart.'

'I must go,' Joe says, quickly kissing me goodbye on the cheek.

I lift Alfie into my arms. 'Wait!' I call out. Joe turns. 'I've missed you, Joe.'

'I've missed you too.'

Michel catches me watching him leave. 'He's a special man, that Joe. Works too hard, that's his trouble. It'll be good for him to take a long break.'

'Long break?'

'Didn't he tell you? He's going away,' Michel says, making it sound so final, as if he's about to disappear off the face of the earth.

I see Joe standing in front of me today, holding me close, saying how sorry he was about Janet. I haven't just missed him. I love him. I'm such a fool.

'Going away? Where, Michel? Where?'

46

Early evening: Alfie and I play sharks and crocodiles in the bath. 'He's coming to get you! He's going to eat you all up!' I say, holding the crocodile over Alfie's head before plunging him into the water.

Michel told me Joe moved house well over a year ago. He gave me his new address, but he's off to Australia to visit his Uncle Tom, who is now well into his eighties. 'Other than that, I have no more details, Rebecca.'

I fear that if I don't tell Joe tonight that I love him, I never will. I need to take a risk. I know what I have to do.

I scoop Alfie out of the bath and put on his favourite shark-print pyjamas. Olly must be thrilled that his son hasn't yet shown any sign of interest in ladybirds and bugs but loves sharks, crocodiles and snakes.

*

I join Mum and Dad in the kitchen. It's 6.30 on the dot. My father is on drink duty.

'Can you read to Alfie tonight?' I grab my car keys. 'I'm going out.'

'Out?' Mum asks, vodka in hand, as if I've said I might climb Mount Everest. 'Where? Is something wrong?'

'Don't have time to explain,' I say, already halfway out the door. 'Though nothing's wrong. In fact, I've never been so sure of anything in my life.'

'What's she on about?' I overhear Dad saying.

'Why won't you put your hearing aid in, Harvey?'

I slam my foot on the accelerator, but my dilapidated old Ford Focus (bought third- or possibly fourth-hand) grunts in protest.

What if he isn't in love with me any more? What if I've left it too late? What if he's going on this Australian trip with someone else? Maybe he has a new girlfriend. I haven't seen him for eighteen months, anything could have happened . . . But it doesn't matter any more. I have to do this.

I'm stuck behind a bus. Passengers get on and off so slowly, as if the world isn't in a hurry.

*

Joe's new flat is in Oram's Arbour, close to the train station.

Flat 5B.

I take a deep breath and press the buzzer.

No answer.

I try again. He could be in the shower?

No answer.

Maybe he's at Maison Joe.

Why didn't I think of that?

Edoardo gives me a great welcome and wants to hear all my news. 'Sorry, but not now,' I tell him. 'I need to find Joe.' Then Adam emerges at the top of the stairs, dressed in smart trousers and a spotted tie. He gives me a big bearhug. 'I'm working here, Rebecca,' he says proudly. 'Helping Joe with the wine courses.' He sticks his thumbs up.

'Oh, that's wonderful, Adam,' I say, cursing myself for sounding so rushed, but . . . 'Do you know where Joe is?' I ask both of them. 'I'm sorry, but this is kind of an emergency.'

Edoardo shrugs. 'Probably packing,' he suggests. 'He's off to Australia early tomorrow morning. Why don't you call him?'

Outside I call his number, my heart racing.

'Think, Edoardo. You really don't know where he might be?' I ask, when I return to the bar. 'He's not picking up.'

Luis joins us with a couple of empty glasses, a pen tucked behind his ear. 'Joe? I think he's eating out tonight. Said he didn't feel like cooking.'

'Where?'

I race up the high street, turn right towards the library, fling open the doors to every single bar and restaurant. I scan the tables. Joe is nowhere to be seen.

It's now close to ten. I'm sitting on the steps outside Joe's flat.

Passers-by return from their evening, warmed up by the company of their friends and the food and wine. A group of students are singing drunkenly as they zigzag across the road. I'm losing my nerve. I can't do this. Defeated, I head back to my car, turn on the engine. I'm about to drive home when something tells me to switch on the radio.

It's Bob Dylan singing 'Make You Feel My Love'.

Some might say it's a coincidence.

I turn off the engine, taking it as a signal to stay.

47

'Becca?' I feel someone shaking my shoulder. I open my eyes and see Joe standing next to a tall, dark-haired woman. I stand up, flustered. I'd sat down on the steps outside Joe's front door, can only have been asleep for a few minutes.

'Becca,' he repeats, 'what are you doing here?'

'Um, I was just passing and . . .'

'It's nearly eleven.'

'You must be freezing,' the woman says with concern.

'How long have you been waiting?' Joe asks.

'Not long!'

He introduces me to Helen.

Helen says how much she has heard about me, and how lovely it is to meet at last. She's nothing like Peta. I can feel that she and Joe fit together this time. Helen kisses Joe on the cheek, says she will give us some time alone. 'I'll call you later,' he promises her.

Joe unlocks the door to his flat. 'Come in. You need warming up,' he says, entering the sitting room. The first thing I see in Joe's new apartment is a framed photograph of Helen on the mantelpiece. But on the wall above it is my painting of the lemon tree. He insists on making me a cup of tea. I ask him if I can use his bathroom. I see her make-up bag by the sink, along with a flowery silk dressing gown hanging on the back of the door.

When Joe hands me a mug of tea we sit side by side on the sofa. 'Why are you here, Rebecca?'

'I'm sorry,' I begin. 'So sorry for what I said to you that night.'

'Don't be. I shouldn't have–'

'Hang on. Let me say this, OK. When I said you couldn't replace Olly, well, it was an unforgivable thing to say but the thing is, it was too soon and–'

'I know it was too soon, and I've hated myself ever since. What was I thinking? I should have known better.' Joe is pacing the sitting room. 'It was insensitive and stupid and impulsive.'

'Joe, sit down. Please sit.'

He joins me on the sofa again. I turn to him, hands placed awkwardly on my knees, when all I want to do is reach out and hold him. 'I've missed you. I wanted to get in touch long before now . . .'

'Me too.'

'Why didn't you?' we both ask together.

'I wrote to you,' I say. I sent photographs.'

'I didn't get them, Becca! 'I never received a letter, otherwise of course I would have replied. You must have sent them to my old address and they didn't forward them on. I just assumed . . .'

We both speak at the same time again.

'You first,' he says, 'seeing as you've waited outside my front door all night.'

I look at him, knowing there's no point trying to pretend any more. 'After the way I'd left it, I thought of a million excuses not to call you, but when I saw you today . . . Over the last year I've begun to dare to think of a life without Olly. I don't want to waste any more time. You and I, we've had so much time apart already, but I'm too late, aren't I . . . ?' I get stuck on the words. I daren't look at his face. I know he is going to tell me that he has moved on.

'Becca, look at me.'

I stumble on, terrified of hearing the truth. 'When

I said you couldn't replace Olly, that was a stupid thing to say, because I don't want you to. No one can replace Olly. I just want you, Joe Lawson. You're a special person in your own right. But I see you've met someone else.' I smile. 'I had to say it, otherwise I'd never have forgiven myself for being such a coward, for being so scared of falling in love again. Because I do love you, Joe.' I reach out and stroke his cheek, look into his eyes. 'There . . . I've said it. Now I'll go.' I attempt to stand up, but Joe grabs my arm, pulls me back down on to the sofa.

'Becca. I haven't met anyone else. Helen's my half-sister.'

'Your half-sister?'

'My family has doubled in the last eighteen months. She's the product of one of my father's affairs, but I'll tell you all about that later. It's a long story.'

'She's your half-sister,' I repeat, unable to disguise my relief.

He nods. 'She's staying here while I'm away, looking after the flat and working in the bar. You'll like her, Becca, and the reason she feels she knows you already is because –' he runs a hand through his hair – 'all I talk about is you. I've been out with her this evening, talking about you again, the poor long-suffering girl, asking her advice because after today I didn't know what to do.' He edges towards me, brushing a strand of hair away from my eyes.

'When I saw you today, at the church, all my feelings came back. I don't think they'd ever gone away, but I didn't know how to deal with them this time.'

Our faces are only inches apart. 'And what advice did she give you?'

'To tell you how I feel a second time, because if I didn't, then I'm an idiot for giving up. I haven't met anyone else. You know me. I'm a messed-up soul, can't commit to anyone.' He holds my face in both hands. 'How can I when I'm still in love with you?'

48

San Miniato al Monte, Florence: a Year Later

Alfie runs up the steps, Joe close behind. I walk past artists in floppy hats, sun-worshippers and photographers taking pictures of the spectacular view across the city.

I'd talked to Kitty about returning to Florence. Was it strange to come back here? Something told me to revisit our special place; it was time for me to say goodbye to Olly properly.

As we get closer to the top I see Olly and me all those years ago, when he'd flown out to see me after his finals. We were young and carefree twenty-one-year-olds.

'This is the place I was telling you about,' I'd called over my shoulder to him, running up the steps. 'Where my Great-Aunt Cecily painted. Isn't it beautiful up here?'

'Hang on!' Olly was saying breathlessly behind me.

'Come on, you old-age pensioner!'

Olly and I sat inside the church and listened to the peaceful music. 'I love it here. This is where I come to think,' I whispered, holding his hand.

'Becca, I'm going to marry you.'

'I know.'

'And we'll be so happy.'

'Have children and a lovely big house.'

'We'll have wild parties with our arty bohemian friends . . .'

'Barbecues with pigs roasting on a spit.'

'Snail!' shouts Alfie, way ahead of me, jolting me back to reality.

I take out my bottle of water, dehydrated from the heat. It's a scorching day. I watch Joe playing with my son. This past year has flown by so quickly that at times I have wanted to press 'pause' because I have felt so happy.

Joe and I don't live together. I spend most of my week in London, painting for my new agent, who holds exhibitions. Alfie goes to a morning nursery round the corner from home, called the 'Little Ladybirds'. We spend each weekend with Joe, at his flat. Slowly I have left an imprint of myself at number 5B so that it feels like my home, rather than just a place I stay. 'As long as we don't have too much pink,' Joe had laughed, 'I don't mind what you do.'

Joe gives Alfie a piggyback up the final steps. I hear them laughing together.

Joe has been happy too. 'You're the reason,' he says to me. His relationship with his half-sister has also opened up another chapter in his life. Out of the blue, Helen's mother had told her that her father wasn't her real dad. She'd met someone at a conference in Nice, a man called Francis Lawson. He was an eminent breast-cancer surgeon. Helen was too late to get to know her father; his illness was too far advanced for him to understand. He barely recognized Joe towards the end. But Helen and Joe have become close, especially when they supported one another after Francis's funeral, a year ago.

I look down to my hand. Today I'm wearing Janet's aquamarine ring that she left me in her will. 'Olly would not want you to mourn forever,' she'd said to me the very last time I saw her. 'I loved my fiancé, but he died in the war, Becca. After Gregory, I fell in love, in a different way, with Michel. There came a time when I no longer felt sad about Gregory, only lucky to have known him.'

*

I wonder what Olly would think of Joe and me. I've asked him many times, but it's been four years now since I've heard his voice. All I can hope is to have his blessing.

'I want someone to kick a ball around with Alfie. You never had any coordination skills.'

I stop short. 'Olly?'

'Joe makes a great dad, Becca.'

'Olly,' I repeat, choked with tears.

'Alfie's the best. Don't make him play the piano. Don't force him to be anything but himself.'

'I won't.' I look at my son with pride. 'He's his own little person.'

'I'm proud of you. I knew you'd be OK.'

'I'll always love you, Olly. You know that, don't you?'

'Even though I didn't tell you about my job and–'

'It doesn't matter, Olly. I don't care. We've both done things we regret.'

'I didn't want you to think I'd failed you.'

'Never. I love you. None of this means–'

'I know. I love you too. Now, you tell Joe he'd better look after you, and please tell Alfie I love him.' I stand still. I can't walk on. There's something about the way he says it. He really is saying goodbye to me this time. 'Catch up with them, Becca. Life is for here and now.'

*

Joe is at the top of the hill. He's pointing out the view of Florence to Alfie, the Duomo always taking first prize in the picture.

'Wait! I'm coming!' I shout, running as fast as I can, the sun shining on my face. I almost trip up on the final step before throwing my arms around them.

'What's Mummy in such a rush about?'

'I have something I want to tell you both.' I recover my breath before standing in between them and taking their hands. 'Alfie, this is where your father and I began our adventure together, a long time before you were born. We came here on our honeymoon.'

'Mummy, I'm thirsty,' Alfie says, and Joe and I smile at one another.

'You're too young to understand, but one of these days we'll come back here again –' I bend down to him – 'and I will tell you all about your wonderful daddy, I promise,' I say, before handing him a carton of apple juice with a straw.

I get up, brush the dust off my knees. 'Hang on, Joe, I have a question for you.'

Joe takes his sunglasses off, looks at me curiously. I dig into my pocket to find the small box, with a gold wedding band inside. 'Will you start a new adventure with me?'

49

Six Months Later

'Is that Rebecca Lawson?' says a curt voice.

'Speaking,' I say. I'm in Maison Joe, having a birthday lunch with my parents, Olly's parents, Alfie (now aged three), Joe, Kitty, Annie and Pippa. Tonight a large group of us, husbands and all, even Todd, are going out for supper and dancing. Carolyn and Victor are staying with Mum and Dad for the weekend. I've told Joe that turning thirty-five is a big deal and we *have* to dance.

'It's Nathalie Jackson calling.'

Nathalie Jackson, I think to myself. Nathalie Jackson?

'You sent a script to me. I'm a literary agent,' she reminds me, when it's crystal clear I don't recognize her name.

'Oh yes, of course. I'm so sorry,' I say, getting up from

the table and walking towards the bar. The truth is, I'd lost heart with Olly's novel. I'd sent it to publishers, and over the course of the year we'd had ten rejections, the script returned each time with a comp slip, so I decided to try and find an agent, but I hadn't had much luck in that area either.

'Well, it was a long time ago.' I can hear paper shuffling. 'Yes, you sent Oliver's script months ago, but as it was unsolicited it went straight to the bottom of my slush pile. I was about to throw it away, but I have to say, your covering letter moved me.'

My heart is beating fast. Does she like it? Why is she calling? Is she going to represent us? I try to keep calm.

'Anyway, I think Oliver's script has real potential. It's very funny, and rather charming. In fact, I couldn't put it down.'

There's no hope remaining calm. 'Nor could I! Oh my God!'

Friends and family stop talking. I catch Joe looking over towards me.

'I happened to show it to the senior commissioning editor at Oak Tree and she loved it, thought it was a highly original concept.'

'Oh my God!' I repeat, wanting to jump on to the table and dance.

'I'm not promising anything just yet, but perhaps we could meet?'

After I hang up, Joe approaches. 'Who was that?' he asks. When I tell him, his face breaks into a smile. 'That's amazing,' he says, pulling me into his arms and kissing me. 'Olly would be really proud of you, Becca, for never giving up. And *I'm* so very proud of you too.'

I take his hand and together we return to the party to share the news.

There's silence, everyone waiting . . . except for Alfie, who charges up to me and throws his arms around my legs, as if we've been parted for a year.

'Come on you two,' Kitty urges. 'What was all that about?'

'Olly's script.' I tell them how I'd kept his last novel under my bed at home, couldn't bring myself to read it for ages, but when I did . . .

'A publisher's interested. I'm meeting an agent next week!'

'Isn't it incredible?' Joe says, before turning to me. 'In fact, that's the best possible news we could have had on your birthday, my darling.'

I hug Carolyn and Victor. Carolyn bursts into tears. 'I loved it too, but I thought I was just being biased.'

'Alfie,' I say, 'your daddy is so clever! And Olly, if you can hear me, your dream might yet come true.'

My friends cheer again. Mum, Dad, Victor and Carolyn clap their hands. Alfie runs up to the bar, tries to climb on to one of the stools. Adam brings over a chocolate cake lit with thirty-five candles, persuading Alfie to give him a hand. 'Come on, monkey,' he says. 'It's time to cut the cake.' Luis and Edoardo bring over the champagne. Everyone sings Happy Birthday. As I blow out the candles, everyone shouts that I must make a wish.

Later, when we're dancing, Joe whispers, 'Did you make a wish?'

I shake my head.

'Oh?'

'I didn't need to. It's come true already.'

ACKNOWLEDGEMENTS

Firstly, I am so grateful to Naik and Gillie of Winchester Bereavement Support. They gave me the confidence I needed to write about grief, both a sensitive and challenging subject. I'd also like to thank Judy Simmons, for sharing with me her personal experience of loss.

Many thanks go to Berrys' Wine School Manager, Rebecca Lamont at Berry Bros. & Rudd. I took part in one of her wine tasting courses, which inspired me to write about this subject. The course was great fun and Rebecca was a wonderful teacher.

There are friends who have helped in many different ways with this novel, from describing antenatal classes to confiding what it is like to return to your childhood home. Lots of thanks go to Caroline Tyree, Sarah-Jane Petherick (SJ), Vanessa and Nick Morris, Sophie Gilbart-

Denham, Clare Camacho (Griz), Juliet Howland and Juliet Geddes.

To Mum and Dad, as always, for being the most supportive parents.

Diana Beaumont. Thank you for reading through the script at a later stage & inspiring new ideas – and for your continuing friendship and guidance.

To Charlotte Robertson, the best of agents.

Finally, *Ten Years On* would not be the book it is without Jane Wood at Quercus. Jane's skilful editing has been invaluable. Thank you, and the team at Quercus, for all your hard work.